MY
MOTHER'S
SILENCE

BOOKS BY LAUREN WESTWOOD

My Mother's Silence

Moonlight on the Thames
Finding Dreams
Finding Secrets
Finding Home

MY MOTHER'S SILENCE

LAUREN WESTWOOD

bookouture

Published by Bookouture in 2019

An imprint of Storyfire Ltd.
Carmelite House
50 Victoria Embankment
London EC4Y 0DZ

www.bookouture.com

ISBN: 978-1-83888-046-0
eBook ISBN: 978-1-83888-045-3

The Selkie

"The cold winds twine the strands of her hair,
She smiles and beckons you to her lair.
Leave your house and leave your lands,
Leave the shore with the pearl grey sands.
Forget your love, and promises made,
Follow her voice to a watery grave."

Music and lyrics by Skye Turner, age 17

PROLOGUE

My sister stands out on the rocks. Her head tipped back, her arms outstretched. The sky pulses with the beam from the lighthouse. The wind lashes her hair, a golden halo against the dark horizon. Behind her the sea is a seething cauldron, the waves booming their terrible heartbeat. The water rises, arcs above her, the air heavy with spray. Her eyes shine with a strange fire.

I begin to tremble, the blood thrumming in my veins with fear and pent-up rage. I've been here before, too many times. Gone out to the edge, held out my hand. Listened to her laugh at me, but in the end, felt the relief and warmth of her hand in mine.

'Come on,' I shout. 'I'm taking you home.'

She does laugh, but at the same time a tear trickles down her cheek. And I almost go to her then. I almost let myself be pulled back into her relentless orbit. I take a step forward, over the barrier. She takes a step backwards to the edge.

'No,' she says.

This is all part of her game. My loyalty, my dignity pushed to the limit. This is where I'm supposed to take charge, become the protector, pull us both back from the brink.

A giant wave booms against the rocks with a shaking force. Icy water rains down on my head pricking my skin like needles.

This is where it ends.

CHAPTER 1

The mists are closing in. Swirling down from the barren hills, creeping out of the glens. The light is fading fast, and with it, my resolve. This is wrong. I shouldn't be here.

I wrap the tooled leather strap of my handbag tightly around my palm, cutting off the circulation. But I can't stop the tide of memories, growing stronger by the mile as the coach heads west.

Some of them are beautiful and shiny: memories of my childhood, especially at this time of the year. The buttery smell of shortbread in the oven; the dogs sleeping on a rug by the fire. Guests arriving for dinner; Dylan songs on the guitar; board games and laughter. Snow, falling in great white flurries onto the beach.

I unwrap and examine each one like a child on Christmas morning. Dad stringing lights on the tree, Bill, my little brother, held up to put the star on top. Mum at the hearth lighting a fire to stave off the cold that was forever seeking a way in through the nooks and crannies. The warm glow of being together. A long time ago.

The coach turns northward and I catch a glimpse of the sea. Mauve-grey, almost purple, with a ghost of orange haze on the horizon as the sun slips away. I see my own reflection in the window, the image sharpening as darkness sets in. For a moment, it's as if I'm seeing someone else's face, Ginny's face, staring back at me from the darkness. Daring me to unwrap those other memories, the ones in the package with no bow and the tag that's fallen off. Remove the tissue paper, look inside...

'Eilean Shiel,' the driver calls out.

I free my hand and untie the scarf around my neck, struggling to breathe. I should have called out and asked the driver to stop, to let me off miles back – anywhere but here. Now, though, it's too late. A middle-aged woman across the aisle looks at me and frowns.

'You OK, love?'

'Yes,' I say hoarsely, though it's probably obvious that I'm not. Since I made my escape fifteen years ago, I suppose that I have been 'OK'. I've had good times that have nothing to do with this place. I've seen the sunrise over the Mojave Desert, driven the Sunset Strip with the top down. I've lived in Vegas and Nashville, and lots of places in between. I've got good memories that I can unwrap and relive when I need them most: on a sleepless night in a dive motel, in a car driving mile after mile down a long, lonely stretch of highway. Dad used to say that without the bad times, you'd never know how good you have it. Dad said a lot of things, most of which I've learned the hard way. But in the end, I can look back and say that I've done the best I can. Done my best to live a life for both me and Ginny.

The coach pulls up at the bus shelter across from the village hall. The door opens and the woman opposite stands up, collecting her bag from the overhead rack. I sit there, not moving, staring out towards the dark, infinite sea. The woman walks to the front of the coach and stops, looking back in my direction. I'm worried she might try to talk to me again. I make myself stand up and move forward.

I step off the coach onto the pavement. The orange sodium lights can't even begin to dispel the darkness. I'd forgotten about the darkness, so heavy and eternal this time of year. But it's the cold that's truly shocking. I pull my scarf back around my neck and clench my teeth to stop them chattering. The wind lashes at my skin, my thin coat unable to keep out the chill.

The driver opens the bottom of the coach to unload the baggage. I look out along the curve of the bay to the dark headland opposite the village. Through the drizzle I can just make out the pinprick glow of lights. The cottage where I grew up. In a few minutes, once I get a taxi, those lights will be my reality. Out there, no amount of shiny memories can make up for what's coming. I'll be seeing Mum again; I'll be coming *home*.

As the driver unloads the baggage, fifteen years seems like yesterday. I'd just turned twenty and was going the other way: Eilean Shiel to Fort William, Fort William to Glasgow, and, eventually, a plane to America. Yesterday for me. But what will it seem like for Mum?

We've been in touch – of course we have. A hurried postcard, the odd strained phone call on birthdays and Christmases. My brother, Bill, acts as the messenger between the trenches, supplying regular updates by email. I'm grateful that he makes the effort, and sorry that he has to do so. When he contacted me in late November to say that Mum had had a fall and fractured her ankle, I was worried. I sent flowers, chocolates and a nice card. When he wrote again and told me where it happened, I cried. And then, on a lonely November night when I was dying for a different town, a new lover – something, anything – to make a new escape, Bill rang me. Mum, he said, had asked for me. *'She wants to know when you're coming home.'* He didn't know that those were the only words that could ever make me come back here; the words that I'd been waiting for all these years. I packed up my things, and booked a flight…

The woman from the coach is still watching me. I take out my phone, pretending I have an important text to send. There's no signal. No pretending here.

'What you got in there, lass?' the driver says, bowing under the weight of my wheelie case. 'Gold nuggets?' His accent rings in my ears. The rich, almost sing-song voice of the Western Highlands. Over the years, I've met people who've thought my accent was 'cute', 'sexy', 'melodic', 'weird'. To me, though, it sounds like home.

'I thought I was travelling pretty light,' I say.

He sets my case on the pavement. 'In my day, all we needed was a toothbrush and a change of knickers.'

I laugh at that, which warms me up inside. A little.

The driver closes the hatch and I wheel my case to the side. It's heavy because I threw in a few books at the last minute, but it's small considering that I don't know how long I'll be staying. Before I left, I gave notice on my rental house in Vegas. As I was packing, I discovered that I had almost no warm clothing. A few cotton jumpers, a pair of boots, some scarves, and a knit hat with sequins and a fake fur pom-pom. I shoved what I could into the suitcase, left my guitar with a friend, and gave everything else to charity. I'm used to being a nomad, a vagabond. My roots have shrivelled up and died.

The driver climbs back aboard and the door shuts with a hydraulic hiss. The engine judders to life. There may still be time. This is the end of the line, but if I gave him twenty quid, I'm sure he'd let me back on. Drop me at a different village, a different cove, maybe take me all the way back to Fort William.

Too late. The coach pulls away. The woman is still hovering about. I stand up a little straighter, like I know what the hell I'm doing next. In fact, I've no idea. There are no taxis. There used to be a village taxi that met the coach, I'm sure of it.

'Would you be needing a ride, love?' the woman says. 'My other half will be here in a few minutes. He's meeting me.' She smiles and, in the glow of the lights, something about her looks familiar. I don't want familiar.

'No, thanks,' I say. 'Someone's meeting me too.' The lie comes easily.

'Right,' she says. Car headlamps come towards us, blinding me for a second. 'This is me, then. You sure…?'

'Yes, I'll be fine. You have a good evening.' I take advantage of a well-practiced 'have a nice day' American answer to everything.

As the car pulls up, the woman cocks her head. 'It's good you've finally come home,' she says. 'Your mum will be glad to see you.'

I stare at her as she gets in the car. If only I knew for sure that that was true. Her words poke at the place inside where my guilt is coiled, lying in wait. She doesn't know anything – can't know anything. About the things that can never be unsaid, the wounds that time can plaster over but never heal.

The car drives away and I'm left standing in the wind and the darkness, feeling utterly alone.

CHAPTER 2

The drizzle is becoming a steady rain and I can no longer see the lights on the headland. I take a breath and steel myself. It's fine that there are no taxis. It's late afternoon, not the middle of the night. I haven't eaten for over six hours, not since the airport at Glasgow. I'll walk into the village, get a coffee, warm up, and call for a taxi. I'll be half an hour at most. It will be good to get the lay of the land again before going to the cottage. I've rehearsed my reunion with Mum many times in my head, but it won't hurt to go through it again. What's another half hour when it's been fifteen years?

I walk quickly, hunched over as the wind blows the rain into my face. The village is only a few streets, all of which lead down to the harbour and the promenade along the front.

I head towards Annie's Tearoom. I can't remember a time when it wasn't there, and the summer before I left, I worked there part-time serving tea and cakes and clearing tables. It's owned by a woman called Annie MacClellan, whom everyone in the village called 'Aunt Annie', probably because she knew everything about everyone, and was everyone's best friend – *if* you stayed on her good side. Annie made melt-in-the-mouth cranachan from wild raspberries and fresh cream, and in winter her clootie dumpling, rich and heavy with dried fruit and spices, was the toast of Hogmanay. Cranachan, clootie, black bun... all those remembered tastes and smells... My senses go on high alert.

My bag rumbles behind me along the uneven pavement. I pass a row of gabled, whitewashed cottages and as I get nearer the water, a small parade of shops. Most of them are closed, but the Spar is open, along with a general store selling fishing supplies, souvenirs and so-called antiques. A signboard outside, optimistically advertising ice cream, creaks in the wind.

The harbour is deserted. I pass the boat-launching ramp, strewn with fishing traps and nets. The breakwater juts out into the gloom and a few wind-tossed boats are moored along the front. My eyes are tearful from the salt and the sharp gusts of wind. I turn onto the promenade looking for Annie's Tearoom along the row of buildings. Where is it? It can't be… gone.

I come to the place where I know it must be. The teashop is dark and there's a sign in the window. Closed. I shut my eyes until the irrational sense of despair ebbs away. Regroup, start again. I'm good at making new starts. Not so good at making them last. I don't need a coffee and a cake anyway.

I walk on. A little way further down the front there's a lit up sign: The Fisherman's Arms.

Fish and chips – now there's a thought. The proper kind, wrapped in newspaper, doused so thoroughly with salt and vinegar that the flavours stick on your tongue, making you thirsty for hours afterwards. Dad used to take us for them on Saturday evenings in summer. We'd find a bench along the front, and the gulls would swoop and dive, squabbling over dropped chips. Bill would chase after them, leaving his chips on the bench to be attacked by other birds. The batter was crisp and the fish was so moist it would just flake apart. How could I have forgotten those fish and chips?

I hurry towards the lit up sign. The pub is neatly whitewashed, and there's a strand of Christmas lights strung inside the bay window. As soon as I open the door, my senses are assaulted by familiar smells: frying food, beer, and wood smoke. The warmth draws me in. I shiver from the sheer pleasure of it.

The pub isn't crowded. A few tables are occupied by couples and families eating fish and chips, and an old man is playing a fruit machine by the door. The room is lit by lanterns and wall lights made from old glass fishing floats. In the corner at the back there's a carved figurehead of a woman with flowing hair trimmed with rose garlands. I recall the odd prickly sensation I had, aged twelve or so, when I first noticed the bare breasts of the figurehead. Even now the carved woman strikes me as garish and risqué.

I approach the bar. Most of the stools are taken. The bartender's back is to me as he pours a measure of whiskey into a glass. But even before he turns around, I *know* him. I had no idea he worked here now, or else I wouldn't have come inside. I should have arranged for a taxi before I arrived, or better yet, rented a car in Glasgow. Now, it's too late. He turns around and spots me. *Byron.*

He stares at me. Long seconds pass. I don't know which is worse: that he recognise me, or not recognise me. Surely, I haven't changed that much…

A smile blooms across his face. He begins walking towards me. His fair hair is longer than it was back then, his skin tanner, like he's been somewhere getting winter sun. He's still big, and though he's wearing a woolly grey fisherman's jumper, looks very fit. His features are bold and handsome, the years making the planes and angles more defined. Byron…

Once I would have done anything for Byron.

'Skye! Skye Turner – it's you, isn't it?'

'Guilty,' I say, then instantly regret it.

Byron engulfs me in his strong arms. He smells of beer and man and it's so familiar that my knees wobble.

'So let's see you.' He holds me at arm's length. 'You look great. What's it been? Ten years?'

'Fifteen,' I say hoarsely.

'Fifteen! Did you hear that, Lachie?'

A ginger-haired man with a scraggly beard turns around on one of the bar stools. I know him too. Lachlan McCray.

'Yeah,' Lachlan says. He doesn't smile or look remotely friendly.

'And you're a celebrity now!' Byron's voice is loud enough that people are starting to look over. He's still holding on to my shoulders.

'No.' I take an awkward step back. 'No, I'm not.'

'Oh, come on,' Byron teases, 'don't be modest. Wee Bill keeps us updated. We've all seen you on YouTube.'

This is getting worse and worse. When I left here everyone knew that I had big dreams. Singing my songs, on my terms, conquering the world with elegant poetry and haunting melodies. Instead I've spent most of the time tarted up in denim and diamonds, singing country music classics in tacky shows and cheap nightclubs. I suppose it was too much to hope for that they didn't know that.

'Great.' I manage not to wince.

'Our own hometown girl made good,' Byron says. 'God, fifteen years! I can't believe it's that long since…'

I brace myself. He cuts off. Lachlan's eyes meet mine. There's a moment of recognition: that this conversation can go nowhere, other than down paths that are best left deserted and overgrown with weeds.

'… since *I left*,' I finish for him.

'Hey, are you staying on for Hogmanay?' Byron deftly changes the subject. 'We could use you. You remember the fire festival, right?'

As if I could ever forget. The fire festival is a big local event that takes in five villages on New Year's Eve. There's a bonfire on the beach, food stalls along the front, carnival rides on the sports field, and a parade of boats trimmed with lights in the harbour. The boats are blessed for winter by the vicar, and one lucky teenage girl gets crowned Queen of the Fleet. The year we turned eighteen, it was Ginny. I remember how beautiful she looked as she sat on the bow of the first boat, her long hair billowing behind her. Not my sort of thing, but I guess I was a little jealous that it wasn't me. And then later on that evening, Byron took my hand by the bonfire. Kissed me and told me that to him I was Queen of the

Universe. And even though I knew we couldn't be forever, it was enough. I wonder if he even remembers that night.

'I'm helping organise the stalls and the entertainment,' he says. 'We've got a ceilidh band lined up. It would be brilliant if you could perform with them. Just a song or two. Our own celebrity!'

I doubt he remembers, and I wish he would drop the groupie act. Byron always had the knack for saying what you wanted to hear exactly when you needed to hear it. I can't let him strip away my defences and reduce me to that needy teenage girl again. The one who wanted praise and recognition for herself, not just to bask in the reflected light of her twin sister. The one who was proud that he loved me best.

'I'm taking a break from performing just now.' I smile casually. 'Recharging my batteries.' Now it's me who's sounding fake, like this is all some kind of restorative trip before I'm on to the next big thing. But what am I supposed to do? Trot out the fact that my Vegas gig dropped me a few months ago? Does that constitute small talk among old friends – first loves – who haven't seen each other for years?

'Right, well, speaking of recharging, what can I get you to drink?' He stands back and peers at me. 'Let's see, what was your poison…? Ah, yes: whiskey and Coke.'

Bile rises in my throat, though I know he's just being hospitable. I like a drink or two – maybe more than I should. But I haven't had so much as a drop of whiskey since leaving here.

'Just a beer, please. A half.'

Byron frowns like he's expecting me to stay all afternoon for a piss-up instead of going to Mum's. Then again, maybe he suspects that I'm here at the pub to delay the inevitable. And maybe I am.

'Actually, I came to find a taxi,' I say. 'There weren't any at the bus stop.'

He goes behind the bar, takes a half pint glass and fills it with rich, amber beer. I take out my card to pay, but he waves it away.

'Lachie can give you a lift,' Byron says. 'Whenever you want.'

I glance over at Lachlan. He's talking to an old man in a deerstalker hat on the stool next to him. He doesn't break off his conversation.

'I don't want to be a bother,' I say. 'Isn't there someone I can call?'

'Lachie's the cabbie,' a woman at the end of the bar says. 'Officially.'

I look over her way and do a double take. She's about sixty, with a wrinkled, heavily made-up face and dyed orange hair that's loose and unkempt around her face. She's wearing a big necklace with macramé beads, and chunky rings on every finger. She wouldn't be out of place at a trucker bar in Tennessee or Arizona, some sad dive where a man passing through can get almost anything for ten bucks. I feel guilty for thinking that, because I also recognise her.

'Aunt Annie?' I say. Byron hands me the half pint.

The woman gives a phlegmy laugh. 'More like grandma now.' She bats a ringed hand in my direction. There's a big gap in the front of her mouth where she's lost a tooth. 'It's been a lot of years, love.'

'I know!' A tiny tear forms in the corner of my eye. Somehow seeing Annie MacClellan makes my being here seem real, even more than seeing Byron.

She cocks her head to look at me. 'You were always in such a hurry to leave. Why bother to come back now?'

There's a barb in her voice that puts me on edge. It's true that when I worked for her, I was always banging on about the life I was going to have once I escaped the misty veils of Eilean Shiel. How Ginny and I were going to become big stars, somewhere better than here. But that was so long ago…

I give her a warm grin to dispel the tension. 'I missed your clootie and black bun, Aunt Annie. They were calling to me from across the miles.'

She laughs again, but her kohl-lined eyes are guarded. I hold the half pint of beer up to my nose and breathe in the hearty, yeasty smell. I don't really want it, but I drink it anyway. I should have laid low and avoided the pub. Eased into things more gradually. Byron, Annie, Lachlan – all here, all different. What will Mum be like after fifteen years?

I choke down the dregs of the beer and put the empty glass on the counter. 'I just need the loo,' I say. 'And then I'm really sorry, Lachlan, but could you give me a lift to the cottage?'

Lachlan turns back, studying me in a way that's a little uncomfortable. We used to think of him as an 'almost' kid. He almost played football at the regionals, got a couple of A-levels and almost went to university. He was never as cool as Byron, or as rich as James. He was never as fun, witty, or clever as the rest of us – or as vain and conceited. Yet Lachlan was always there in the background. Observing. Judging. I'm not looking forward to getting a lift with him.

'Sure,' he says.

'Thanks.' I go to the other side of the bar where a door leads to the loos and the pool tables upstairs. The corridor is unheated and the cold is startling after the warm bar. In the loo I stare for a long time at my reflection in the mirror. When I left here I had just turned twenty. Now, I'm thirty-five. My face is thinner, my dark hair longer. My eyes are my best feature: green flecked with hazel. But in this light, they look almost blue. More like Ginny's.

For the most part, Ginny and I never looked that much alike. She was blonde and fair, and stunningly beautiful. Most people were surprised to learn that we were sisters, let alone twins. Though most people weren't surprised that I was the eldest, if only by a few minutes. Dad used to say that I had an 'old soul'. Ginny, in contrast, was like a little girl who didn't want to grow up. A free spirit; unruly and untameable.

I splash water on my face and put on lip gloss. It's time to go. I can't delay any longer. I need to see Mum. Face Mum. Find out if it's really possible to come home after all the years.

As I re-enter the noisy bar area I imagine that, just for a moment, there's a hush. I hear a voice: Aunt Annie talking to the man next to her: '… dead sister.'

I need to get out of here. Panic begins to well up inside of me, just like earlier on the coach. Panic laced with resignation. Here, I will always be *that* girl, even when I'm as old as Annie MacClellan. Some things you can never escape. I should know. I've been running away for fifteen years. Now I'm right back where I started.

CHAPTER 3

Outside the pub the wind is relentless, whipping the rain diagonally. The boats at anchor creak and groan, and waves batter the stone wall along the front. Almost as soon as I step outside, my coat is soaked through by rain and spray. The good thing about the weather is that there's no question of idly shooting the breeze with Lachlan. Both of us bow our heads and hurry along as quickly as we can.

Lachlan's vehicle, a Nissan Qashqai, is parked up near the bus stop. He beeps the locks and I heft my bag into the back. The Nissan is freezing, but at least it's dry. As soon as I close the door, I experience an odd sensation of light-headedness. I hate being a passenger in a car, with someone else driving. It gives me a panicky sensation of being out of control. At least it's a short journey.

When Lachlan starts the car, the stereo blares on. I recognise the CD: 'Capernaum' by the Tannahill Weavers, a traditional Scottish band. I feel an unexpected rush of nostalgia. When we were teenagers, Ginny knew the words to all their songs, and I'd pick out the chords on the guitar.

Lachlan switches off the music abruptly. 'So how long you back for?' he says. He turns the windscreen wipers on full tilt, but there's still a wall of water in front of us.

'I don't know yet.'

He nods. We drive out of the car park and turn onto the main road that hugs the coastline to the north. I don't need to look at the road signs, written in English and Gaelic. I know the way in my sleep.

'Been a long time that she's been gone,' he says.

It takes me a second to process that he said 'she' instead of 'you'.

'Gone?' I say. 'You mean Ginny? Ginny's dead.' The word echoes through the car, drowning out the sound of the rain. I grip the door handle tightly wishing I could get out and walk.

'Yeah. That's what I mean.' He sighs. 'A couple days ago on the radio I heard that song you two used to sing. You know, "The Bonny Swans"? Man, that is some dark shite.' He gives an awkward laugh. 'The part about the harp?'

I laugh too, because it's either that or be freaked out. 'The Bonny Swans' is based on a traditional murder ballad called 'The Cruel Sister'. In the song, the dark-haired eldest girl drowns her sister because she wants her lover, a prince, for herself. A miller makes a harp of the dead girl's breastbone, using strands of her golden hair for its strings. He takes the harp to the castle and sets it before the king and the dark sister who is now the queen. The harp begins to play alone, singing that the queen murdered her sister.

The version we used to sing was by Loreena McKennitt, the Canadian folk singer. Ginny had a pure, clear voice just like hers – a special voice that was destined for great things. We'd sing that song, and we'd laugh, and it would be funny and silly. We loved to sing macabre songs. Back when we had no real experience of death.

'It's a very old song,' I say. 'A lot of them were pretty dark.'

'Yeah,' Lachlan says. 'Maybe I'm too sentimental, but I like the old songs. I wish they had a traditional music session here. I keep telling Byron he should start one at the Arms. But he's tone deaf. Not interested.'

'That's a shame,' I say. In truth, I'm relieved that there isn't a local session. When Dad was alive we went to one nearly every week at a nearby pub or village hall. Musicians would come from miles around to play music, talk Gaelic and have a few laughs. People took turns leading and calling the tunes. There was no written music; if you didn't know the song, you improvised.

Depending on who turned up, the same tunes might sound completely different from one week to the next. As the night went on and the pints flowed freely, the songs would start. I remember Dad, tears running down his face as he sang 'Ae Fond Kiss', or 'Ye Banks and Braes' in his raspy voice, while all the other stalwart, hard men joined in. Those nights were magical. The best of my life, I think.

Thanks to Lachlan, 'The Bonny Swans' lodges itself firmly in my head and repeats over and over in an endless loop. I sit in silence as we continue to drive. The road weaves its way around small coves dotted with houses and then turns to single track as it curves out towards the headland. As the rain sheets down in front of the headlamps, it's as if we're driving to the edge of the world.

'I've thought a lot about that night,' Lachlan says. 'I guess it changed me. It was such a terrible thing. So… unexpected.'

I don't answer. I suppose I have to accept that this is all part of my punishment. For staying away and… for coming back. In a way it's a relief to have it out in the open. That he's not simply going to pretend, the way Byron did, that we're all just old friends, happily reunited.

'I mean, you probably don't want to talk about it,' he adds. 'But sometimes I wonder what *really* happened, you know?'

'No,' I say flatly, 'I don't. We all know what happened.'

Everyone but me, I don't add. I have no memory at all of that night.

'Yeah, you're right…' He hesitates for a second. 'It's just that there was some talk in the village, a while back now—'

'Please, Lachlan,' I say. 'Can we talk about something else?'

'Sure, sorry.' He squints at the dark road ahead.

'No, it's fine.' I swallow hard. 'It's just that I'm here to see Mum. Not to dredge up what happened back then. I miss Ginny every second of every day. She was my twin. And I don't know – maybe it sounds harsh – but I've tried to move on. You know?'

'Yeah, I get it.' He glances at me with a smile that's almost wistful. Byron used to tease that he had a crush on me. I never believed it then, and it's totally irrelevant now. 'Anyway, it's good to see you.'

'Thanks,' I say. I can't quite bring myself to return the compliment.

'I'm sure your mum will be happy you're back,' he adds. 'We haven't seen much of her lately. Not since her fall.'

The mention of Mum's fall catches me a little off guard. I know I shouldn't be surprised – in a place like this there are no secrets. In fact, he probably knows much more than I do about Mum's general 'state', which my brother has alluded to in his emails without saying very much at all.

'Yes, well, I'm hoping I can help her out while I'm here.'

'Yeah. I guess she keeps busy with the holiday lets,' he says, signalling a clear change in subject. 'Good decision she made on those.'

I know a little about Mum's renovation of the two stone farm buildings on the property that she did a few years back. Apparently she took out a mortgage on the cottage (that in itself was a big deal: my parents always despised things like banks and debt) and got a local builder to gut everything other than the outer walls. She got planning consent and the necessary licenses all on her own. I'd thought at the time that if she did all that, she must be fine. I wanted to believe it…

'She's had them rented out all summer,' he adds. 'One's even rented now.'

'Really?' I manage a little laugh. 'Who'd want to come here in December?'

'Some artist from down south.' He wrinkles his nose dismissively. 'Haven't seen much of him.'

'He's probably frozen solid.'

'Yeah.'

Lachlan turns onto a gravel road that runs along a narrow neck of land jutting out into the sea. Beyond, the dark hills of the headland rise up. Technically, the headland where Mum's cottage is located was once an island, but a nineteenth-century crofter filled in the narrow inlet with boulders and rubble to build the track. On the other side of the inlet, there's a small tract of woodland: mossy oak and rhododendron. The track dips down into a little sheltered area where the cottages are located. We reach a gate. I'm about to brave the rain and climb out to open it – something I've done thousands of times. This time, though, Lachlan jumps out first.

He opens the gate, gets back inside the car soaked, and drives through. I stay put as he gets out again and closes it. No point in us both getting wet. A few minutes later, we pull into the yard of Croft Cottage. There's a yellow glow of light coming from inside. A figure at the kitchen window. My stomach is tied in knots. *Mum.*

CHAPTER 4

Lachlan parks in front of the cottage and tosses my bag out onto the wet gravel. I sit in the car staring at the rain streaming down the windscreen. Now that I've come all this way, it seems impossible to go the last few metres that will take me back to the place where I grew up and reunite me with the most important living person in my life. My own mother, whom I've conveniently allowed to slip into the mists of the past like those childhood memories... because that's the way she wanted it.

The words that were spoken so long ago gouge their way into my head:

I know it's wrong, but I do blame her...

My hand is clamped to the door handle like a claw. Lachlan frowns as he comes back to the car. 'You OK?' he says.

'Fine.' I loosen my grip; make an effort to smile. 'Just delaying the soaking. How much do I owe you?'

'There's no charge.' I sense he's not fooled by the brave act I'm putting on. I'm terrified. I'm sure he's noticed. 'Buy us a round down the pub when you get settled in.'

'I'll do that,' I say. 'Thanks so much for the lift.'

'Sure thing.'

'And now... I'd better make a run for it.'

I get out of the Nissan, grab my bag and run to the porch. I'm relieved that he doesn't wait around until I'm inside. The yellow beams of the headlamps pass over me as the car reverses and drives off with a crunch of gravel.

The cottage is different than when I was here last. The door is painted a pretty shade of cornflower blue, and on the step there's a pair of floral-patterned welly boots and a basket with seashells and pebbles from the beach. Before, there were always pairs of muddy boots, old skates, fossil rocks and bicycles cluttered around the porch. Even the stream of water coming from the gutter seems orderly. I guess that's what Mum's like now that she's been living on her own for all these years. The tide of guilt surges again and I close my eyes until it passes. I've done what I've done, and I have no idea what kind of reception I'm going to get. Will I see judgment in her eyes, recriminations? Will she look at me and immediately think of Ginny? Or will there be no recognition at all?

It's time to face up to the answer. I focus on the one solid inimitable fact, clinging to it like a little plant on the edge of a cliff.

She's my mum, and I love her.

I knock on the door. The dripping rain marks time as I wait. There's no sound from inside. Another change from when I was growing up and we always had at least one dog, sometimes as many as three, who used to bark when people came to the door.

Now the silence is unsettling. Mum was in the kitchen, surely she saw the car pull up. With every long second, my heart beats faster. In years past, Bill's emails were usually along the lines of: 'I know you're busy, but it would be great if you could give Mum a call,' or 'Just a reminder that it's Mum's birthday next week.' But in the last few years, they've been more carefully worded. 'Mum's having a little trouble remembering things.' 'Mum sometimes gets disoriented.' And in the last few months, more pointed: 'Look, we need to talk. I can't do this alone.' I never knew how to respond to those messages. It hurt knowing that my brother probably thought the worst, thinking me callous and indifferent. And maybe I should have told him the reason I stayed away for all those years. Maybe it's not too late…

I knock again, harder this time. I begin to shiver and not just from the cold.

And then finally I hear it: a sound from inside. Slow footsteps approaching the door. A dull thudding in between each step. The chain rattles. The door opens.

'Mum,' I say, my voice hoarse.

She's smaller and slighter than I remember, with bobbed hair that's gone completely white. But the warm scent of lavender and apple hasn't changed. Her face is lined, but her hazel-green eyes are the same.

'Skye…?' She lifts a hand almost to my face, and I can see that it's trembling. And then I lose it completely. I open my arms, and crush her inside of them. My tears fall into her hair, and she's shaking as I hold her. But I'm smiling too, and somewhere inside of me the sun is trying to burst through what had seemed like impenetrable clouds.

She recovers before I do, pulling away to hold me at arm's length. 'It really is you,' she says, a quaver in her voice.

Whatever I was going to say at this moment – whatever I'd rehearsed – all falls by the wayside. Right now there's no room for all the apologies that will need to be said, on my part at least. It's as if a bubble has closed around us, two people whose lives are inextricably linked. At this moment, I am glad that I am alive.

'Yes,' I say. 'It's so good to see you.'

'You're soaked through.' She falls into the role of caregiver. 'I'll put the kettle on.'

She begins to move towards the kitchen and I realise why it took her so long to answer the door. She's leaning on a wooden cane, her left foot in a dark nylon sock but no shoe. Her walk is slow and stiff, her back hunched over. I'm a little shocked. Mum was always so robust. A pillar supporting our family, almost frighteningly strong. Now, though, she looks… old.

I take off my wet coat and hang it on a peg beside the door, adding my boots to the neat line of shoes underneath. The cottage too seems smaller, the ceiling lower than I've remembered. Certainly, it never used to be so tidy. When I was nineteen and Bill was sixteen, our stuff was everywhere. Bill was into racing bicycles and wanted to compete in the Tour de France – a goal that ended as soon as he got his driving license. I remember his huge bike parked in this room, along with his shinty stick, ice skates, and rugby kit. There was also the music equipment: guitars and stands, amps, cases – it's a wonder that there was room for any furniture or people.

Now all of that is gone. There's a sofa along the far wall and two armchairs in front of the fireplace. It might be our old sofa and chairs, but if so, they've been recovered with blue corduroy fabric, accented with blue and white floral cushions. The nostalgic part of me had hoped to see a tree up; Mum went all out for Christmas when we were growing up. Now, though, it could be any time of year.

In a way, I'm relieved that so much has changed. Maybe Mum felt the need to extract and extinguish the memories and grief of that time, just like I did. She didn't have the luxury of running halfway around the world to do it. She had to be content with new sofa coverings and cushions.

My eye is drawn to the photos on the mantle shelf. However long I stay, there will be many things that I have to face. This is one of them.

I look at each photo, trying to remain impassive. If we were a normal family, I might be a little put out that most of them are of Bill, his wife, Fiona, and their three kids. There's a wedding photo; a photo of the five of them on a beach holding up a huge fish; Bill holding a baby in his arms; two toddlers and a little girl together in a bathtub making funny faces; the same little girl sitting at a piano. As I move down the row to the last three photos, my throat tightens. There's a photo of Ginny and me on a stage singing into microphones, and our school photos from our last year.

I stare at Ginny's school photo. Maybe it's the fact that no one ever looks good in a school photo, but she seems somehow *less* than the girl in my memory. Less beautiful, less talented. It's as if the camera couldn't capture the essence of her: her wonderful spirit, the light in her eyes. I feel an overwhelming surge of grief. The real Ginny – my Ginny – is gone.

'I've got shortbread and ginger biscuits. Which would you prefer?'

Mum has come back into the room. She leans on her cane and watches me looking at the photos. The crinkle between her brows gets a little deeper. But biscuits is a topic I can handle. 'I'll have shortbread,' I say. 'But I can get it.'

She waves away my offer of assistance. I follow her into the kitchen. Over the years, I've bought Scottish shortbread occasionally from the supermarket, or else people have given it to me as a gift at Christmas thinking that I would enjoy a little 'taste of home'. But it's never been the same as Mum's shortbread, so rich and melt-in-the-mouth buttery.

Mum leans her cane against the sink and pours boiling water from the kettle into the teapot. It's the same teapot with pink roses on a gold trellis that I remember from my childhood. It looks out of place, unstuck in time. Everything else has changed so much. The walls that were once yellow have been repainted a neutral cream. There are new worktops, and the big wooden table that took up almost the entire room has been replaced by a smaller one made of light wood. The front of the fridge that used to be covered with certificates, reminders, and letters from school is now bare except for a red-striped tea towel hanging on a magnetic hook. Near the back door, there's a recycling bin. On top is a tartan packet: Walkers Shortbread. Was Mum's shortbread always from a packet? Did I only imagine that it was homemade?

I hover awkwardly. 'I love what you've done with the place,' I say, trying small talk. Mum puts the teapot on a tray, along with two cups and the plate of biscuits. I angle in to pick up the tray, but Mum blocks me. The dishes rattle unsteadily as she takes a tentative step towards the table without her cane. I hold my breath, ready to catch her...

She brings the tray to a successful landing on the table.

'Please sit down,' she says.

I sit. She scrapes back a chair and lowers herself down on it. I can see the sharp bones of her shoulders underneath her blue cotton blouse.

'The house needed doing.' Mum sets out the cups: white with gold rims, not the blue stoneware mugs we had before, and pours the tea. 'Annie, from the village, helped me. She's remarried now to a carpenter. Greg.'

'I saw her in the pub when I was getting a taxi.' I take a sip of the tea: a mix of rosehip and Earl Grey. 'She seems, um... different.'

'Well, I guess we're all different.' Mum winces as she takes a sip of her tea, like she's burned her throat.

'Yes.' I'm not sure how to respond to this undeniable fact. Older, sadder, and probably not an awful lot wiser. In my case, at least. 'I saw Byron too, tending bar. And Lachlan is the taxi driver. But I'm sure you know that.'

She stares down into her teacup like she doesn't know what to say. Any more than I do.

'Yes,' she says. 'And there's a man staying at one of the cottages. The smaller one: "Skybird".'

Skybird... Why did Mum choose that name? 'Skybird' was one of the last songs Ginny and I wrote together. It was our eighteen-year-old take on the legend of Tristan and Isolde. Isolde stands by the shore waiting for her lover to return. She sees a boat on the horizon with black sails, which means that Tristan is dead. As Isolde throws herself into the sea and drowns, a flock of crows flies off the masts to reveal white sails. Tristan sees Isolde floating on the water, the birds circling around her body.

Most of our songs from back then were laughably bad. But we were proud of 'Skybird'. I can still hear my sister singing the chorus, in her high, pure voice: *Fly bird, skyward, bring my love home to me.* When Ginny sustained a note, the vibrato sounded as if something was spinning, like a perfect snowflake whirling and turning carelessly as it falls from the sky.

I shudder and take another sip of tea. Mum too seems stunned by a memory. I surreptitiously push my plate of shortbread towards her and she eats it without realising. 'It will be nice to have music again in the house now that Skye is home,' she says. 'I'm looking forward to that. You can sing…'

My hand pauses with the teacup raised halfway to my mouth.

'I've missed hearing your beautiful voice, Ginny.'

The words from Bill's last email flash into my mind. 'Most of the time she's fine. But sometimes, she loses the plot.'

My hand jitters and I set down the cup. I wish I'd emailed back and asked what to do. Do I take the tough-love approach and calmly inform her that she will not be hearing Ginny's beautiful voice ever again because Ginny is dead? Or do I change the subject and hope she snaps out of it?

I try the latter approach.

'So when is Bill coming? I'm really looking forward to seeing the kids. It's been a while.' I ramble on. 'I saw them about eighteen months ago, did he tell you? They went to Disney World in Florida. I had a gig in Charlotte – that's in North Carolina – so I popped down and saw them for the weekend.'

I watch her face. Whatever temporary bubble world she was in a moment ago seems to have shattered. Her face goes blank and she looks confused. She opens her mouth and closes it again without speaking.

'I got a few gifts on my way here,' I continue. 'Just little stuff. And do you think we might have a tree? I mean, I don't want to add extra work for you – or me—' I laugh awkwardly. 'But it would be nice for the kids. Are the decorations still in the attic? I could get them down…'

Mum sighs. I sense that she's fully back now and reality is not as nice as the fugue world. 'Your dad used to hit his head every year on that beam getting those boxes down,' she says. 'Do you remember?'

'I do,' I say, feeling a sharp pang of loss. Dad was a gentle, unassuming man with a kind word and comforting saying for every situation. He drove almost a hundred miles each day in his little red van, delivering the post to the villages and farms near the coast. He never missed a day of work no matter what the weather. Music was Dad's passion. He played guitar and whistle, and we spent a few summers in ear-splitting discomfort when he tried and failed to learn the pipes. He loved a good rousing Jacobite song, belting out in his terrible singing voice the praises of Bonnie Prince Charlie, while the rest of us tapped our feet and laughed. Like Dad, I took to playing instruments. By the time I was twelve, I could play guitar, mandolin, fiddle, bodhrán, and keyboards. Ginny played guitar and she taught herself to play a Celtic harp that someone in the village was getting rid of. But mostly, Ginny was the singer, the star performer. We made a great team.

And then, when I was sixteen, Dad died. One morning on his rounds, he stopped to help a farmer deliver a breached calf in a driving rainstorm. That night he came down with a cold that turned into pneumonia. He tried to joke about it: 'Feels like an elephant on my chest,' and 'Caught a wee nip, but I'll be right as rain.' We believed him: Dad never lied, and no one dies of pneumonia in this day and age. The doctor came and Dad was taken to hospital. I think his greatest tragedy was that he died there, instead of at home. He was lucky, though, to be spared what happened later.

Mum accepted Dad's death with a stiff upper lip wrought from Scottish steel. I remember her standing next to his coffin during the service, her mouth in a thin, flat line. Maybe it was Dad's death that began our family's slow, downwards spiral. I don't know. When Dad died, I lost the person I loved most in the world. But when Ginny died three years later, it was like half of my soul was extinguished forever.

And Mum… Dad's death affected her more than she let us see. She became harder, sharper – on the outside, at least. At night, though, I'd sometimes hear her talking to him, as if he were there with her in her room. I'd sometimes hear her cry.

She didn't cry when Ginny died. Maybe she did, later on. I didn't stick around long enough to find out.

I smile wistfully at Mum. 'I do remember. It was the only time he ever swore.'

'Yes, your dad didn't like swearing.' Mum pours the last of the tea into my cup. 'He used to say that we're smarter than that, we have a better vocabulary and don't have to use that kind of language.'

'Yeah,' I say fondly. That was such a *Dad* thing to say.

'Anyway…' Mum shrugs, 'the boxes are still there if you want to get them down. Obviously, being here alone most years, I haven't bothered.'

I analyse her manner to see if that's meant as a dig or a guilt trip. As far as I can tell, though, she's just stating a fact.

'I understand,' I say neutrally. 'Can I do anything else? I'd like to help out while I'm here.'

Mum gives me a sideways frown almost like I'm a stranger. Is this how it's going to be? Am I going to worry over each look, each cloud passing over her face? Worry that she doesn't know me; that she doesn't want me here after all?

'I mean, that way you can rest your leg,' I continue. 'I can go to the shops for you or help with tidying up. I must admit, though, I'm still a terrible cook.' I give her a sheepish grin. 'So you might not want to delegate that.'

I begin piling the dishes onto the tray. I'm trying hard. Too hard. Mum doesn't respond. It's killing me that she seems so bland. So entirely lacking in any kind of sparkle or warmth or wit – not like I remember her at all. Mum was always the smartest person I knew. She taught maths at the local school up until the time Dad passed. I was never very good at schoolwork, and I was a genius compared to Ginny. No, in our family, Mum was the quick, intelligent one. But time, grief, and tragedy seem to have dulled that edge, put out that fire.

I stand up to take the tray to the sink. Mum pushes her chair back too, as if she's trying to beat me to it.

'It's OK,' I say with a brittle smile. 'I can do the washing-up.' In my peripheral vision, I'm aware of her levering herself to her feet, gripping the edge of the table and the chair. The chair wobbles precariously. A knot of tension forms in my chest. Her cane is still leaning against the cabinets near where I'm standing. I grab it and hold it out to her.

'Here, Mum,' I say. 'Do you need this?'

She ignores me again and hobbles over to the sink, wincing a little. She props against the edge and runs the water, waiting for it to get hot.

'You must be tired after your long journey,' Mum says, not looking at me. 'Why don't you have a rest? I'll heat up some stew for supper.'

'I can do—' I start to say. Her shoulders stiffen. I break off, leaning the cane back where it was. 'That sounds good, thanks.' I hold in a sigh. It's clear that the only way to end this odd little power struggle is for me to give in.

For the first time since I arrived, a smile ghosts across her face. Mum squirts soap in the sink. I notice that her good ankle is shaking a little from the effort of supporting all of her weight. I look away. I can't watch. I need space… air…

'You're in your old room,' Mum says.

My old room. I was expecting that, and yet, the words make my skin feel clammy.

'Um, OK.' I squeeze out the words. 'And I might have a quick shower. Travel makes me feel so grimy.'

'Yes,' she says. 'Fine.'

'Thanks.'

I'm in such a hurry to get out of the kitchen that I trip over the little ridge of carpet on my way to the sitting room and I have to grab the wall to steady myself. I get my suitcase and handbag to take upstairs. My eyes snag once again on the photos. *The* photo. Yes, it's a terrible school photo, and we always hated having those taken. But from this angle, I get the feeling that Ginny is looking back at me… and laughing.

CHAPTER 5

Mum asked for me: she must want me here. So why not accept my help? It's painful to feel like such a complete stranger, especially in a place that's so familiar. Too familiar...

As I climb the stairs, my suitcase feels heavier with each step. There's a hallway at the top that leads to the three bedrooms and the bathroom. The hall has been repainted, the white walls bare, except for a few framed needlepoints and an oil painting of Glenfinnan that looks like it came from a charity shop. The old burgundy carpet runner has been replaced with one in dark beige. For a second, I allow myself to feel hopeful. Maybe Mum's redone all the bedrooms too, making each one into a neat, cosy space with white walls, flat-packed furniture, and a pot of heather on the windowsill. If that's the case, then maybe everything will be fine. Maybe...

I continue past Mum's room, Bill's old room, and the bathroom. Each step is unbearable as I approach the room at the end of the hall that I shared with my sister for almost twenty years. The moment I see the sign on the door, all hope evaporates: *Stage door*. My hand shakes as I turn the knob and switch on the light.

Mum hasn't changed one single thing. The room is a time capsule, a wormhole to a different decade. It's a shrine not only to my sister, but to our lives back then. A memorial to everything that was lost.

I feel sick as I step inside, leaving the door open. There are two single beds, one on either side of a gabled window. I go over to the bed that was once mine and fling my bag onto it. Above the pine headboard there's a poster of Bob Dylan and Joan Baez, an original from the 1963 civil rights rally. Dad won it in a raffle. When Bob Dylan was awarded the Nobel Prize for Literature in 2016, I thought of that poster and about getting another copy. But seeing it here now, I'm glad I didn't. There are other posters and flyers pinned to the wall around the room. Ginny's Oasis poster: when she was sixteen, she had a mega crush on Noel Gallagher. There are also flyers for pub gigs that happened years in the past, a poster for the Hebridean Celtic Festival, and a picture of Billy Ray Cyrus torn from a magazine. I have the urge to rip them all down, but the memories seem tainted and I don't want to touch them.

I venture across the braided rug to Ginny's side. Her Celtic harp is in the corner next to the wardrobe. I pluck one of the red strings: 'C'. It's flat. I think of that awkward conversation in the car with Lachlan: 'The Bonny Swans' and the chilling sound of the harp as it magically weaves its tale, unmasking the guilt of the cruel sister. I shudder. Maybe I can move the harp up to the attic while I'm here.

I go back to my own side and open my suitcase. I unpack a few books, setting them on the bedside table. They look unfamiliar and out of place. I take out a change of clothes and my toiletries bag. A shower is what I need. Or better yet, a hot bath.

When I'm back out in the hallway, I feel an almost giddy sense of relief. I've stayed in lots of dive motels when I've been between gigs, flats, or men. Some places were so bad: noisy, grubby, lonely – or all three – that they were almost worse than having no place to sleep. Right now, any of them seem better than my old room. If I'm going to stay here, even for a short time to help Mum out, then I'll have to do something about it. I can't live in a shrine.

I carry my things to the bathroom. What does that room say about Mum's state of mind? Does she keep it that way because she's afraid of the memories slipping away? I think of how Mum used to talk to Dad after he died, and her earlier 'slip of the tongue' about Ginny singing. Is there a part of her that honestly believes that one day, Ginny might miraculously return from the dead and need a bed for the night?

No. I don't believe that. Mum's too strong, too stoical for that. Too much of a realist. At least, she *was* back then.

In the bathroom, the avocado sink and toilet have been replaced with white, which is a big improvement. The cast iron bath on claw feet is still there. I turn on the taps and wait until the water runs hot before putting in the plug. Mum used to bath all three of us kids together in this tub until we were about nine years old. Even after that we all had to use the same water. The cottage has a rainwater cistern, and even though it rains a lot we still had to ration the water. Maybe that's no longer the case, but I'm not taking any chances.

I undress and slip into the water. It's so hot that it's almost scalding. I quickly run some cold water and swish it around to the back of the tub. I don't want to use too much. Once the hot water is gone, it's gone.

When the temperature is right, I put a towel behind my head and stare at the steam rising upwards to the ceiling. The light fitting is the same: a round half-globe letting off a pale yellow glow, speckled with shadows of dead moths. I've lain here so many times, warm and contented. But the last time I lay here was the night before I left for good, six weeks after my sister died. I had already packed my rucksack and my guitar. The coach ticket was in my bag, my place at the audition in Glasgow confirmed. And yet, I was wracked with indecision. How could I leave Mum after everything we'd been through? How would I ever be brave enough to make my escape, like I'd dreamed of doing for so many years, without my sister by my side?

In my mind's eye, I can see my younger self. Getting out of the bath, my mind made up. I'd tell Mum that I wasn't going. That my place was with my family, together in our grief. Maybe there'd be another opportunity. Eventually… someday. But deep down, I knew that my chance was unlikely to come again.

I went downstairs. I'd planned on making Mum a cup of tea, sitting her down, having a conversation. She'd said precious little to me after I came home from hospital after my car accident. She'd gone about the necessary tasks: arranging the memorial service for Ginny, graciously accepting casseroles, pies, and condolences. Even six weeks on there was a steady stream of visitors and well-wishers. People who 'couldn't believe it' and 'couldn't get over such a terrible tragedy'. The kettle was on permanent boil. But *we* hadn't spoken, not really. Because what was there to say?

I paused at the door to the kitchen. Mum was talking on the phone to someone. Normally, I would just march in and make myself a snack or a cup of tea, leaving the dishes by the sink for Mum to wash. But this time, something held me back.

'… seeing her, I'm just constantly reminded…'

I knew I should go back upstairs, or else come into the room and have Mum alter her conversation accordingly. But I stood rigid, rooted to the spot.

'… off to live her dream, and that's for the best.'

I gripped the edge of the doorframe, my pulse exploding in my head.

'Yes, I know it's wrong, but I do blame her…'

I'd run outside then. Banging the front door. Waiting for her to suss out that I'd overheard. Waiting for her to follow me. Take it all back. What she said, and what she… felt.

She didn't do so.

The light shade blurs as my eyes fill with tears. In a way, Mum's icy arrow of blame was the thing I needed to set me free. I'd felt like I was doing the right thing when I got on that coach and passed through the misty veils of Eilean Shiel. Mum was right to blame me. I'd failed to protect my sister.

CHAPTER 6

'Skye?'

I jolt upright with a splash of cold water. The bath... I'm in the bath. A moment ago the water was steaming, now it's cold and filmy. A moment ago I was standing outside the kitchen door overhearing that awful conversation. A moment ago... fifteen years ago.

I've rationalised it over and over, many times. Mum was grieving. She didn't mean what she said. Or if she did, it was just at that particular moment, the hurt and pain frozen like a fly in a bubble of amber. She didn't know I overheard, so she didn't know how it affected me, how deeply it lacerated what was left of my heart. In my darkest times – and sometimes happy ones too – I've thought about coming home. Dreamed about having a normal life: laughter, tears, arguments and hugs with what was left of my family. But each time I came to the same conclusion: Mum was better off without me. Better off without my presence bringing back bad memories. After all, she had Bill, a much more complete human being than I'll ever be; she had her friends and her charity work at the church and the WI. She never asked for me, or expressed a wish that I return. I concluded that she too thought it best that I stay away.

And now I've been back for less than an hour. It's little consolation to feel that maybe we were both right.

'Hi, Mum,' I say, loud enough for her to hear through the door. 'I think I must have nodded off. Jet lag's a killer.' I feel awful that

Mum's had to come all the way up the stairs to get me, when I'm supposed to be helping her.

'Supper's ready,' she says.

'Sure, I'll be down in a minute.'

I sweep the bad memories from my mind. The fact is that after her fall, she *did* ask for me. That's a positive thing. Something to grab and hang on to. This will be the first Christmas we've had together as a family since before I left. Mum, Bill, his wife Fiona and their three kids, me. When I embarked on the long journey from America to Eilean Shiel, I even dared to hope that if we were all together once again, then maybe we could make some shiny new memories. Maybe I'm just being daft, but I'm determined to try.

I get out of the bath, dry off and put on clean clothing. Mum's gone by the time I leave the bathroom. I can hear her footsteps as she makes her way slowly down the stairs. *Cane, foot, foot, cane.* Her fall happened almost three weeks ago, so I guess she must have decided not to move downstairs to sleep on the sofa, like I would have done. According to Bill's emails, she's had a nurse from the local GP practice looking in on her, as well her best friend Lorna and a gaggle of church and WI friends. Does she accept help from them? Let them make the tea, carry the tray, and do the washing-up?

I put on a pair of furry slippers and pad downstairs, pausing just outside the door to the kitchen where I stood all those years ago. I steel myself; I'm going to make this work. I want to be here – home after so long. I want to get to know Mum again and not be strangers. More than anything, I just want things to be 'normal' between us.

Whatever that means.

I enter the kitchen, noting that Mum's set everything out on the table already, the food in blue and white stoneware dishes. 'It smells delicious,' I say, keeping a smile on my face even as I watch the excruciating process of her sitting down in the chair again.

'I remember you always liked your stew,' she says.

I feel happy hearing that. She's made an effort – a huge effort in her current state – to make my favourite meal. Maybe I need to stop over-analysing everything and let her treat me like a guest if that's what she wants. In addition to the stew, there's also neeps and tatties – turnips and potatoes – and parsnips. I haven't had a parsnip since I was here last: I don't even know if they have them in America. Maybe they're called something else like courgette is called zucchini and aubergine is called eggplant. I say as much to Mum, more to make conversation than because I expect her to be interested in the international nomenclature for root vegetables.

'Your dad loved parsnips,' is all she says. That ends that conversation.

Mum is quiet as we serve ourselves. I feel nervous and on edge and ramble on making small talk. What's the weather supposed to be like? Is it still possible to take the path out to the beach? Oh, and by the way, Byron asked me to play at the festival. (Nervous laugh.) *As if.*

Mum answers in a patient monotone. Whenever I pause to take a breath, the silence is heavy and cloying. I wish I knew how to dispel the tension, but it's hard when I don't want to bring up anything relating to the time when I left, or my fifteen year exile, or… much at all really. Maybe that's how she feels too. If so, this is either going to be a very long visit… or a very short one.

Mum is animated only on two topics of conversation: the cottages and Bill's upcoming visit. She fills in more details about the refurbishment of the old farm buildings. 'The Stables', closest to the main house, now sleeps eight people, and the smaller cottage – 'Skybird' – sleeps four; six if you use the sofa bed.

'What about the chap who's there now?' I ask, hoping to keep her talking. 'How long is he staying?'

'Through the holidays,' Mum says. 'I gather that he's been through a nasty divorce. That sort of thing is difficult this time of year.'

'I'm sure.'

'He keeps to himself.' Her brow wrinkles. 'He didn't even want to come in for a cup of tea when he arrived.'

'Sounds dodgy.'

She shrugs. 'I don't think so. I've seen him on the beach a few times with his dog. I guess he's just… grieving.' Her eyes glaze over. 'Everyone does that in their own way, in their own time.'

'I guess so.' Once again it feels like we're being sat on by the elephant in the room. I pounce on the other 'safe' topic of conversation.

'So are Bill and the family, um… all going to stay upstairs?'

'Oh no. There wouldn't be room.' Mum spoons the last of the vegetables onto my plate. I hide a wince. Parsnips are one of those things that taste better in my memory than they do in real life. 'They'll stay in the Stables. It will be much more comfortable.'

I wish I had a family of eight so that I could stay in the Stables. I'm tempted to ask if I can sleep in Bill's old room, but I know it's best to leave it for now. There will be plenty of time to broach uncomfortable subjects if and when they come up. Right now, I just want to get through dinner.

Mum pushes her chair back. I abandon the parsnip. I simply *cannot* watch her clear away and wash up these plates. The battle lines are drawn and I'm going to cross them. Mum makes to stand up, but I'm faster.

'Let me.' I practically grab her plate away and whisk it over to the sink.

Mum sighs. 'Don't be silly, I can do it later.'

I feel a satisfied flash of victory as she lowers herself back down in the chair.

'There's no pudding,' she says. 'I don't eat many sweets. I hope you're OK with biscuits. The ginger ones are home-made.'

Why didn't she say so before?

'Great, Mum,' I say. 'Your ginger biscuits are the best.'

'Yes, well. Ginny used to think so. I always thought *you* preferred shortbread.'

My sister's name is like a flare fired across enemy lines. It catches me off guard. Is Mum admonishing me for liking shop-bought biscuits better than her homemade ones? Is this yet another way in which I was an inferior daughter to her than Ginny?

'I like both,' I say. I fill the kettle with water and switch it on. I let the water run and squirt suds into the sink to make a start on the dishes. 'But I don't eat many sweets either.' I give her a quick glance over my shoulder. She's frowning in my direction.

'Yes,' she says. 'You do seem very thin. I suppose it's that glamorous lifestyle, or whatever.'

I don't really know what to say. I take one of the used knives and scrape just a little harder than necessary at the black residue at the bottom of the stew container. I must stop thinking that everything is a little dig. She's probably struggling too as to what to say to me, how to talk to me after so long. How to broach the pile of unspoken issues, that with each minute of small talk is growing higher, like a rampant weed.

'I do have a busy life,' I say. 'And I eat on the go a lot.' The kettle switches off. I dry my hands and pour water into the teapot. It's a relief to be able to make the tea and do the washing-up, anything to be useful. Anything to prove that I have a place here. 'But I really want to slow down a little while I'm here. And also help you out.' I take a breath. This feels like one of those now or never moments. 'I mean... umm... is your leg going to be OK? Are you in any pain?'

'It's fine,' Mum says with a little tsk. 'It was only a hairline fracture and some pulled ligaments. Your brother shouldn't have made such a fuss.'

Ask her... A voice screams in my head. Why did she go there? What was she doing? Why did she go out onto the treacherous rocks below the lighthouse at Shiel Point? The place where my sister died. I have to know, and yet, I don't want to. What if she…? What if the person who found her, crumpled in a heap in the freezing rain, hadn't come along?

'Um, I'm really glad you're OK,' I say. My small victories topple, shot through the heart. I can't do it. I'm too much of a coward. I have no right to ask her about… anything really. Not now, when I'm less a welcome guest than a total stranger. 'I hope you'll let me help out while I'm here,' I repeat dumbly.

Mum purses her lips. 'And how long exactly are you staying?' she says.

I take the teapot over to the table. My hands shake as I put it down and bring over the milk and sugar, and the plate of ginger biscuits. 'I don't know, Mum,' I say. 'I'm kind of… at a crossroads right now.' I don't elaborate. She doesn't ask me to. My life in America is riddled with things I'd rather Mum didn't know about. I've literally had nightmares over whether she's seen the tacky videos on YouTube that people have occasionally posted of me performing in some dead-end gig. But that's just the tip of the iceberg. There's the fractured relationships, the substance issues, the frequent 'lack of a permanent address' that sums up my lifestyle. My propensity to run away from my problems, rather than face them. And here we are, case in point…

'I definitely plan to stay through the holidays – if that's OK,' I say. 'But if you don't need me here after that, then I can… make other arrangements.'

I wait for her to answer – it's killing me that she's taking so long. I feel a pesky bout of tears coming on.

'You know that you can stay as long as you like,' she says.

I'm so grateful that I want to hug her. I pour the tea and put a splash of milk in Mum's cup, and two sugars in mine. How Mum takes her tea seems as familiar to me as my own reflection. That gives me a glimmer of hope.

'Thanks,' I say. I take a long sip of tea. This time when I look around the kitchen I notice the things that are familiar. The recipe books on the shelf of the china cabinet, a vase filled with shells and sea glass, a framed needlepoint of thistles and forget-me-nots that one of Mum's friends did for her when Dad died. Little things that make a place feel like home.

I take my cup over to the sink and finish the washing-up. I'm aware of Mum hoisting herself out of the chair. This time, though, she seems resigned to using her cane. As I'm drying the last dish, she comes over and takes a cloth from a pile by the sink. She goes back to the table and wipes it down. I don't try to step in. Maybe in order for her to accept any help, she first needs to prove she doesn't need it. Fair enough.

'Good,' I say, hanging the tea towel back on the fridge to dry. 'Job done.'

'Do you need anything else?' Mum says. 'Hot milk? A hot water bottle?'

'No, thanks,' I say. 'I think I'll go to bed if that's OK? Do a little reading, and then, hopefully I'll sleep.'

'Of course,' she says. 'Whatever you want. You have enough towels?'

'Yes, Mum. I have enough towels.'

'OK, well…' She sets the cloth down and wipes her hand on her woollen skirt. 'I'll probably watch some TV in my room. That's not going to disturb you?'

'No. I'll be fine.' I try to smile reassuringly. This is all going awkward again, like a frame of snooker where someone has pushed all the red balls up the wrong end of the table.

'Thanks for making supper. It was delicious.'

I smile at her, hoping to see even a glimmer of warmth reflected back. But her eyes have taken on that cloudy, dazed appearance from earlier. It's clearly going to be up to me to bridge the gap. I step forward, take her arms, and give her a light kiss on the cheek. 'Goodnight,' I say.

'Goodnight… um… Skye,' she says.

That pause… it's almost like the gears in her mind are recalibrating to get the name right. Well, she's done it. This time.

CHAPTER 7

I'm exhausted. Every molecule inside of me is crying out for sleep. And yet, as I lay curled up in the narrow bed, I can't switch off my thoughts, can't dispel her 'presence' from the empty bed across the room.

Ginny, my twin. The girl with the golden hair and the silver voice. We were born together, raised together, spent most of our waking hours together. And yet, we might as well have been from different worlds.

When Ginny walked into a room, people took notice. Her beauty, her smile, her voice, and when she sang, the other emotions that would play across her face like clouds across a full moon. Always changing, always captivating.

And she was my sister.

When Ginny and I were teenagers, sometimes we barely slept because we'd be up so late talking about our dreams, which, as time went on, became plans. We were going to be famous, a double act. My songs, her voice. We'd see the world, go to New York, we'd meet our favourite boy band members, we'd be celebrities. I was going to make it happen. Once we escaped Eilean Shiel, the sky was the limit – we were going to fly.

On her eighteenth birthday, I gave Ginny a bracelet and matching earrings that I'd made for her from silver wire, shells, blue and green sea glass, and a golden heart charm. I remember how she'd smiled and told me they were the most beautiful things she had ever owned. That she'd take them with us, wear them when we were in America together. I'd felt so proud that she liked them, so proud that she was my sister…

She was wearing the bracelet and earrings the night she died. Out on the rocks below Shiel Point Lighthouse. There were two eyewitnesses who saw her out there, twirling around; singing; happy. And then, she was just… gone. Swept into the water by a wave. Her body was never recovered.

The rain batters down on the roof and a loose shutter bangs outside the window, almost like someone knocking, trying to get in. I bury my head under the blanket, praying for sleep. I wish that I hadn't flushed all my sleeping tablets down the toilet before I left Vegas. I wish that I had brought her home that night like Mum asked me to. And I wish we hadn't had an argument, right here in this room, before she left for the party out at the lighthouse. It was the last time I saw her alive.

I turn on the bedside lamp, staring at the circle of light on the ceiling. In the background I can hear the drone of Mum's TV and the ticking of the travel alarm clock that's still in my suitcase. How cruel life is that we never know when the seconds will begin ticking down to something that changes us forever.

That night I sat on my bed watching her getting ready for the party: combing out her hair and putting on her Aran jumper and polka dot scarf. I felt so happy. In only six weeks' time, we'd finally be leaving; finally off to begin the wonderful life that I had planned for us. The life I'd been working so hard to achieve. For two years I'd been sending out demo tapes to agents and record companies. I'd got used to the crushing silence, and had even begun to lose hope. But something that Dad used to say kept me going: 'The only way you're sure to fail is if you don't give it a try.'

The letter arrived in late September. It was from one of Dad's musician friends who lived in Glasgow, and had stayed in touch over the years. I'd sent him one of our tapes in case he happened to know of anyone who could help us. He'd enclosed a flyer that he'd picked up for open auditions. A Glasgow-based band was looking for a female singer and back-up musicians for an upcoming American tour. When I saw the flyer I felt a surge of hope stronger than anything I'd ever experienced. I screamed and jumped up and down. I picked my sister up like she weighed nothing and whirled her around. This was it – the opportunity we'd been waiting for our whole lives. And Ginny had been happy too. Her eyes had shone with pale fire as she'd laughed and twirled around.

The audition was in early January. On the night of the party, there were only six weeks to go. Our coach tickets had arrived by post earlier in the day. I'd shown them to Ginny. Kissed them, I was so excited. I had them out on my bed as she got ready. I was telling her about the hostel I'd found for us to stay, I was going to call and book it… Ginny put on the bracelet I made for her and put the earrings in her ears. And then she turned to me: 'I'm not going to the audition, Skye,' she said. 'But you should go. You'll be brilliant.'

My first reaction was to laugh in her face like it was all a great big joke. If I had, then maybe things would have turned out very differently. But when I rewind the conversation in my head, even after all these years, I still feel the same icy ball of anger forming in my stomach.

'No…' I'd said. 'You're not serious. You… can't be serious.'

Her smile faded. 'I am serious,' she said. 'I'm not going. I want to stay here.'

'Stay here!' The very idea filled me with dread. There was a world out there. We only had to take the first step. Together.

'Yes, Skye. I'm sorry to let you down.'

'No… you… can't…'

She came over to my bed and picked up the coach ticket I'd bought for her. The glass earrings flashed as they caught the light but her eyes were dark and cold. She looked at the ticket, then at me.

Then she ripped it up.

She put the pieces in a little pile on my bed. I stared at her, stared at the pieces of my dream in a little white heap.

'I'm sorry,' she said, and left the room.

I was fizzing with anger and disbelief. I curled up in a ball on my bed facing the wall. I stayed there until I heard Byron's Jeep pull up outside to give us a lift to Shiel Point. I heard voices downstairs, the front door close, and the car drive away.

My sister was gone.

And then she was dead.

I roll over, away from the empty bed. My pillow is damp with tears. The shutter bangs again in the force of the wind.

'Why?' I whisper into the darkness.

I pull the pillow over my head to drown out the silence that's the only answer.

CHAPTER 8

When I wake up, the room is bathed in pearly morning light. It takes me a moment to realise where I am, and that I haven't gone through some kind of time warp. All of my old things in this room now seem strange and remote. I glance at Ginny's empty bed and feel an ache of sadness. But it's a familiar sadness tempered by years, not the dark, gaping hole of loss that I felt last night. I get out of bed and go to the window. The rain has stopped and the wind has blown away the clouds to leave a perfect ice-blue winter sky. I crack open the window and take a deep breath. The air that fills my lungs is cold and bracing, but with a freshness like nowhere else. I smell mossy earth and sea air. It's the kind of morning where it's impossible not to feel a sparkle of optimism.

I come away from the window. My suitcase is on the floor near the bed. I dig through it and put on a black roll neck and a pair of jeans. There's a chest of drawers in the room and two identical pine wardrobes. If they're empty, I could move in my things. But what if they're not? I don't want to face any more memories right now, so I zip up my suitcase and put it back on the bed. Seeing it there, knowing that I can run away again if I choose, gives me that little bit of extra resolve I need to face the day.

I smell fresh coffee as I go downstairs. Mum's not in the kitchen, but I find a big pot of coffee in a drip coffee maker. When I was growing up, Mum and Dad drank instant coffee. This is another definite improvement. I pour coffee into one of the old mugs from the back of the cupboard. Cradling it to warm my hands, I go to the window at the back of the cottage. Outside is a panorama of land, sea, and sky. The grass behind the house stretches about thirty metres to a wooden fence with apple trees planted along the side. Beyond the fence, huge rocks jut up from the water below. The sea is a milky blue-grey, the fragile sunlight shimmering on the water like diamond chips. Across the bay, the village is still mostly covered in mist. A fishing boat slowly makes its way out of the harbour towards open water, seagulls circling the deck.

The view is so familiar, and yet it's like I'm seeing it for the first time. Appreciating the remoteness of this place, hours away from the nearest city. Here, we live at the mercy of the sea and the wind. Any impressions we leave behind are shallow and delible, like footprints in the sand. Fifteen years is a blink of an eye; the land doesn't care that I once went away, or that I've come back again. My life is small, my little dramas and struggles unimportant against the vastness of sea and sky.

There's a kind of comfort in that.

I sit down at the table. The door to the shed off the kitchen is slightly ajar, and I can hear the sound of running water. Dad built the shed in part for his tools, and in part for the times when he was banished by Mum outside with his bagpipes. After he died, Mum turned it into a greenhouse, growing tomatoes, broad beans, and strawberries for planting outside in the spring. She must be watering them. I decide not to disturb her.

As I drink my coffee, I wonder about Mum in a way I haven't done before. In the way of an adult, not just a spoiled teenager. Back then, Ginny and I mostly relied on her to do the cooking and the laundry. Though she was quietly supportive of our interest in music, she also encouraged us not to neglect our studies so that if our big break never came, we might be able to go to university. Neither of us listened to her.

Now, though, I wonder about what hopes and dreams she had. A family, children, and a quiet, authentic existence, or something else? Did she ever dream of escape, or was she content with her life until tragedy struck? I've never asked her. Would I have asked her if things had been different and we'd been able to have a real mother-daughter relationship? Would I have got to know her as a friend? Is it too late to do so now?

I hear a noise in the shed; slow, laboured footsteps coming towards me.

Instantly, I feel anxious. Dinner was so awkward last night; feeling constantly on edge for the next mention of my sister's name, the next invocation of her memory. And that awful moment when Mum mistook me for Ginny and spoke to her like she was in the room…

I need to know a lot more about Mum's mental state before I can assess what our future relationship might be. Whether there are too many bad memories lurking in the shadows for us to have *any* relationship whatsoever. I have to believe, though, that she wants me here. She asked for me… To me, that makes all the difference.

The footsteps stop, recede. She begins to hum. I hate the sense of relief I feel that Mum seems to be occupied at the moment, and there's no need for a repeat of last night's tussle over the teapot. I finish my coffee (washing out the mug before putting it back), eat a banana and then go upstairs to get the decorations down from the attic. Maybe I'm living in cloud cuckoo land thinking we can be like a normal family and have a normal Christmas. It might cheer up Mum, though, so I may as well have a go.

The attic is accessed from a hatch at the end of the corridor. I find the long stick to open it in the airing cupboard, and the hatch comes down with a creak and a cloud of dust. I unfold the ladder and climb up.

I know about the low beam and even put my hand up over my head so as not to hit it. I wiggle into the hatch, feeling for the light switch. As I do so, I hit my head on a second beam that's hidden behind the first. I swear out loud, feeling close to Dad.

The fluorescent light hums and flickers like it's awakening from a long sleep. I get onto one knee and then manage to stand up, taking care not to get another bump on the head or cobwebs in my hair. The attic is full of boxes labelled in Mum's neat writing. The Christmas boxes are near the hatch: she must have had them down at some point in the last fifteen years, probably another time that Bill's family came round for the holidays.

Snooping around makes me feel like an intruder. Everything seems to invoke a past that's no longer mine. There are boxes labelled 'School workbooks: Skye & Ginny', and 'Sports trophies: Bill'. There are old amps, cables, and broken microphone stands scattered haphazardly. There's a box marked 'music books', and another box of books without a lid. On top is a book called *Celtic Myths and Legends* that I must have read a hundred times when I was growing up. I based a lot of the early songs I wrote on those stories. Songs of giants, fairy worlds, and Selkies: sleek, seal-like sea creatures who could shed their skins and become human, their voices luring unsuspecting fishermen to their deaths.

I toss the book over near the hatch. Maybe I'll read those stories again, see if they might provide inspiration like they used to. In the last few years, I've barely done any songwriting. I turned away from my Celtic heritage even before leaving here, trying instead to write catchy country and western songs in the usual theme: my man left me, my dog ran away, my pick-up died, but my boots are good as new. It wasn't difficult, and I even had a few successes. But it was never really *me*.

I'm about to go back down the ladder when something catches my eye. Dad's guitar case, shoved under the eaves behind the amps. The case is covered with stickers from various folk festivals, and the handle is taped with black electrical tape. The handle broke one night when we were dashing from the car to a pub in the middle of a rainstorm. He kept saying that he was going to get it fixed, but he never did.

I stoop down to pull out the case. Once, my hands were too small to play Dad's guitar, but no longer. I don't have my own guitar here so if I'm going to do any songwriting, I'll need to use Dad's. As I pull it out, another box shifts. It's labelled: 'Old Journals'.

I stare at the box. The only one of us who kept a journal was Ginny. She used to get a new one every Christmas and wrote in it almost every day. I never read her journals, but then, we were so close that I felt I already knew what she was putting down on paper. Now that she's gone, though, it's a bit chilling. Has Mum read her journals? Did she read through the details of her daughter's life, trying to keep her memory alive? At least they're up here and not downstairs on a bookshelf. Maybe she hasn't read them.

I leave the journals where they are and take down the Christmas boxes and the book. I go back up for Dad's guitar. As I'm taking it through the hatch, something gives way. The taped-on handle finally breaks. The case crashes to the floor, squashing two of the Christmas boxes. There's a discordant vibration of strings… and then silence.

In that moment, something cracks inside of me. All the negativity, pain, and regret I've been holding inside come rushing back. I've tried so hard to put on a brave face and keep moving forward. Tried to get over the death of my sister and build a life without her. I did what Mum wanted and stayed away – so long that it seems like forever. Or it did, until I came back. Now, though, I realise that I never escaped anything. Not the memories, and certainly not the regrets.

I come down the ladder and slump to the floor. I think of my suitcase, zipped up on my bed. A voice inside my head screams that I should just leave. Escape again, keep on running…

But there's nowhere else to go.

CHAPTER 9

I sit staring at the wall, fingering the broken handle. In all the years that I was away, there was a part of me that yearned to come home. A prodigal daughter, returning to find peace and forgiveness. When Mum asked for me, I thought that might finally be possible. Now, though, everything still seems broken. There's no peace or forgiveness here.

Dishes clatter in the sink downstairs. Mum: pottering about on her bad leg, getting on with life's chores. As she's done for all these years, even though she lost a child and her surviving daughter left home six weeks later. I wipe away a stray tear. Mum's never been much of a crier, and neither have I. I'm beginning to see that there's more of Mum in me than I've ever consciously admitted. A core of steel tempered by loss. I guess that's what comes of having an 'old soul'.

Ginny was a crier. She had big emotions written there on the surface for everyone to see. She would cry loud tearful laments whenever she was sad. When she was angry she would go outside and scream into the wind. When she was happy she would run down to the edge of the garden twirling and singing. Ginny said 'I love you' easily and frequently. All that emotion, all that changeability, could be endearing, but it was also exhausting. Ginny was an exhausting person.

I open up the guitar case, breathing in the scent of varnished wood. I run my fingers over the steel strings, the small dots of mother-of-pearl inlay and the intricate pattern of Celtic symbols around the tone hole. The guitar is a beautiful instrument, handmade on the Isle of Harris. Dad bought it at a festival. We sat together in the guitar maker's tent as he tried each instrument out to find the one that was right for him. Ginny had got bored and went off with Mum. Dad had strummed the guitar, and I'd sung, and then we'd switched. The maker had joined in and people had stopped to listen, almost like we were one of the acts. And I'd felt so happy and proud that I was musical like Dad. I was part of a tradition that was important, something larger than just my own life. Thinking back, that must be why Dad bought the guitar, even though it cost a lot of money. The guitar had given us joy.

I continue staring at the guitar even as I hear footsteps on the stairs: slow, arrhythmic. Mum. I should get up, save her the effort of climbing the stairs. I don't move. I pluck the low 'E' string. It twangs and slackens. The guitar is hopelessly out of tune.

'Skye, what are you—?' Mum comes to the top of the stairs. 'Oh.'

'I'm sorry, Mum.' I don't look at her, but at my own, hazy reflection in the high gloss wood of the guitar. 'So sorry.'

'For what?' Mum sounds a bit cross.

I don't know. It's not a specific sorry as much as a deep, existential sorry.

But it's something that I feel needs to be said between us. *I'm sorry that I didn't protect Ginny that night. I'm sorry you blame me for her death. I'm sorry I've stayed away for so many years, not facing up to things. Sorry that I still can't do so now.*

'I accidentally dropped the guitar on the Christmas boxes,' I say. I set the guitar case aside and get to my feet. 'The handle finally broke.'

A phantom smile crosses Mum's face. 'That guitar was so expensive. It should have been more sturdy.'

'Yeah,' I say. 'But the case was probably made in China.'

'Probably.' She shrugs. 'Have you had breakfast?'

'I had some coffee.'

'I can make you an egg.'

'No really, Mum, that's not necessary.'

She stands there staring at me, the frown etched on her face. I've made a mistake. I should let her make me an egg, fuss over me – whatever it takes to make her look at me the way she used to, when I knew she loved me and was proud of me. She gives a little shake of her head and begins to turn, agonisingly slow and with a wince of pain. I hate seeing her like this. She takes a few steps towards the stairs, then stops and frowns. She's caught sight of the book of Celtic legends on the floor.

'That was Ginny's,' she says, almost like she's talking to herself.

I decide not to point out that the book belonged to both of us, and I was the only one who ever read it.

'We used to write songs about the stories in this book,' I say carefully. 'Do you remember?'

'Of course,' she says. '"The Selkie" – what was that one?'

The words to the song materialise from the ether, shape themselves in my head and demand to be spoken: '"She calls to you from upon the rocks, the maid with the silken hair. Leave your home, leave your lands, leave behind your care. Follow her down to the depths of the sea, your little boat adrift. Drown yourself in her deepest love, your human life forfeit."'

My throat constricts as I finish speaking. Mum's face is frozen, the cane juddering as her knuckles go white. 'Yes, that was it,' she says quietly. 'I remember now.'

'You went out there,' I say. 'To the lighthouse. To the place where she died. That's where you had your fall. Bill told me.' I try to find the courage to continue. 'Why did you do that? Why put yourself through that?'

Mum stares down at her hand on the cane as it begins to steady. I hold my breath, thinking she isn't going to answer. Then, she sighs. 'Lorna and Annie wanted to have a remembrance service in the village. To mark fifteen years. A special mass, and a reading at the grave.'

I nod. I recall Bill mentioning something about that, a few weeks before Mum had her fall. At the time, I'd thought it sounded like a nice idea.

'But when the day came, I just couldn't... do it.' Her voice is laced with anger. 'It seemed like a joke, standing by that grave. Some kind of sick joke. I mean, she's not there, is she? She's still...' She sweeps her hand. 'Out there.'

I stand very still, worried that maybe Mum is losing the plot and has somehow convinced herself that Ginny is alive. The comment about the singing last night, the room kept as it was... what else might there be that I know nothing about?

She frowns like she's guessed what I'm thinking. 'I don't mean that she's alive.' Her eyes darken with pain. 'I know she's... not.'

I nod, wishing I knew the right thing to say. The empty grave has haunted me too, across all the years and miles. Ginny was officially declared missing at the time because they didn't find her body, just her jumper out on the rocks below the lighthouse and her scarf washed onto the beach by the old jetty. They searched by helicopter and lifeboat and the friendly, if not particularly sensitive, lifeboat captain gave us a fifty-fifty chance of recovering her body depending on the ocean currents, which were 'complicated'. We were told we might be 'lucky': she might wash up on a beach near civilisation. Or, she might wash up on a remote inlet or skerry somewhere on the coast and never be found. Or, she might have been sucked straight down to the bottom. As it was, we were unlucky.

Maybe Mum's right – the grave in the village is a joke. And even if her body had been found, Ginny wouldn't have wanted to be buried in a dark hole. But at the time, it had seemed the right thing to do to get closure: for Mum, for Bill, for me, for the entire village that was so shocked and shaken by the tragedy. Mum made the decision almost as soon as the lifeboats called off the search. It had seemed part of her coping strategy, and I for one was too dazed and numb at that time to question it. There was a memorial service for Ginny at the churchyard, and a little headstone erected next to Dad's: black granite flecked with iridescent blue.

I am lucky: I haven't had to see that grave every week for fifteen years like Mum has had to. Knowing that Ginny isn't there. The only real closure of sorts came when Bill took care of having Ginny legally declared dead after the seven year 'in absentia' period.

'I understand, Mum,' I say. I decide that I'll give her the benefit of the doubt… for now. That she went out to the cliffs to remember Ginny, not to try and find her – and failing that, to try and follow her.

'Yes, well…' Mum draws herself a little straighter. Maybe it's because we've finally made a start – though a very small one – at breaking through the wall of silence. 'Let me know if you change your mind about that egg.'

Mum continues her journey to the stairs. I wait until she's out of sight and I hear the kitchen door close. I move the Christmas boxes down to the sitting room and go back upstairs and take the guitar to my room. My mind rewinds back to the night when Ginny left for the party. I'd stayed in my room, still so angry. I didn't believe that Ginny meant what she'd said, but with her, you never knew for sure. I got out my notebook and went back over the calculations I'd made on the cost of our trip but the figures swam before my eyes. I knew then why I was so angry with her. It was because I was a coward; I'd never have the courage to leave without Ginny. The flyer that Dad's friend had sent us was folded up between the pages. I ripped the flyer in two, balled it up, and threw it.

A while later, Mum had come into the room carrying a basket of laundry. As soon as she saw me, her face went pale. 'Skye?' she'd said. 'What are you doing here? I thought you were going to the party?'

'I decided not to.' I'd crossed my arms.

'But... you were both going. I thought...'

'I'm done playing babysitter,' I'd said sharply. 'It's about time Ginny learned to look after herself, don't you think?'

Mum sat down on Ginny's bed, frowning at the mess of discarded clothes on the floor. 'You know what she's like. She needs you.' Mum seemed oddly upset. 'I'd just feel a lot better if you were with her. Those boys will be drinking...'

'So now I'm supposed to be her taxi service? Is that all I am?'

'Don't be ridiculous,' Mum snapped back. 'Fine. If you won't go collect her later, then I will. I just want to see her safe home.'

I shook my head, the fight draining out of me. 'You hate driving in the dark. I'll go get her.'

'Thank you.' Mum had seemed a little overcome. I had no idea why she was making such a fuss this time. We'd been out to parties loads of times. Yes, Ginny usually ended up doing something stupid, like riding on top of a moving car or jumping off a roof. But that was just Ginny.

'You're welcome,' I'd said with a shrug. I'd collect Ginny, bring Ginny home, keep Ginny safe, just like so many times before. But as Mum left the room and I got ready to go, I swore an oath to myself.

That this would be the last time.

CHAPTER 10

Far away out of time there's a knock downstairs on the front door. I wrest myself back to the here and now. I'm in my old room, but I'm a different person. I went out to the lighthouse that night to bring Ginny home, but I didn't do it. I don't know the how or why – I got in a car accident on the way back and suffered a head injury that took away my memories. Others who were there filled in the details. When I arrived at the party, I was annoyed that Ginny wasn't with the others. I was told she was off with James, her boyfriend. I had a few drinks. Decided that someone else could bring her home. And then I left. Ginny ended up dead. Mum blames me, and I will always blame myself.

I stand up; I need to get out of this room. I go out into the hallway as Mum is answering the door. 'Do come in,' I hear her say. A moment later she calls up to me: 'Skye, Byron's here.'

Byron. I suppose I should be glad to see him, glad of a distraction from my own thoughts. But I feel so raw and unsettled, and would rather not see anyone. Still, he's made the effort to come here, so I should make an effort too.

I make my way downstairs. Mum offers him a cup of tea, which he declines, and he compliments her on how well she's walking after her fall. She thanks him, and I'm a little surprised that she's being so friendly. When I was seventeen and Byron and I started dating, Mum was less than enthusiastic. He was the boy from the wrong side of the tracks, or more accurately, the wrong side of the docks, coming from a family of fishermen. In contrast, Mum loved James, Ginny's boyfriend, who was polite and polished. It was another way in which I could do no right and Ginny could do no wrong, in Mum's eyes at least.

But all that is ancient history. She and Byron seem perfectly amiable now as I go into the sitting room. Byron is standing just inside the door. He's so tall that he could easily reach up and touch the ceiling. He's wearing a black knit cap over his fair hair, and there's rough stubble on his chin. He's an attractive man.

'Hi there.' He bridges the gap between us and gives me a kiss on the cheek. 'Thought I'd see how you're settling in.'

'Thanks.' I resign myself to pretending. 'Everything's good. Right as rain.'

'Grand.' He turns back to Mum. 'So Bill and the family are coming?'

'Yes.' Mum gives him a rare smile that makes her look years younger. 'It's going to be chaos. So we thought we'd get the decorations out before they get here.' She indicates the boxes. 'Skye wants to get a tree.'

'Good idea.' He smiles at me.

'Yes, well, I haven't had a tree for a few years,' I say. I'm pleased that Mum seems on board with my idea of decorating the house. 'I thought it might be nice, especially for Bill's kids. Though…' I hesitate, thinking through the logistics, 'I'm not quite sure where to get one this late. And I'll need to borrow the car…'

The car. For a second it feels like the air has been sucked out of the room. Why did I mention the car, and in front of Byron too? He was the one who found me that night after I'd had the accident. He called for emergency services and I was taken to hospital. The car was a complete write-off. I didn't drive again until I got to America. But since then, I've driven a lot. In fact, I'm a very good driver.

'Of course,' Mum says through her teeth. 'You may as well. I can't drive yet with my ankle.' I get the distinct impression that she's seeing everything through a fifteen-year-old lens, just like I am.

'Why don't I give you a lift?' Byron comes to both of our rescues. 'I could use a tree too. My son's coming for Christmas.'

'Your son?' I say.

'Yeah,' Byron says. 'His name is Kyle. He's seven.'

'Seven.' I consider this. Byron, who is stuck in my mind as forever twenty, has a seven-year-old son. Mum, I note, is watching me and my reaction. I go with: 'Wow, that's... um... great.'

'Yeah.'

'So you're married?'

'No,' he says. 'His mum, Cath, is a nurse in Glasgow. We're separated. He lives with her most of the time.'

'Oh.' I don't know what to say. I glance over at Mum. She's leaning against the back of the sofa, resting her leg. She's frowning down at a tiny stain on the upholstery, almost like she's not paying attention to the conversation. I'm sure, however, that she's listening intently.

He shrugs. 'It's not ideal, but it's the way things are. So, should we go now and get that tree?'

'It sounds like a fine idea,' Mum says, looking up at me. 'I can give you some money, if you need it.'

'I'm fine,' I say. I put on my coat, checking to make sure that my phone and credit cards are in the pocket. I may not have returned home rich and famous, but I have enough money to pay for a Christmas tree.

'Great,' Byron says.

As we're leaving, Byron gives Mum a gentle hug goodbye at the door. I smile and give her a kiss on the cheek, refusing to acknowledge the relief on her face that I'm going out, or the relief I feel when the door is closed behind me.

If Byron notices anything is wrong, he doesn't let on. As soon as we're outside, he turns to me. 'They may still have trees out at MacDougall's. We can go there, get a coffee.'

'OK, sure.'

We cross the yard to where Byron's parked his vehicle: a dark green Land Rover. On the night she died, Ginny got a lift with Byron to the party. He was driving his uncle's beat-up Jeep with no shock absorbers back then. If Ginny and I hadn't quarrelled, if I'd gone with them instead of driving myself, would things have turned out differently? I get in the vehicle and slam the door hard.

Byron whistles a little tune as he gets in the driver's side and turns on the engine. In a way, I'm grateful that he seems so relaxed; like the sight of me hasn't immediately made him think of *her*. 'Nice Landy,' I say, matching his casualness. 'Must come in handy.'

'Yeah,' he says. 'It does the job. Towed a carful of tourists out of a ditch not a fortnight ago.' His eyes twinkle as he reverses in a three-point turn. Then, in a gesture I remember, he reaches behind me and pushes down the door lock. 'Keep you safe,' he says. 'Seat belt's broken.'

'Oh…' This is the excuse I need to get out of the car. Stop this 'old friends' charade right now. My Uncle Ramsay broke all his teeth when he was flung out of the car as a boy, and Mum and Dad drilled that story into us to teach the importance of wearing a seat belt. When the emergency services found me that night, I apparently wasn't wearing one.

'Drive carefully,' I say with a shudder.

'Always,' Byron assures me.

As we approach the gate, Byron slows down. Another car is coming towards us and reaches the gate first. I feel lucky. It's twice now that I haven't had to open the gate. We all hated doing it as kids, and when we got older, we traded gate duty. 'You get the gate this week, and I'll do the hoovering,' and so forth. Maybe, while I'm here, I could get Mum an automatic gate opener. Surely, that wouldn't count as meddling with her independence.

The other car is a silver Vauxhall Estate covered with mud. A man gets out, raising his hand in a wave to show that he's got this. He's as tall as Byron, but less broad-shouldered, with a clean-shaven face and dark hair. He's wearing a red ski jacket, blue hat and mud-splashed waterproof trousers. He looks a few years older than us: maybe fortyish. I don't recognise him, but I assume he must be Mum's guest – tenant? – the artist who's renting Skybird.

'Odd bloke,' Byron says. He gives the man a quick wave and we go through.

'Odd how?'

'Keeps to himself. Never seen him down the pub once. Like he's got a stick up his arse. I guess he's an artist…' he pronounces it 'ar-teest', 'so he thinks he's too good for the rest of us.'

'Maybe he's here for peace and quiet,' I say. 'Or maybe he doesn't drink.'

Byron snorts, like either of those possibilities make him a lesser mortal. 'Maybe.'

It's strikes me that Byron has a chip on his shoulder that wasn't there before. When I knew him, he was always so sure of his place in the world – a big fish in a little pond. He was the centre of the working-class cool crowd at school, which was nearly everyone other than James and his mates. If there was a party to be thrown, he was the go-to man. If there was a bully to be sorted, he wasn't afraid to use his fists. He's distantly related to Annie MacClellan, so he had clout in the village. The Fraser twins, Jimmy and Mackie, who saw Ginny swept away by the wave, are his cousins.

I'd fancied Byron from the time I was fifteen. When at seventeen he asked me out to the mobile cinema and we spent the entire film snogging in the back, I felt like I'd died and gone to heaven. I started writing cheesy love songs, one after the other. Ginny laughed at me. She thought Byron smelled of beer and fish, and wondered if he ever bathed. I was a little offended by her reaction, but not put off. Not long after, James asked Ginny out, and *she* started singing cheesy love songs. I said that James was too straight-laced, a mama's boy, and wondered if she worried about mussing up his hair or crinkling his shirt when they made out. She was a little offended, but in a light-hearted way. It was nice to be us: the Turner girls, both sorted with the hottest boys in the village.

The track is bumpy, and without a seat belt, I bounce up and down uncomfortably. Byron comes to a sudden stop at the main road and I'm pitched forward. My hands are clammy, my pulse unnaturally fast. He turns onto the main road, which is smoother but full of twists and turns. I tighten my grip on the handle of the door, hating this feeling of panic. As the road levels out, Byron seems to notice my disquiet.

'Sorry,' he says. 'Too fast?'

'A little,' I say. 'And besides, I'd like to see the view.'

'Yeah, fair enough.' He slows right down as we reach the lowest point of the road and drive along the rocky coastline. As we curve around, the village gradually comes into view. In the slanting sunlight, the little white houses seem almost cartoonish against the dark hills. Byron pulls off at a layby where there's a fringe of white sand and some flat rocks that are perfect for sitting on. 'Shall we stop for a minute?' he says.

'OK.'

The discomfort of being with Byron is outweighed by my eagerness to experience the beauty around me that my soul remembers, but my eyes are appreciating for the first time. I unlock the door and get out. It seems a long way to the ground.

As he gets out, Byron takes something from behind the seat. A red and green tartan rug. He spreads it over one of the rocks. I stare at the orderly geometric pattern that's so familiar.

I lost my virginity on that rug.

I sit down cross-legged, determined not to think about it, or wonder whether or not he's thinking about it. It might not even be the same rug.

The air shimmers above the horizon as the sun dispels the last of the mist. The sea is a pale, milky blue and, at the horizon, I can make out the hazy shapes of the islands far out to the west. In the middle distance, a CalMac ferry is slowly making its way from port. The sea air is bracing, and I pull my coat tightly around me.

'Nice, isn't it?' Byron sits down on the rock, close, but not too close. 'I never really stop and take a look.'

'I never did either,' I say with a little shrug. 'It's just being back after so long.'

He nods. 'I get it. I went away for a few years too. To Glasgow. I guess you inspired me to leave. To escape. That was the word you always used, wasn't it?'

'I suppose it was.'

I watch as a gull lands on a nearby rock, observing us with a shifty eye. I realise now how my constant talk of 'escape' was not only ridiculous, but callous too. It wasn't like I had a terrible life – far from it. I had loving parents, a sister and brother I adored. And in Byron, I had a boyfriend who treated me well. Loved me, even. Why wasn't that enough?

I sigh as the gull hops away, landing in a nearby rock pool. The year I turned nineteen, we didn't see each other much at all. He was off working on boats and I was sending off demo tapes. Each time we were together, and he smelled of fish and sweat and man, I pulled away just a little more.

He, in turn, seemed more keen. When I told him about the audition, he said that he was happy for me. And then, he asked me to stay. He said he loved me, and that he wanted me to include him in my plans.

I was surprised and taken aback. If I'm honest, Byron was part of the reason I didn't want to go to the party at the lighthouse that night. I was trying to distance myself, and I knew that we'd likely end up drinking whiskey and having sex on that tartan rug…

'It was a long time ago,' I add, as if that makes the slightest difference.

'Yes,' he says. 'That's for sure. And has life treated you well since you left?'

'I'm doing all right.'

'So you're not married? No kids?'

'No,' I say. 'Hasn't happened. I'm too much of a gypsy. Travelling around, touring with bands. It's not a lifestyle that lends itself to that sort of thing.'

'Sounds exciting,' he says.

'It has its moments,' I say. 'Ups and downs.'

He fiddles with the fringe at the edge of the rug. It *is* the same rug, and he *does* remember. I'm sure of it.

'I always knew you had it in you to be a success,' he says. 'Even more so than Ginny. You were just as talented, but unlike her, you worked your socks off.'

'Thanks,' I say, 'but we both know that isn't true. Ginny was special.'

'Well… she was a bit of hard work. I remember that.'

I stare at him. Even when she was alive, people rarely had a bad word to say about Ginny. She was fun and charismatic, the life of the party, everyone's friend. 'What do you mean?' I say.

'Well, she always had to be the centre of attention, didn't she? Everything was about her.'

'I… don't know.'

'Do you remember that time she stood on the top of Archie Kirk's car? Arms out, singing at the top of her lungs? He must have been going thirty miles an hour.' He shakes his head and laughs. 'You were right to lay into her for that.'

'Yeah, I remember.' I feel a familiar sinkhole opening up in the pit of my stomach. The fear I felt. The anger. Of course I remember that incident – and others. Ginny 'flying' off Dougie Lyle's roof and breaking her wrist. Ginny racing Rosie Morrison off the edge of the breakwater. Always testing limits and pushing boundaries – usually mine. I was the one who would get in trouble at home for her antics. I was the eldest, and we all knew what Ginny was 'like'. There was only one time that I wasn't there for her: the time when it mattered most. I think of a dream I've had in the past; almost like a vision. My sister out on the rocks below the lighthouse, waves crashing behind her. Arms outstretched, her hair whipped by the wind…

'Ginny was a free spirit.' I default to the euphemism that I, and everyone else, used whenever Ginny did something silly or dangerous.

'Yes, she was,' he says. 'And I guess that for someone like her, there were worse ways to go. I remember what Jimmy and Mackie said when they saw her out there. Even over the noise of the waves they could hear her singing. She was happy; in her element.' He smiles wistfully.

'I don't think it was a great way to go,' I say. 'It would have been cold, and frightening and horrible. Her body would have been bashed against the rocks and she would have drowned. That's what the lifeboat man said.' I take a breath. 'And then, a few days or weeks later, the gasses inside the corpse would have made it rise to the surface. She probably washed up in a cove somewhere and rotted.' I scrape my fingernails against the hard, unforgiving surface of the rock.

'Well, since you put it that way…' Byron winces.

We both fall silent. This is exactly why I feared coming back here – one of the reasons, anyway. Everything here reminds me of my sister and my presence is reminding everyone else too. It's pointless having this conversation. And yet, if there's anyone I can tell, anyone who might take my side, then surely it's Byron.

'Mum blames me,' I say. 'Did you know that? She blames me for Ginny's death.'

'Hey, no…' He holds out his hand, tries to take mine. I pull away. My nails are jagged now.

'Yes, she does.'

I stare straight ahead at the horizon and tell him what I overheard before I left. The anger in Mum's voice. The fact that she'd never be able to look at me again and not think about my dead sister. The daughter she loved the best. Byron is silent for a long moment. I can almost sense the conflict in him as he tests each possible response for the right answer. When there can't be a 'right answer'.

'Does she know you heard?' he says softly.

'No. I… don't think so.'

He shifts his body so that he can look me squarely in the face. 'She was grieving, Skye. Fifteen years ago it was the most terrible, unendurable thing for her.' He shakes his head. 'And I can't speak for her, obviously. But I did help out Greg – Annie's other half – with some of the work on the cottages. We got to talking quite a bit. When I mentioned you, her face lit up. And then, when I asked what you were up to, her eyes died again. It seemed to me then that it was hurting her that she didn't know. And to tell you the truth…' his brows narrow '… I felt angry. Angry that you were putting her through that. I mean, she lost Ginny. You're the only daughter she had left.'

I swallow back a tear, wishing instead for the familiar cloak of anger. But if any person has a right to speak to me like this, I suppose it's him. Byron lost his father when he was fourteen. Losing our fathers was one of the things we had in common and that brought us together in the first place. But whereas mine died of an illness, Byron's dad committed suicide. Hung himself from the boom of his boat, one winter when the catch was particularly bad. Byron's dad was a drunk, and more besides. By all accounts the family was better off without him, but still… it's hard to get past something like that.

'I may be the only daughter she has left,' I say. 'But she'll barely even let me make her a cup of tea. So far, I feel like I'm a complete stranger.'

'No,' he says. 'Now that's not true. I'm starting to see that you haven't really changed that much.' His eyes soften and for a second

I'm transported back in time. To the days when the tartan rug got a lot of use. I look away.

'Just give her time,' he says with the hint of a sigh. 'Unless you're planning on leaving soon?'

'I don't know how long I'm staying,' I say.

'Fair enough. I guess the longer you stay, the more you'll be part of things again. If you want to be. Then, it will just be you.'

'It will never just be me,' I say. 'I'll always be the twin that didn't die.'

I regret the words as soon as they're out of my mouth. Now I'm sounding like I've got a chip on my shoulder. Maybe I do. Ginny liked to be the centre of attention. And she certainly is managing that – even fifteen years on.

'Come on, now. That's not true.' His fingers brush mine. This time I don't move my hand away.

'Shall we go?' I say. 'I want to hear everything about Kyle.'

CHAPTER 11

Byron folds up the rug and we get back into the Land Rover. As we drive inland to MacDougall's Farm Shop, I stare out of the window at the bleak, craggy moorland of the hills and glens, coloured in soft tones of brown, grey and gold; the shimmer of waterfalls and swift-flowing streams, and the occasional tantalising glimpse of a distant snow-capped mountain.

Byron accepts my invitation and talks about his son with relish. He tells me about Kyle's football, his ice hockey, his Year 3 teacher and the park nearby where his ex lives. He's lively and animated when he talks, but it's all kind of heartbreaking.

'How often do you see him?' I ask.

His strong face wrinkles into a frown. 'About twice a month,' he says. 'I go there for the weekend and stay with my cousins. Jimmy and Mackie both live there now. Kyle comes up for school holidays and the odd weekend.'

'That's...' I want to say 'good', but it's obviously terrible.

'Yeah.'

'So I mean, what happened? You said you're separated?'

'The problem was that I hated Glasgow.' He gives a little laugh. 'All those cars and people, all that noise. It was OK when I met Cath, but I always knew I'd end up back here. I never made that a secret.' He shrugs. 'Then she got pregnant, and my granddad died, and Mum inherited the pub. Cath and I came back here together. But she's a city lass at heart.' He sighs. 'Out here it was too small, too isolated, too rainy, too… everything. It was a case of right time, right person, wrong place.'

'I understand.'

And I do understand, in a way. When people look at a map of Scotland, they see Glasgow, and they see the western highlands, and it doesn't look that far away. But for anyone who lives in either place, it's a world apart. Like many young people, Ginny and I wanted to leave as soon as we could. But there's something about this land that gets in your blood. Even when I thought I might never come back, I still felt the pull of this place. No matter where I was in the world, if I listened hard enough, I could hear the whisper of home.

'So right now,' Byron continues, 'everything's in limbo. I just want Kyle to have a good Christmas. That's all I'm focused on at the minute.' He glances over at me and raises an eyebrow. 'That and the festival. Are you sure you can't be persuaded?'

'I'm sure,' I say quickly. 'I need to focus on Mum right now. She's… not entirely well.'

'It was a bad fall,' Byron says. He obviously knows much more than I do. 'She was found by Kitty Reid and her husband. Complete chance that they happened to be out there that day. They said she was calling out for Ginny. Telling her to come home.'

I feel a little nauseous. If Byron knows, then everyone knows. 'Mum's having a bit of a problem with reality right now.'

'Yeah,' Byron says. 'That must be tough.'

'It is.' Having someone – him – acknowledge what I'm feeling brings the tears close to the surface again. I'm grateful that he seems content to leave it there. We reach a crossroads on the shores of a long inland loch with a few scattered farms and bothies. A sign points down the glen: *MacDougall's Farm Shop*. Half a mile on, we turn onto a gravel lane. At first glance, the tiny farm shop, surrounded by barns and paddocks is much as I remember it. However, when I look closer, I see that the largest of the old barns has been restored and there seems to be a construction project underway. A canvas sign reads: 'Coming soon, Indoor Adventure Park.'

'Adventure Park?' I say. 'That's very grand.'

He laughs. 'Daft, isn't it? Old man MacDougall died and his family sold up. Now James has got grand plans for the place.'

'James?' I say. 'James Campbell-Ross?'

'The very one.'

Another name from the past, coming up like a bad penny. Or, in this case, a very good shiny copper one. James was lovely. Kind and caring, a boy you'd be proud to bring home to meet your mum. Given how Mum felt about Byron, I think Ginny felt a little proud of herself when she did just that.

'Where's he getting the money to do all this?'

'Worked as a banker for a few years,' Byron says. 'In London.'

'London?' Right now, London sounds as far away and exotic as it used to.

'Yeah. Made a packet,' Byron says as he parks next to a coach. 'He's doing up the old hunting lodge down the glen too. Like he's some kind of laird.' I sense that chip on his shoulder again.

'Good on him.' I get out of the car and look at the signboard. The farm shop now specialises in 'Locally sourced, organic products'. There's also, apparently, a little train that kids can ride to see the animals: sheep, deer, and highland cattle, along with more exotic animals like alpaca and emus. It's not exactly Disneyland, but I can definitely bring Bill's kids here for an afternoon.

We walk to the farm shop. There are still a few trees for sale under an awning in the back, and I find a fat, bushy pine that Mum will like. I check the tag. 'Crikey!' I say.

'Yeah, I know.' Byron snorts. 'James always did know how to make a quid or two.'

Byron chooses a smaller, less expensive tree, and an employee puts his tree and mine through a big metal ring, where they come out the other end bagged up in netting. Another great invention they didn't have before. We pay for our trees and I buy us both hot chocolate with whipped cream and cinnamon sprinkles from a trolley near the till.

He holds up his cup. 'To coming home,' he says.

I clink my paper cup against his. 'To old friends.'

He gives me a kindly smile but looks a little sad as the little train rumbles by with a few kids and their parents going off to see the animals. The situation with his son sounds impossible unless he's willing to move back to the city.

'Do you want anything else?' I say when we've both tossed away our cups.

'No,' he says. 'I'd best be getting back. I'm working the afternoon shift at the Arms.'

'OK. Let's go.'

He hefts my tree onto one shoulder, and his onto the other. He walks ahead of me, and I wonder if I'm supposed to be impressed by this manly show of strength and muscle. I feel a touch of regret that the physical spark there once was between us has entirely died out. I know I didn't treat him with the respect he deserved: he always came second to my dreams, my plans, and my sister. Realising that we wouldn't have had a future even if I'd stayed is probably for the best. It makes me feel less guilty.

But only a little.

CHAPTER 12

Rainclouds are gathering overhead as we drive away from Mac-Dougall's. There's still a glimmer of light towards the sea to the west. Dad said that he always liked driving towards the sun. 'Always go towards the light,' he'd tell us. He meant it literally, but it's a good enough lesson for life.

Though the landscape is impossibly beautiful, as the first drops of rain fall on the windscreen, a sadness overtakes me. Byron too seems lost in his own thoughts, and we drive on in silence.

I stare out of the window thinking that I could have stayed in America, with its vast skies and reliable sun. For the most part, I had a good life there. I didn't get the part with the Glasgow band, but I worked there for a few months and then bought a one-way ticket to Nashville. When I arrived on the scene, a fresh-faced twenty-year-old girl, I got lucky. My accent made me exotic, my instrumental skills made me useful, and I had a tush that looked good in Levi's. I met people who knew people, I got a few opportunities and I took them.

In the years I spent there, I had many love affairs, mostly short-lived and insignificant, like a stone gathering no moss. My lifestyle lent itself to transient flings with fellow musicians and hangers-on. Since the day I left home, I've not been one to gather moss.

I had two longer-term relationships, which were significant, if only for the scars they left. The first was with Justin, a Nashville boy. We spent two years together in L.A., until our relationship ended when I found him in bed with a friend. I left. I got in my car and drove all night to Vegas. I spent a week holed up in a motel room with a bottle. Eventually I pulled myself together and got a gig at one of the hotels on the strip.

I hated Vegas from day one. The drunken stag dos, the tourists, the glitz, the no-hopers pouring their dole money down slot machines. The strip malls, the heat. The only thing I liked was the desert. It was possible to drive out to a lonely place where I could scream at the top of my lungs. I got good at screaming.

I did some songwriting too: songs of lost love and being lonely. Songs of missing home and not having a place to call home. They weren't the kind of songs that a Vegas audience wanted to hear, but I wrote them anyway, in my beige living room in my beige house in a development surrounded by a high beige wall.

Then, my second relationship came along. John was an older man, a doctor. I could be forgiven, I think, for falling for him. For a while it was a nice life: skiing in Aspen, weekend breaks to the Grand Canyon. But everything fell apart when he was found out to be falsifying prescriptions and taking drugs. I spiralled downwards into depression. I didn't leave my house or return phone calls. I missed a few gigs and got dropped by my management. I was at a crossroads, with all directions leading to a bad place. And then I got the emails about Mum's fall. I was told that Mum had asked for me. *'When is Skye coming home?'*

The words I'd been waiting to hear.

I glance over at Byron, and instantly my time in America becomes a figment of my imagination, a shadow at the edge of my memory. But instead of a new beginning, I feel like the clock is running backwards, rewinding itself until the distant past looms larger than life.

Instead of seeing him now, I picture him on the day I left home. Standing next to Mum, putting his arm around her as the coach pulled up. Seeing that gesture gave me the strength to get on the coach, even without my sister. I loved him a little for that.

But now, I wonder why I've never been able to love anyone since I left home, or care very much whether anyone loved me. Is that down to losing Ginny? Dad? Was it guilt for choosing to 'escape' rather than stay with Byron? Disappointment that the reality of my career never lived up to the fantasy? Is it because Mum blames me for Ginny's death, and I lost her along with my sister? Is that why I squandered the chances I was given?

I don't have the answers, but I need to find them if I'm ever going to make something of my life. I suspect that many of them they lie here in Eilean Shiel.

When we get to the gate on Mum's property, I jump out to open it. I get wet, but the rain feels refreshing after being in the car.

'Thanks,' Byron says when I get back inside. 'Your mum really ought to get an automatic opener.'

'Agreed,' I say. 'Know where I can get one in time for Christmas?'

'Try Amazon. They deliver out here, you know?'

I laugh. I'm not surprised. We pull into the yard, where there's a green car parked next to Mum's Volkswagen. The windows of the cottage are warm squares of yellow light. My melancholy evaporates. *Home...*

Byron unloads the tree and offers to bring it into the house. 'That's OK,' I say. 'I can handle it. I'm really grateful for the lift... and the chat.'

'Yeah, it was good to catch-up,' Byron says. 'And maybe, we can do it again. Like over dinner.'

I'm a little taken aback. Given everything that happened before, can he really be asking me out? 'Um... maybe,' I say, non-committal.

'Think about it,' he says. 'That and the festival. Remember, it's all about making new memories.'

I think of Mum and the awkwardness between us. Her break with reality last night. The room she's left untouched for so many years. 'I wish it were that simple,' I say.

He looks at me with an expression I can't quite read. 'It can be, Skye. Remember that.'

He gives me a kiss on the cheek and gets back into the Landy. I have an uncomfortable feeling that maybe we're talking about different things.

CHAPTER 13

I haul the tree inside. The door to the kitchen is closed, but I can hear Mum's muffled voice, no doubt talking to whoever came in the green car.

The strong sense of déjà vu makes me feel light-headed. Like a child reaching out a hand to touch a hot stove, I can't resist moving closer to the door.

'... feel it's wrong that I never told her. Do you think it would have made a difference?' Mum's voice is slightly raised.

'Come on, Mary, that's not helping anything.'

'I know.' A sigh.

I've no idea what Mum's talking about – it could be any sort of local gossip for all I know. Or, it could be something about me. All I know is that I lost fifteen years of my life and my family from the last time I listened at the door to one of Mum's conversations. I'm not going to let it happen again. Without knocking, I turn the handle and fling open the door.

'Hi, Mum.' I smile, taking in both her and her visitor. It's the middle-aged woman from the coach. I was right, she was familiar. I've no idea what her name is, but she's wearing a white smock, and has a small bag of dressings with her. The nurse from the local doctor's surgery, I assume.

'Skye,' Mum says, a frown tightening across her face. 'I didn't hear you come in.'

'Sorry. We just got back.'

The other woman looks a little like a deer in the headlights, but only for a second. It's enough, though, to conclude that they were talking about me.

'Hi, again,' I say.

'Skye, do you remember Alice Thomson?' Mum says.

'Of course,' I lie. I hold out my hand and shake hers. 'Nice to see you.'

'Yes,' the woman says. 'Glad to see you made it home. In fact, we were just talking about how good it is that you're around to help out, weren't we, Mary?'

Mum nods. I sense that she'd like to give Alice a good slap across the face. Whatever they were talking about when I came in, it wasn't that.

'Yes, well, I'd like to help.' I punctuate my response by going over to the hob and putting the kettle on.

'Good. Your mum obviously wants to be up and about, and that's a good sign,' Alice says. 'But for now, she should stay off the leg as much as possible.'

'That's ridiculous,' Mum says. 'I'm fine.'

Alice pats her hand as she rises up from the chair and gathers her things. 'Now, now, Mary. None of that.'

I admit it's a little satisfying to hear Mum get her comeuppance and to know that, like it or not, she *does* need me here.

The kettle boils and I take out a cup. There's a plate of sandwiches wrapped in cling film on the worktop. Mum looks like she's just sucked on a lemon as I make her tea and put it in front of her.

'You needn't have bothered,' she says. 'I'm going out. To the WI fundraiser. Lorna's due to collect me any minute.'

'Just make sure they give you a nice comfy seat,' Alice says. She gives me a wink. 'I'll show myself out.'

Alice leaves the kitchen and then goes out of the front door. Outside I hear the crunch of gravel as another car pulls up. I don't want to be paranoid, and I don't want Mum to drop everything just because I'm here, but I feel a little hurt that she seems to have orchestrated the day so as to spend as little time as possible with me. Some stupid part of me thought that maybe we could put up the tree, decorate it together. It will have to remain in its netting for now.

Mum stays where she is and takes a sip of her tea. I grab a cloth and begin wiping down the table. She doesn't speak to me. The silence is empty and disheartening.

'I assume you've been over to MacDougall's,' I say, for lack of anything else. 'It's changed quite a bit since I was there last. Maybe we could take the kids to see the animals.'

'I haven't been out there.' Mum purses her lips.

'Really?' I say, surprised. 'The shop is quite nice. Byron says that James owns it now.'

'Yes,' Mum says tightly. 'He does.'

I study her reaction. Why is she so down on James? Maybe the locals objected to his planning application for expanding the farm shop – that would almost certainly have been the case. Maybe Mum joined in. Maybe she thinks it's kitschy, or too high and mighty. I could let it go, but I can sense the pile of unaddressed issues growing between us again. I don't want that.

'You always liked James,' I press. 'Didn't you—?'

'He should have protected her,' Mum blurts out. 'He was her boyfriend.'

I shudder a little. Part of me wishes that Lorna would hurry up and come in. But I can see through the kitchen window that she's outside in the yard, having a chat with Alice.

'Maybe,' I say, carefully. 'But there were lots of people there that night.' *I was there*, I don't add. 'Unfortunately no one saw her out there until it was too late.'

'So they say.' Mum frowns, staring at the steam rising from the cup.

I put down the cloth and stare at her. 'What do you mean?'

She shakes her head. 'Nothing. I shouldn't have brought it up. But you're right, no one saw anything. That's for sure. And none of you should have been there in the first place. You all… she… should have been more careful.'

My mind rushes to analyse the meaning behind her words. I know she blames me, but it seems that others bear some responsibility in her mind as well. Apparently James bears quite a bit.

'Yes, Mum,' I say, backing down. 'You're right about that.' I turn away. Through the window I see Lorna on her way to the door.

'Leave it,' Mum says. The burst of emotion seems under wraps now, her stiff upper lip firmly back in place. 'I don't think it helps to dredge all of that up again. I don't want to think about what… happened.' She pauses for a moment. 'I'd appreciate it if you would respect that.'

I sigh. 'OK. Fine,' I say. 'I understand.'

And I do understand – sort of. For fifteen years I've tried not to think about what happened that night, though I've also discovered that trying is pointless. But now that I'm here, surrounded by things that remind me of my sister, I'm not sure I agree. How can Mum and I have any kind of relationship when there is so much unspoken between us? Surely at some point we'll need to clear the air, hang out the dirty laundry, not be allowed to change the subject. At the very least, I'll need to talk to her about clearing out the old room. But maybe neither of us is ready for that yet.

'Hello?' Lorna calls out from the porch.

I feel a further little jab when Mum abandons the tea I made for her and levers herself to her feet. She hobbles over to the worktop to collect the tray of sandwiches but I grab them away before she can try to carry them one-handed. 'I'll take them,' I say. Before she can object, I go through to the front room.

Mum comes in behind me, hobbling with her cane. I have a brief reunion with Lorna, Mum's oldest friend, whom I've known all my life. We exchange hugs and as Mum puts on her coat and scarf, I chat with her about my journey and what her two sons and four grandchildren are up to.

As they're about to leave, Mum turns to me. 'There are some extra sandwiches in the fridge for you.'

I smile gratefully. Things between Mum and me are strained to say the least, but the fact that she's made me some sandwiches says something too. That underneath the guilt and the pile of unsaid things, there is love too. Something to cling to.

'Thanks, Mum,' I say. 'Have a good time.'

When they've left the house, I stand in the sitting room staring at the Christmas tree, trussed up in its netting. It looks sad, like a caterpillar curled up too long inside a cocoon. I find the tree stand in one of the boxes and lift the tree into it, tightening the bolts at the bottom to hold it in place. Then I go to the kitchen and find a pair of scissors. As I cut through the netting, it feels like I've thrown a party and no one has turned up. Under the watchful eye of the school photos of Ginny and my younger self, I fluff the branches out, dark green and thick. The scent of pine fills the room.

I go back to the kitchen and find the sandwiches. I eat an egg and cress and half of a ham sandwich. The ingredients are store bought, but the sandwiches still taste better than if I'd made them myself. The silence, though, is unnerving; I don't think I've ever been in this house when it was this quiet. I check my watch: it's nearly three in the afternoon, so there's about an hour of daylight left. I go to the door and put on my coat. The rain has stopped and a walk will do me good. And I know exactly where I'm going.

CHAPTER 14

The path to the beach is one I could walk in my sleep. I go out of the house and down the new gravel track that leads to the cottages. The refurbished buildings were once part of the old croft that's stood on this site for generations. When I was a child, the whole area was wild and derelict, the old stone paddocks having been taken over by bracken, broom, gorse, and rocks. The hills rise behind to form the backbone of the headland, giving it the form of a giant, beached whale.

I pass a windbreak of trees and The Stables, the cottage where Bill and his family will be staying. Beyond that, in a little sheltered glade, is Skybird. There's a grassy area at the back going down to the water, and a gravelled yard at the front where the silver car is parked. The lights are on inside the cottage. A dog barks and a man's voice silences it. I quickly move on.

The rocky path rises sharply as I head for the pass in the hills. It takes about fifteen minutes to make the ascent, by which time I'm breathing hard. The wind has picked up and the tops of the hills are shrouded in mist. The path levels out around a tiny lochan and then descends a boggy slope of bracken and dead heather. On the other side of the headland, there's another bay. In the distance, a long white sand beach curves along the shore with a few caravans scattered among the dunes. The horizon is covered with cloud except for a sliver of light to the west where the sun will be setting in less than an hour. *Always go towards the light.'*

As I skid down the steep path, the sound of breaking waves grows louder. The path ends at a little cove sheltered by a cliff on one side and huge grey boulders on the other. The beach is mostly shingle with a small crescent of white at the water's edge, the sand made up of millions of tiny, iridescent seashells. The waves froth and foam, making a pattern like lace as they pull back from the shore. I walk up to the high tideline marked by a fringe of brown sea kelp. The wind is bracing, and my hair whips sharply into my mouth and eyes.

I love this place. Though I haven't been here for years, everything is familiar, as if I've come here regularly in my dreams. I go along towards the huge boulders at the water's edge, embedded in the sand like the tips of an iceberg. Every whelk and barnacle, every tiny plant clinging to the rocks, every sea bird circling overhead, seems like one I've known before.

I listen to the shucking sound of the waves pulling back from the shingle. The rocks are dark and shiny, smoothed by the relentless tide. By force of habit, I look out for a pretty pebble or a bit of sea glass.

The patch of silver at the horizon is larger now than it was only a few minutes ago. It's like the saying printed on tea towels, mugs, and T-shirts around here: 'Don't like the weather in Scotland? Wait five minutes and it will change.' The light is like a tantalising glimpse of another world far off to the west.

I continue on towards the cliff and the little caves that we used to explore looking for pirate treasure and Jacobite gold. I sit down on a small, flat rock near the foot of the cliff. There are literally hundreds of coves like this, some on the tourist route, others almost inaccessible from the shore. Any one of which could be my sister's final resting place. I shudder and pull my knees to my chest, as if the rocks scattered around me might conceal her bones.

When Ginny was alive and we came here, she would go out to the furthest, wettest, most slippery rock. I remember how my heart used to race and I would get annoyed, telling her to be careful, and that if she fell in, I wouldn't be pulling her out. And she would just laugh and sit cross-legged with the spray washing over her.

There's a thin, howling sound as the wind changes direction again. I shiver with a sudden, aching sense of loss. Like a ship drawn into peril by a siren's song, my sister followed the voice in her head, the one that lead her out onto the rocks and away from me forever. What was in her mind when she was standing out there that night, the sea roaring furiously below? What did she feel as the wave took her legs from beneath her, and she slid into the cold abyss?

The glimmer of light on the horizon is fading and thin tendrils of mist have begun to creep across the beach. The air seems to grow opaque, almost solid around me. And that's when I see her, a shadow projected from my memory. Ginny running down the beach, her arms outstretched, her hair flying behind her. A flock of gulls at the water's edge all took flight together. I thought she'd never stop running, even when she reached the end of the beach. I thought she might take to the air and fly away.

I taste salt on my tongue: a tear that has run down my cheek into my mouth. Out here, I understand why Mum went to the cliffs. Somewhere in that deep, ever-changing water, there is a part of my sister: the atoms of her body, the life force that was Ginny. If I try, I can almost reach out and grab hold of it… her freedom, her happiness…

I take off my outer clothing and leave it in a pile by the rocks. The shingle stings my feet as I begin to run towards the water, wearing only my bra, long-sleeved top and underwear. The cold water flays my skin and a million nerve endings scream out with shock. I run out to waist-depth, and then I dive in.

There's a rushing sound in my ears. Under the surface, the sound is gentle, almost womblike. I open my eyes: bubbles of green water flow over my head as a wave breaks above me. Strands of kelp and seaweed brush my face. The cold is shocking, and my lungs are full to bursting. I swim underwater for as long as I can, and then surface to take a breath. But as I do, a wave crashes over me and the breath is half air and half water. As the undertow grabs hold of me to take me away from the beach, I'm seized by a coughing fit and I swallow more water. I have a fleeting thought: this is ridiculous. I've swum out here many times before. I just need to get to shore and everything will be fine.

I surface again, try to breathe, swallow more water. My body kicks into panic mode. I flail with my arms and legs, but there's another wave and I go under. My lungs fill with water.

And then there's something there, sleek and dark underneath me. I gasp and flail, but the cold is overwhelming. I seek out her voice, her face, the kiss of death that is upon me. I stop moving and let her pull me out to sea...

CHAPTER 15

The shingle cuts through the skin of my knees. I'm lifted by strong arms. I'm cold, so cold, but the arms are warm. I feel a dark, languid sensation as my body succumbs to lack of oxygen. And then a pain as something pounds my back.

Salt water trickles from my mouth but it's like my chest is wrapped in tight bands of iron. I can't breathe… There's another thud on my back and, this time, water spurts from my mouth, making me gag and cough. But I'm going under again and everything begins to slip away…

I'm jolted back by more pain. Sharp rocks under my back, my nose pinched tight, and then warm lips against mine. Breathing into my mouth… beloved air. I'm coming back to my body. But I'm so cold, and the weight on my chest is so heavy. The world is sharp and painful and I can no longer hear her song—

'Breathe, for fuck's sake!'

Her voice… it isn't a her at all. A man's voice, deep and angry. I have to get away. I sputter and gasp… and draw a breath. And then another and another. Gradually, the dark blur before my eyes becomes a lighter one. The world judders into focus. A white sky. A swirl of mist moving against the dark cliff. And the cold. Shivers wrack my body and I try to curl up in a ball. But it's too painful. Something wet and rough touches my forehead. I gasp and try to wriggle away.

'Stop it, Kafka. Go find her clothes.'

I try to lift a hand. Nothing happens.

A sharp bark.

'OK, OK,' the voice says. 'Good boy.'

There's a crunch of shingle. He's going. Good, I'm fine. I'll just sit up, get my clothes on…

I can't move except to shiver. Why can't I move?

'We need to get this coat on you. I'm going to lift you. Are you ready…?'

Before I can even process what's happening, he lifts me onto something soft. My coat. Why is my mind moving so slowly and my body not moving at all?

'Good,' he says. 'That's better.'

The voice… I must stay with the voice.

'And now we've got two options,' he says. 'Option A, I leave you here with Kafka and I go for help. But that could take some time.'

Leave me here… no…

I open my mouth but all that comes out is a splutter.

'Or, I can carry you up.'

No… he can't possibly carry me…

'And as you're in no fit state to respond, I think we'll have to go with Option B. Your body is in shock. I don't want to leave you here on your own.'

'I…'

'You can thank me later.'

The next thing I know, I'm being lifted again. I'm still shaking, but his arms are strong and his chest is warm. The man sinks deeper into the shingle with the double weight. I try again to see him, but my vision is blurry. Dark hair, a blue cap. I'm fairly sure it's the man from Skybird. With that thought, I sink down again…

'Stay with me. You're heavier to carry when you're out cold.'

Focus. I try to memorise the outline of his face. The silhouette of his chin, with a dark dusting of stubble. His nose, his cheekbones. Deep set blue-grey eyes. For a second I want to laugh; this is ludicrous. I don't need rescuing…

I drift off again. He's huffing now. We've reached the steep, uphill path. I have to stay with him. I can't let my muscles go slack.

Focus. He's speaking again. Trying to distract himself from the climb and the weight. Follow his voice.

'… so incredibly stupid. I mean, if you were trying to do yourself in, you very nearly managed it. I ran as fast as I could, but I wouldn't have got there in time. If it hadn't been for Kafka, then you would have succeeded…'

Succeeded? Wait no. I realise now that Kafka was in the water, not pulling me under but nuzzling me to get my head back above water. And this man thinks that I was trying to drown, that I'd gone in deliberately to… do myself in. But that wasn't true. Just like Ginny going out on those rocks… I was stupid. I went into the sea in the middle of winter. Stupid, but that was all.

'I mean obviously, I would have called for help, but there's no reception here so I didn't even have my phone with me. Practically broke my ankle scrambling down the damn path.'

He's labouring now, his brow glistening with sweat. He should rest. I should walk. I think I can walk. I squirm a little in his arms. 'Walk…' I sputter.

'No. You can't walk.' He pauses for a moment, leaning against one of the huge rocks embedded in the cliffside. I can feel his breath on me when he speaks, feel the rise and fall of his chest.

'We're almost there anyway.'

We're moving again and this time, he doesn't speak. I try to breathe in time with him. The path descends sharply. He slips and for a second, we teeter. But then, in front of the white sky is the blurry haze of trees. The cottages. I close my eyes… I can't help it.

'Stay with me.'

I try, but I can't do it. 'Thank you…' The words form on my lips, but the light fades away before I can give them voice.

CHAPTER 16

It's warm when I awake. Warm and dark and it's a struggle to draw precious breath. My eyes adjust. Black and white lines. Beams on a ceiling. Flickering shadows. Everything hurts.

'Where am I?' I rasp.

'Shh, don't try to talk. The paramedics are on the way. You may need to go to hospital.'

That voice again. His accent is from down south. I don't even know who *he* is. I see him, sort of, over by the fireplace. He bends down and picks up a log, throwing it on the fire that's roaring in the grate. He's tall and leanly built. His hair is dark and a little shaggy, his face has that tanned weathered look of someone who spends a lot of time outdoors. He's good-looking, but there's a sort of arrogance about him that's off-putting. I should get up. I don't want to go to hospital. I'll thank him and then get the hell out of here.

I try to sit up but my body simply won't co-operate. My hands are at my side under the blanket. I move them up. My skin is soft, cleansed by the sea. My skin…

Oh God.

'Um, excuse me,' I say. 'Where are my clothes?'

I'm naked. I'm fucking naked. This man pulled me out of the freezing water, and carried me up here, and then…

'Your clothes are in the dryer. You were soaked through. There was no other option.'

Yeah, it's all coming back to me. Mr Option A and Option B, and, it seems, Option C. Rescue the damsel in distress and then undress her.

'I've got a T-shirt here that you can put on. It's mine, I'm afraid.'

'Yeah, I'm afraid too.' I may have nearly lost my life, but my sarcasm has remained intact.

He has the nerve to laugh. Then he walks away, to the kitchen, I think. I stare at the fire; the wood crackles and the flames hum as the oxygen is consumed and the smoke goes up the chimney. It's mesmerising to watch, especially as I'm still having trouble focusing my eyes.

Something moves in front of the fire. A dark blur lifting its head, looking at me with shiny glass-like eyes. 'Kafka?' I whisper. The tail thumps. Kafka is quite a large dog. Maybe some sort of husky, Labrador mix. 'Thanks, old chap.'

The dog came into the water to try and help me, and that says something about both the dog and the owner. And as I really have no other choice in the matter, right now I'll have to go with this.

A kettle switches off. I'm consumed by a terrible thirst. I've swallowed so much salt water that my cells must be ready to burst. My rescuer returns with a cup of tea and a glass of water. I try to sit up again.

'No,' he says. 'Which one do you want? Tea or water?'

'Water,' I croak.

I suffer the indignity of him kneeling down next to me, bringing the glass to my mouth and holding it while I drink. I try to grab it with both hands and my fingers brush his and I pull away like I've got an electric shock. His grey-blue eyes have a spark of amusement in them that annoys me no end. As I drink, the pain in my chest intensifies, and for an awful second, I think that I'm going to spit all the water back up. I grip the edge of the blanket and pull it to my chin until the feeling passes.

'I… it hurts to swallow,' I say.

He frowns, the amusement gone. 'You really did a number out there,' he says. 'Your lungs and your chest are not going to thank you. I had to try CPR when you weren't breathing. So your ribcage is going to be sore.'

Jesus. His lips. I don't want to look at them, but of course that's exactly where my eye is drawn. Wind-chapped but soft. The kiss of life. I look away, staring up at the ceiling. I need to leave here as soon as possible. I wonder when Mum's coming home…

It seems I've spoken aloud. He sets the glass back down on the table. 'Is your mother Mrs Turner, in Croft Cottage?'

'Yes,' I manage.

'After I called for the paramedics, I went over and knocked on her door. She wasn't home. I left a phone message, but I think it's a landline not a mobile.'

'She went to a WI thing,' I say. 'I'm not sure when she'll be back.'

He raises a single wry eyebrow. 'I guess you'll just have to stay here, then.'

He stands up with the empty water glass and moves out of my sight line again. My senses are gradually coming back to life. The awful salty taste in my mouth. The smell, not just of burning wood, but of something… paint? Turpentine? I look around but I can't see any paintings. But before I can wonder any further, the dog gets up and goes to the door, giving a short bark.

'Settle down, Kafka,' the man says. 'It must be the paramedics.'

I try to wriggle up into a sitting position and end up coughing. This is not good. I *cannot* cause Mum more worry. I can just picture her face when she hears the news: 'Your daughter almost drowned. She's fine now, breathing on her own, but we had to take her to hospital.' It's really the last thing she needs – *we* need – when our relationship is so fragile.

There's a knock on the door.

'DCI Nicholas Hamilton?' a female voice says.

'Come in.' My rescuer opens the door. '"Mr" will do. Or just Nick.'

'Fine, Mr Hamilton.'

'She's this way…'

Nicholas Hamilton. Nick. At least I have a name. But DCI?

A middle-aged woman in a green paramedic's uniform comes around to my side of the sofa. She's followed by a much younger, gangly man who must be straight out of paramedic school. It's some small relief that I don't recognise either of them.

'Hi.' I force a smile. 'I guess I'm the patient.'

A frown line deepens between the woman's eyes. 'I'm Maureen, and this is Dougie.' She indicates the man. 'Can you tell me what happened?' She directs this last question at Nick Hamilton.

'She was under the water for over a minute,' he says. 'The dog got to her before I could and nudged her face out of the water.'

'Grand dog.' Maureen gives Kafka a pat on the head. The dog licks her hand and thumps his tail. Kafka seems like a nice dog, but so much for hygiene.

'I put her in the recovery position. She wasn't breathing so I gave her CPR.'

Maureen shakes her head and tsks. 'Honestly, lass, what were you thinking?'

'That I felt like a swim,' I say. I'm annoyed that they're talking like I'm not there.

'In December?'

'My grandmother was a champion open-water swimmer. She swam in the sea every morning until the day she died. She was eighty-nine.'

'Aye, but do you swim in the sea every day?' Maureen challenges.

'No.' I lift a hand and let it drop again. She's got me. I never was a patch on Grandma Turner.

'Dougie, can you check her blood pressure?'

'I don't want to go to hospital,' I say, for the record.

'We'll see.'

Dougie bends down and puts the blood pressure cuff around my arm. I'm seized by a coughing fit, my lungs gurgling with liquid.

Maureen comes over with a cylinder of oxygen and puts a mask over my face. 'Breathe,' she says.

I breathe, and cough, and breathe some more. The cuff tightens around my arm. It hurts. I try to pull away.

'Shh,' Maureen says. 'Just breathe.'

My skin feels clammy with panic. I have to breathe in this damn oxygen or else they might take me to hospital. I take a few shallow breaths as the pressure on my arm releases.

'Ninety over thirty,' Dougie says.

I remove the mask for a second. 'My blood pressure is always low,' I say.

'Get a fluid drip going,' Maureen says.

Oh for God's sake. It's embarrassing to be taking up Nick Hamilton's valuable time and his sofa space. But before I can protest further, Kafka jumps up from the rug by the fire, barking excitedly. There's a loud, frantic knock on the door, and then the bell goes.

'Mr Hamilton!'

It's Mum. I can hear the panic in her voice as Nick opens the door. 'What happened?' she says.

'Over here, Mum,' I say, removing the breathing mask. 'I'm fine. So sorry for the fuss.'

'Keep breathing,' Maureen admonishes. A second later, there's a jab in my wrist. I hate needles. I never did any sort of drugs that required them, but I knew plenty of people who did.

'Stay still,' Dougie says. He puts tape over the needle in the top of my hand and brings over a stand with a clear bag hanging at the top like a flaccid jellyfish.

'This'll bring that blood pressure right up,' he says.

Mum hobbles over, her whole wrist shaking as she grips her cane. I try to make room for her to sit down but Maureen helps manoeuvre her to one of the wing chairs by the fire. Her eyes are red-rimmed and have that terrible haunted look about them that I remember from when Dad died. How could I have done this to her? It really is unforgivable. She talks to 'Nicholas' and he repeats the story again. This time, though, he includes one additional salient point. 'She says she was just going for a swim.' I'm grateful to him for that.

Mum opens her mouth but nothing comes out. She tries again, her chest heaving from the effort. She reaches out and grabs his hand. 'If you hadn't been there... then...'

It's true, and I feel all the worse for it. Nick Hamilton must have already been most of the way down the path, maybe even on the beach when I went in. A few minutes either way, and either I wouldn't have gone into the water, or else I wouldn't have come out. My entire life, all the memories, everything... swept away. I shiver and end up coughing again. Life sometimes hangs on a very thin thread.

A cup of tea is brought for Mum. It takes a while for the drip to finish, at which time my blood pressure is taken again and Maureen renders her verdict. I don't have to go to hospital. I set aside the oxygen mask and Maureen helps me into my clothes, which are warm from having been in the dryer. With Dougie's assistance, I get to my feet. I'm relieved that I won't be imposing on Nick any longer. I want to explain to him – and Mum, and the paramedics – that this is not *me*. That this is the kind of thing that Ginny would have done, not sensible, practical Skye. I slump against Dougie. I just feel too exhausted...

As I'm leaving the cottage, I turn to Nick. 'Thank you,' I say. 'I'm sorry for putting you through so much trouble.'

He looks surprised, and then, behind his grey eyes, I see a flash of something else. And I think again of the 'kiss of life' and the fact that he removed my wet clothing to put me under the blanket.

Maybe it wasn't such a huge hardship for him. And probably I ought to find that creepy – and I do – but on the other hand…

'No worries,' he says. 'Take care of yourself.'

He stands at the door and I can still feel him watching as Dougie and Maureen help me down the path, with Mum hobbling along behind.

CHAPTER 17

I'm deposited on the sofa in the sitting room rather than taken up to my room. I'm happy to be home and not in hospital. I'll be right as rain with a cup of tea, and besides, it's me who's here to look after Mum, not the other way around.

Maureen instructs Mum on what symptoms to be concerned about, and eventually, she and Dougie get ready to leave. Mum calls Dougie into the kitchen to send him off with some leftover sandwiches. Maureen comes over, kneels down beside the sofa and takes my hand.

'Lass,' she says. 'You were very lucky this time.'

Actually... I'm about to say, I was pretty *un*lucky. I went for a swim, and if it hadn't been for the cold and that wave and... I hear Mum's voice, muffled in the kitchen, and keep quiet.

'What you put your mum through is really just... well, terrible. Especially now. You owe it to her – and to yourself – to get help if you're feeling this way.'

'Wait,' I say as I realise what she's getting at. 'No, you've got it wrong.'

'There is always help out there,' Maureen continues, ignoring me. 'This is temporary. It will pass.'

'But I just went for a swim.' My voice rises in pitch.

She shakes her head. 'Please don't make your mum suffer any more than you have already.'

'What's that supposed to mean?'

Maureen just smiles and fusses with the pillow to prop me up. I try to wriggle forward and end up coughing; my chest feels like it's being squeezed by a very large fist.

'I didn't try to drown, if that's what you're implying, Maureen,' I say. I'm half aware of Mum and Dougie stopping the conversation they're having in the kitchen. 'And I didn't come back here to cause Mum or anyone to "suffer". For your information, I love that beach. I love the sea, and I like to swim even in freezing cold water. It went wrong, and I'm sorry for that.'

I'm sorry, too, for the outburst. Mum hobbles back over. 'Shh.' She bends down unsteadily and tries to tuck the blanket around me. 'It's OK. You're safe now. Everything is going to be fine, my wee bird.'

That strange, glassy flicker is back in her eyes. But I'm fully back to my senses. There was only one person she ever called her 'wee bird'. And it wasn't me.

The name stemmed from Ginny's roof incident. She was fifteen, and she and some friends were sunbathing and passing a bottle of whiskey around. Someone – I don't remember who – dared her to jump. I remember, because Dad had sent me on my bicycle to tell her to come home. I came just as she stood there with her toes curled over the edge...

My breathing constricts even further. I hate the fact that I've caused Mum stress that's made her lose her grip on reality. She stares at me for a second, and I reach out and touch her hand. 'Thanks, Mum,' I say. My voice seems to bring her back to her senses. Thank God.

'We'll be off,' Maureen says to Mum, seeming not to notice anything amiss. 'Remember, Lorna's coming back to sit with you, and we're just the other end of the phone if you need us.'

'Yes, fine.' Mum insists on walking Maureen to the door where Dougie is waiting. They talk for another minute about Bill and his family. When they're finally gone, Mum comes over to me. I manage to shift so she can lower herself down to perch on the edge of the sofa. 'I didn't... understand.' Her voice is shaky. 'I didn't realise that you were feeling so low.'

'Mum, listen to me...' I reach out and take her hand. Her skin feels like paper, her knuckles hard and gnarled. 'I'm the one who's sorry – it was stupid of me to dive into that water. But I did it because it felt good to be out there on the beach. I've missed the sea – and this place – so much.' Hearing the words, I realise how true it is. 'I wasn't doing anything else.'

She turns away and looks up at the photographs. But she leaves her hand in mine. I wonder how many more times I'll have to have this conversation. She'll no doubt tell Bill and Fiona, and everyone's going to be walking on eggshells. I don't want that. I want to be sensible, reliable, trustworthy Skye again. The less beautiful, less talented sister, but the one you'd go to in a pinch. How can I convince Mum that I'm that person?

'Yes, well...' Mum removes her hand. She traces the wooden veins on her cane. 'It's just awful, you know? To get a message like that. I immediately thought the worst.'

'I'm sorry, Mum,' I say.

'I mean, to do that...' She turns to me, her eyes dark with anger. 'I just don't understand.'

I stare at her, looking for the meaning behind her words. 'What happened was an accident. I didn't do it deliberately, if that's what you're getting at.'

'How do I know that? You've been away for so long. Fifteen years! I don't know you. Maybe I never knew you – or your sister – at all.'

'I left because that's what you wanted.' I lower my voice. 'Because you blame me. You told me to bring Ginny home and I didn't do it. That's why I didn't come back. Because I know that each time you look at me, you think of her, and what happened.'

Mum clenches her teeth and for a second I think she's going to slap me. I wish she would.

'That is simply not true.' She emphasises each word. 'And I don't know how you can believe it.'

'Because I heard you say it. The day before I left. I don't know who you were talking to, but I can remember every word you said.'

She opens her mouth then closes it again. I've struck a blow, that much I can see. Maybe a fatal blow to our relationship. Which was not what I intended.

'I don't know what you're referring to.'

She makes a move to stand up. I can't let her. Can't allow her to go off and make a cup of tea, change the subject, plead ignorance. I *need* this out in the open.

'Look we're both grown-ups here,' I say. 'Can't we talk about it?'

'Talk about it?' She looks genuinely surprised. 'What is there to say? Do you want me to say I'm sorry? That I wasn't there for you, that I couldn't cope with your pain as well as my own. That I pushed you away?'

'That would be a start.'

She shakes her head. 'You didn't have to deal with funeral arrangements, and all that awful business with the grave. You didn't have to talk to people, see people. Put on a brave face. You seemed not really there, like you'd already left to get on with your life. And I was happy for you. Happy that you didn't have to live with her memory every single day.'

'But I do live with it. Don't you understand? She was my twin.'

'She was my daughter!' Mum's anger is flowing freely now. 'And so are you. I lost both of you. Two children, in the span of only a few weeks. You don't know what that feels like, Skye, believe me. Until you have your own child – and don't worry, I've given up hoping for that – you will never understand.'

My throat feels raw, my breathing raspy. There's a faint little voice in my head that's saying 'yes, this is good. Get it out, clear the air'. But my emotions are churning with a sickly, dizzying vertigo. On the one hand, I feel so angry with Mum, comparing her pain and mine like it's some kind of competition. On the other, I feel a whole new sense of guilt at her words. Mum lost Ginny because she died in a terrible accident. But I *chose* to stay away. If I'd faced her at the time, told her how much she hurt me on top of all the other pain, then maybe things would be very different now.

'Maybe I won't ever understand,' I say, my voice hoarse. 'But that's neither here nor there. Ginny's not coming back. But I'm here now. You asked for me…'

She looks at me sharply, and I feel a cold, searing pain in my chest. Bill. My lovely brother. The messenger between the trenches…

No. Surely he wouldn't have lied. Surely! And yet, Mum's reaction tells the truth. She didn't ask for me. She doesn't need me, or want me here.

'I'm sorry,' I blurt out. 'Bill said… I thought…' I can barely get the words out. 'I'll leave again. As soon as I can make arrangements. I think it's better for both of us… I see that now.' A sob catches in my throat. I start coughing again, water gurgling in my lungs.

Mum levers herself to her feet. The argument seems to have strengthened her, because she stands straight, barely leaning on the cane. She goes over towards the photos on the mantle shelf.

'You and she were always so different,' Mum says, her voice softer now. She picks up my school photo and looks at it. 'It was as if you were years older than she was, rather than only a few minutes.' She sighs. 'She looked up to you so much.'

'I don't think that's true.'

She sets down the photo and picks up one of Bill, Fiona and the kids. 'I think the problem between you and me back then was that we were so alike,' she says. 'I saw myself in you. Much more so than Ginny. I guess I paid less attention to you, gave you less praise because of that. I always imagined that I knew what you were thinking and how you would react to things. With Ginny, I never knew, so I always felt worried. She was like the child captured by fairies. There was a part of her that none of us could reach.'

'You think I'm like you?' Of all the things she's said, this is what my mind hones in on. I've always considered myself closer to Dad than Mum, but maybe this explains why. Mum always seemed so strong, logical, and distant. Perhaps we were like two magnets with the same poles. But if that's true, then what future do we have?

'Oh, you're much better than I ever was,' Mum says. 'I'm not talented and creative like you. And I never had the wanderlust either. We're different in a lot of ways. But I always knew that I could rely on you.' She turns back to me. 'I know you didn't go into that water deliberately to drown, Skye. Maureen's wrong about that. I have to believe that lightning doesn't strike twice.'

She turns away again and I hear a strangled sob.

'Mum?' I say, alarmed. 'What do you mean?'

'I… no. Never mind.'

'Please,' I say. 'Whatever it is, tell me.'

'No. It's nothing. I'm just being silly.' She takes a moment to steady herself. 'The bottom line is, she's gone. You're here now, so let's end this silly conversation. Of course you're staying. All these years, I've wanted nothing more than to see you. To have you back. I'm sorry if I never said so. I've got on with things while you were away, as have you. That's the kind of people we are. But that doesn't mean that I haven't been waiting for you. Praying…'

'Mum…' The single word is all I can manage. I'm so tired. I close my eyes…

CHAPTER 18

I wake from a fitful sleep where my dreams are haunted by flashing lights; a girl on a cliff, a dark body pulling me underwater. The first thing I feel, though, when I come back to my senses, is a stifling pain pressing down onto my chest. For a second I worry that I'm coming down with pneumonia, just like Dad. Then I recall what Nick Hamilton said about the CPR and chest compressions that would naturally make me sore. Nick Hamilton: the 'kiss of life'; removing my wet clothes by the fire… I'm ashamed that the righteous indignation I feel is tinged with a frisson of adrenalin.

As the room comes into focus, I feel confused. It was dark out when I was brought here, and, surely, I've only been out for twenty minutes; half an hour at most. And yet outside the curtains, there's daylight.

The room is also different. The photos have been taken down from the mantle and replaced with a set of copper lanterns. There's a garland of pine and holly hanging above the hearth. The boxes from the attic have been neatly stacked to one side. How did Mum manage all this?

I replay the conversation – row, really – over in my mind. I suppose it really was unforgivable, me going into the water like that, given what almost happened – given what *did* happen to my sister. I guess that's what Mum meant by lightning striking twice. But even though it was painful to get things out in the open, we're probably better off for having done it. There's still a long way to go in patching the rift between us – but we've made a start. My love for her is less hazy, less cluttered by unspoken things.

But my brother… Bill lied to me. Mum never asked for me at all. The all-important words that brought me back here were never even spoken. I close my eyes until the wave of anger subsides. I'm sure he had only good motives. He doesn't know what I overheard all those years ago, or why I stayed away. He did what he felt he needed to do for Mum, and for the family. And I'm here as a result. Isn't that an end that justifies the means?

I make an attempt to sit up but the pain in my chest is excruciating. This is stupid… I clench my teeth and just do it. I swing off the sofa and stand up. My breath is raspy as I slowly make my way to the kitchen where I can hear the sound of dishes clanging.

'Oh!' Mum says when she sees me. She grips the edge of the sink to steady herself.

'Sorry to startle you,' I say, smiling.

'Sit down. Let me put the kettle on.'

Walking to the kitchen seems like heroics enough so I pull up a chair and sit down. I feel bad not only for being utterly useless, but now a huge additional burden that Mum doesn't need.

'Maureen gave me some painkillers for your chest,' she says. 'Do you want them?'

'No.' I hold up my hand. 'Just a cup of tea. Please.'

'You should take them if you're in pain.'

'No,' I say. 'Throw them away.'

She shakes her head. 'Your dad was just the same.'

I decide to take that as a compliment. I don't want another row, so I change the subject. 'Tell me about your tenant,' I say.

The kettle boils and Mum takes out two white cups. 'Oh, well, there's not much to tell. You probably know as much as I do.'

'I doubt that. When Maureen came, she called him DCI Hamilton.'

'DCI?' Mum looks surprised. 'Like Vera?'

'I don't know who Vera is,' I say, 'but I mean like, Detective Chief Inspector.'

'She's a TV detective,' she says.

'Right. I thought he was an artist, not a detective.'

'Yes, he is an artist.' She brings the cups over to the table on a tray. This time, they don't rattle at all. She sits down facing me. 'His paintings are quite good, I think. Did he show them to you?'

'We really didn't get that far.'

'Of course.' Her smile is brittle.

'I'll have to go over there again,' I say. 'To thank him for rescuing me.'

'You must take him something,' she says. 'I'm going to start baking now. For when the hordes descend later.'

'Later? I thought they were coming tomorrow.'

She stares at me, her brow creasing. 'It is tomorrow,' she says. 'You slept for almost eighteen hours. Lorna was here, helping me out. I woke you a few times, like Maureen said. But you just went right back out.'

'God... I had no idea.' I can't remember the last time I slept for eighteen hours, if ever. I was hoping that the day after the incident I'd feel a little better than I do.

'What time are they getting here?' I sip the tea, fighting the urge to cough.

'Around two, I think,' Mum says. She finishes her tea and gets out of the chair, her joints creaking as she rises.

I stay in the chair trying to gather my strength, which I'm going to need when Bill and his family arrive. I want to be at my best, to prove that I do belong here, even if he told a lie to get me back. When Bill was growing up, he was a typical wild, energetic boy, three years younger than Ginny and I. When Dad died, he stepped up immediately to become the man in the family, something that I will always admire and appreciate. He buckled down, got an after school job, four A-levels, and eventually a degree in accounting. He met his wife, Fiona, his first year of uni in Glasgow.

Getting married young was the only 'rebellion' that Bill ever did. In fact it wasn't rebellion, but him stepping up once again, because Fiona got pregnant. She was from a well-off Glaswegian family, who didn't exactly approve of my brother who came from the back of beyond. But as far as I know, they're happy, and how many couples who have been married for twelve years can say that?

I didn't go to the wedding. Another black mark against me. I couldn't afford either the cost of the flight or the time off. Bill and Fiona had every right to hold it against me, but they're not that kind of people. Though we were usually thousands of miles apart, Bill was an anchor, reminding me of where I came from, who I was, and that I ought to ring Mum once in a while. Sometimes I resented it, but most of the time, it was just nice to know he was there.

I've seen them in the States a few times when they've travelled over to visit Fiona's parents, who now live in a retirement community in Florida. Each time, I've felt a little nervous: that I wouldn't know how to act around the children, or that they wouldn't know me.

Now, those worries pale in comparison to my new ones about Mum and the effect my presence here is having on her. Reminding her of the past, loosening her grip on reality. The last thing I want to do is ruin Christmas for Bill and his family – or any of us. I'll have to watch my step.

I finish my tea and wash out my cup at the sink. Mum is getting ingredients out of the cupboard: flour, sugar, cans of mince. She's slow and a bit unsteady, but her mouth is set in a determined line.

'So what can I do to help?' I say. If she thinks we're alike, then she'll realise that I'm not going to take no for an answer. 'Do you want me to get out the rest of the decorations, or go check that the cottage is ready?' I give a little laugh. 'Like I said, it's probably best if I don't help out with the cooking.'

Mum leans against the worktop. 'Skye, you almost drowned. I really think it's best if you rest.'

'No, Mum.' I keep my resolve. 'I've slept long enough. I feel fine... much better. I'm going to have a shower. And then, I'd like to help.'

She sighs. 'Didn't you say you'd brought some gifts? There's gift wrap in my room. You can get on with that.'

'That's it?' I feel so useless.

'Really, Lorna has seen to everything. And I think we'll leave the decorations in the boxes for now,' she says. 'The children will like getting them out.'

'That's true.' As a child it used to be so exciting to open up the ornament boxes: like opening up a treasure chest full of jewels and sparkly things. Mum's right – it will be good to have children about the house. I want them to like me. I want them to think: 'That's my Aunt Skye – she's cool.'

'Fine,' I say, giving in. 'I'll go wrap the gifts.'

'Good.' Mum seems relieved. 'There's sellotape and scissors on my work table.'

'OK.'

My breathing is laboured as I go upstairs. I take a shower, and then find the bag of gifts that I picked up at the duty free at LAX during the layover from Vegas. Sunglasses and Mickey Mouse beach towels for my seven-year-old twin nephews, Robbie and Jamie, and a notebook with a picture of the Hollywood sign for my twelve-year-old niece, Emily. There are also some shot glasses, a couple of T-shirts, and an 'I love California' oven glove for Mum.

I feel embarrassed about the gifts. They seem inappropriate, like they don't belong here. Ginny would have laughed if she'd seen what I bought. I can almost hear the sound of it as I go to Mum's room to start wrapping. I push my sister from my mind.

Like most of the house, Mum's room has been revamped. There's a scroll iron bed, a wall of white built in wardrobes, a flat screen TV, and a table in front of the window with her sewing machine and basket of knitting. It's a calm space, without photos or pictures on the pale blue walls. Outside the window, the sky is grey and hazy, but a weak sun is trying to break through. The village across the water looks dull and sleepy, the boats in the harbour stationary, like ships in a bottle.

As I'm laying the gifts out on the table, my eye strays to the bookshelf in the corner. I skim the titles, hoping they'll give me some insight into the person my mum is – or has become. The books are mostly hardback and look like ex-library books. There are a few by authors I recognise, like Maeve Binchy and Joanna Trollope. But then I notice one laid across on top. *No Time for Goodbye: Dealing with the suicide of a loved one.* Frowning, I go over and pick it up. It's been well-thumbed through, and there's a bookmark with the 23rd Psalm printed on it. The words swim before my eyes and I put the book back as I found it. Surely Mum doesn't think… No. She can't…

'*I have to believe that lightning doesn't strike twice.*'

I try to get on with wrapping the gifts: taping, curling ribbons and writing tags. But all I can think about is that book. Why would she have it, and has clearly read it, if she didn't harbour some suspicion? Of suicide…? Even the idea strikes me as ludicrous. Ginny was happy, full of life. The last person who would do something like that. Ginny's death was an accident. I can't believe Mum would let any other thought cross her mind even for a second. But if it has… Is that why she's come unravelled?

I put away the gift wrap and scan the room for anything else I've missed that might explain what Mum was thinking. There's nothing. Just the book. I leave the room and take the gifts downstairs. I set them by the Christmas boxes and go into the kitchen. After what happened yesterday, I can't let this go.

Mum's sitting at the kitchen table spreading melted chocolate over a rectangular tin of shortbread. 'Mum,' I say. 'Can I have a quick word?'

'Of course,' she says, not looking up.

'I found a book upstairs. About suicide. Of a… loved one. And I just wondered, I mean, surely, you can't think that about…' I can't continue.

'Ginny,' Mum says. Her lips set in the familiar straight line. She continues spreading the chocolate. For a long second I think she's completely blanking me.

'Mum, Ginny didn't go into the water deliberately.' I try to sound calm, measured. Inside my heart is racing.

'How do you know that?' The sharpness in her voice startles me. 'How do I? I wasn't there. All I know is that she went out on those rocks. She put herself in danger.'

'Yes, and that was stupid,' I say. 'But that's as far as it went. Jimmy and Mackie said that she was singing out there. Happy. It was just that the seas were so high that night. A rogue wave…' I shudder.

'The "rogue wave".' She gives a grim laugh. 'I suppose you've been gone long enough that you still believe that story.'

'What are you talking about?' I say, stunned. 'There were witnesses. Jimmy and Mackie Fraser.'

'Yes. It was all so very convenient, wasn't it? The Fraser boys just happen to see her swept away by a wave when no one else sees anything.'

'But that's what happened.'

'That's what people *said* happened. At the time.'

'Yes…' I cock my head trying to fathom what's going on in her mind.

'People drink,' Mum says. 'People talk. And people lied about that night.'

'Come on, Mum,' I say, raising an eyebrow. 'Now you're just being paranoid.'

'And you're being obtuse!' She shakes her head. 'Oh – I don't know. Believe what you want – what you need – to believe. It's better that way. Whether it was a rogue wave, or whether she threw herself into the sea – what does it matter in the end?'

I open my mouth but nothing comes out. *It does matter*, I want to say. *It makes all the difference.*

'But Ginny was the last person who would do something like that. She was so full of life. So…' *The ripped up coach ticket. The row we had.* Surely… surely those things had nothing to do with her death.

A wave of dizziness sweeps over me and my head begins to pound. I grip the edge of the table until it passes.

'Like I said, I wasn't there.' Mum backs off a little. 'So obviously I don't know what really happened. Just that the story was a lie. Jimmy and Mackie were up here from Glasgow. Shooting off their mouths down the pub. I didn't hear it first-hand. But the rumour started doing the rounds. That no one saw anything. Anything at all.' She shudders. 'They found her scarf and her jumper when they searched. But no one saw her go into the water.'

'No… that can't be right.' I shake my head. 'When did all this happen?'

'About six months ago.'

Six months. Around the same time that the tone of Bill's emails began to change.

I pace back and forth in front of the table.

'Mum,' I say. 'I can understand how upsetting that must have been. But we know her…' I catch myself. '*Knew* her. She was happy. A free spirit. Yes she occasionally did stupid things, but that was just what she was like.'

Mum shakes her head. 'I don't know anything. Not any more.'

'Yes you do,' I challenge. 'You and Ginny were close.' I go up to her and try to hug her. She pushes me away.

'Please, Mum,' I say. 'You know that she would never have committed suicide. Don't you?'

The pause is a little too long. I feel a tremor shoot down my spine. Is there something she's not telling me?

'Yes, you're right,' she says, brisk now, like she wants to end the conversation. 'It was a terrible accident. That's what I… believe.'

'Good,' I say, allowing no more room for argument. 'I'm glad we're agreed.'

CHAPTER 19

I know it's wrong, but I feel angry at Mum even for listening to the village tittle-tattle, let alone allowing it to affect her the way it clearly has. I'm sure it must have been upsetting: Lachlan mentioned something about 'talk' in the village, and I didn't even let him finish the sentence. But there's always gossip about one thing or another, and this sounds like absolute rubbish. Mum should have known better than to give it any credence. Especially in this case, where there was a proper investigation, with people like Jimmy and Mackie giving formal statements.

I go up to my room and try to read a book, but the conversation keeps going through my mind. I wish we'd never had it. Does Mum know something that I don't? I set the book aside. My head is reeling and I can't focus—

Outside there's a crunch of gravel. A car. The engine goes off and instantly, doors bang and there are excited voices. I leave the room and go downstairs. Mum's already hobbling to the door.

Bill and his family have arrived.

*

It's a whirlwind as the two boys come into the house. They practically knock Mum off her feet hugging her, cane and all, and then run off to the kitchen.

'Jamie! Robbie!' I hear Fiona calling from outside.

It's too late, they're long gone. As Mum turns to follow them, I give her a look of mock horror. 'You'd better make sure they don't eat everything,' I say.

She smiles, looking almost like I remember her from before. My earlier anger evaporates, and I'm just glad to see her happy. 'You're right,' she says. 'Boys…' she calls out, and heads after them with her awkward gait.

I go outside to where Bill is unloading some bags of food. Fiona has her head stuck in the car and I can see that Emily, my niece, hasn't budged, and seems to be lost in her own world listening to headphones.

'Bill!' I say, going up to my brother.

'Skye!' He holds out his arms. I wince a little as he hugs my bruised ribs. 'It's so great to see you here,' he says.

'Um… thanks,' I say. I decide to leave it at that – for now.

'I want to hear everything,' he says, 'but first I need to catch those little blighters. See you inside?'

'Sure. Everything OK there?' I nod my head to where Fiona is clearly having a heated discussion with her daughter.

'Oh, it's fine,' he says with a slight roll of his eyes. 'It's her age. Didn't want to leave her friends back at home. Or her fast Wi-Fi.'

'Right,' I say with a smile. 'I feel exactly the same.'

Fiona gives up the fight. The car door slams shut with Emily still inside. Fiona turns to me and smiles. 'Skye,' she says. 'Sorry about that. It's lovely to see you.' She comes up and hugs me. 'Are you OK?' she says. 'You look a little pale.'

'I'm fine,' I say. 'But I did have a bit of a mishap yesterday.'

'Oh?' Fiona says. 'Is everything OK?'

I give her a very brief account of my 'swim', minus the part about the paramedics and having to be rescued by a handsome, reclusive stranger. I also omit any mention of Mum's reaction. If she's truly been harbouring even the slightest suspicion – no matter how unwarranted – that one daughter committed suicide, then what I did was unforgivable. 'It was pretty stupid,' I sum up.

'Well, I guess you have to be careful this time of year.' She goes to the boot and unloads more bags. 'All those ocean currents and undertow. Not that I would know. I'm strictly a Jacuzzi lass myself. Even a swimming pool is too cold for me.'

I laugh. 'I'm with you,' I say. 'It's just that when we were kids, we used to swim out there all the time. The cold never fazed us a bit.'

'Right.' She grins. 'But don't go saying that around the wee scallywags. I don't want them getting any ideas.'

'Sure. Can I help you with the bags?'

'I've got them,' she says. 'But if you want to have a go with that one, be my guest.' She indicates with her head towards Emily.

Fiona goes off into the house where I can hear the boys yelling and Bill trying to calm them. They sound so happy and excited, and I feel a little bit like a spare wheel. At her age, maybe Emily does too. 'Hey there, Emily,' I say. I knock on the window of the car. 'You OK? Do you need anything? I'm going inside.'

Saying that I won't be hanging around does the trick. Even though I'm almost three times her age, I can still remember what it's like to be in a teenage strop. That feeling of isolation – that everyone else in the entire world is against you and complete morons to boot. But it's only worth keeping up as long as there's an audience.

Emily opens the door. 'Hi,' she says.

I stare at her, unable to tear my eyes away. I last saw Emily just over eighteen months ago. She was ten years old and a bit of a tomboy: with short-cropped strawberry blonde hair, freckles and thin, gangly legs that seemed too long for her body. But now, she looks totally different. Her hair is lighter and long down her back. Her skin is pale, almost translucent, and the freckles have been replaced by a constellation of pimples around her mouth. But it's her eyes that burn into my mind. A pale and striking shade of blue.

Ginny's eyes.

In fact, there's such a strong resemblance, that if they weren't separated by years – and death – *they* could be twins.

She frowns as if it's weird that I'm staring. I guess it is. 'What are you listening to?' I deftly change the subject.

'A pop compilation,' she says.

'Yeah? Who's on it?'

'Um. There's lots. Adele, Katy Perry, Taylor Swift. Some oldies too – like Oasis.'

Oasis. For a second I feel like I'm in a strange time warp. 'I probably know a few of the "oldies",' I say with a laugh.

'Well, you'll definitely know this one.' She scooches over in the seat so I can sit down, takes out an earbud and hands it to me.

The familiar intro… the chord progression… the first riff. 'Warrior Woman'. I can't help but feel a stab of pride that it's on her playlist. It's not me singing but it's my song. My one hit of sorts – not for me but for Chelsea Black, a big country star. She got the fame, though as the writer I still get royalties each time it's performed. I'm proud of that song, and glad that Emily knows it.

We both hum along for a little bit, and I take out the earbud. 'Thanks,' I say.

'Yeah, sure. It's a good song.'

'I'm glad you think so.' I smile. 'Your dad told me that you're learning guitar.'

She flushes a little. 'Yeah. But I'm not very good.'

'Everyone has to start somewhere,' I say. 'Maybe we can do some music together while you're here.'

'Yeah, OK. That'd be cool.'

'Great,' I say. 'Shall we go inside? Mum – your grandma – has been baking all morning. Mince pies, ginger biscuits, shortbread…'

'I don't eat carbs. They make you fat.'

'Oh.' God – twelve years old. I consider giving her a lecture on eating a balanced diet that gives you energy, but then decide to skip it. I won't have many chances to win her over.

'Anyway, I'm going inside.' I get out of the car, relieved when she gets out too. But almost immediately I'm seized by a coughing fit.

'Are you OK?'

'Yeah,' I say, recovering. 'It's just that I'm not used to the cold any more. How about a cup of tea? There are no carbs in tea.'

She screws up her face in an unconscious gesture of distaste and once again I have an uncomfortable flash of recognition. 'Is there any hot chocolate?' she says.

'I don't know. Let's find out.'

Just as we're about to go in, Bill comes back outside. 'There are some carb-free mince pies in there.' He winks at Emily. 'I don't know how your grandma does it. But she's a genius. Packed solid with protein.'

I laugh. Emily rolls her eyes. 'Come on.' I hold out my arm to lock with hers. Ginny and I used to lock arms like that. She looks surprised for a second, then does it. I try not to think about how natural it feels.

We go inside and unlink arms to remove our shoes. I can hear shrieking from the kitchen: the decibel level certainly rises when there are two seven-year-old boys on the scene. Fiona is in the kitchen talking to Mum. I want her to like me and for us to be a normal family. I'm an aunt. I have a brother and a sister-in-law. And, of course, Mum. I am very blessed.

'Nice tree,' Emily says. 'But kind of naked.'

I laugh. 'We thought we'd wait until you got here to decorate it. Maybe later, after you've had time to settle in.'

'Will you show me your room?'

'What's that?' I say, startled.

'You shared with her, right? With Ginny.'

The name seems to come from nowhere, like a noisy ghost playing tricks on my mind.

'I did,' I say carefully.

'I wish I had a twin,' she says.

'Emily?' Fiona calls out from the kitchen. 'Come say hi to your nan.'

Emily tosses her phone and headphones on the sofa and marches into the kitchen like she's off to fight a duel at sunrise. I follow behind.

Mum's sitting at the table with the boys, drinking a cup of tea. When Emily walks into the room, the blood drains from her face. The hand holding the teacup begins to jitter and shake. She opens her mouth and closes it again. I hold my breath, sensing the recalibration process that seems to be going on in her mind.

'Emily,' Mum says, her voice a little hoarse. I exhale, relieved that she's recognised her niece. 'Come here, child.' She holds open her arms. Emily goes to her and gives her a quick hug, her body tall and slender like a willow branch. Seeing the two of them like that, I feel an ache inside. I go over and help Fiona unload the bags of food she's brought.

Mum pulls out a chair for Emily and continues to stare at her. Fiona scolds the boys for not saying hello to me. I go over and give each of them a hug. Robbie, the quieter of the two, pulls away, staring ruefully at the plate of crumbs before him. Jamie gives me a goofy smile. They're both easy to love, and I feel sad for all the time I've missed out seeing them.

'Now can we have more?' Robbie says, his eyes pleading like a puppy.

'Oh, go on then,' Fiona says. 'But just one more biscuit each.'

'Is there any hot chocolate?' I ask Mum. 'I think that's what Emily wants.'

'Of course,' Mum says. 'I'll make some straightaway.' The boys pipe up that they want some too.

'I'll make it,' I say. I put my hand on Mum's shoulder pressing her down in the chair. She scowls at me but I ignore it. I put the kettle on and find the cocoa in the cupboard. Emily comes over and helps me make it. I get the sense that she's disconcerted by the way Mum's looking at her. But I can't blame Mum this time. There is quite a strong resemblance between Emily and Ginny.

When the hot chocolate's made, I go to the sitting room. Fiona follows me. 'Whew, that's them sorted,' she says. 'For now.'

'It's a long journey,' I say. 'They're probably tired of being cooped up in the car.'

'And now they'll be on a sugar high,' Fiona says. 'I'll have to get Bill to take them to the beach.'

'That sounds good,' I say. 'And have they been to MacDougall's Farm? They've got animals and a little train.'

'Really?' Fiona says. 'I'm surprised we haven't been.'

I think back to Mum's negative reaction when I mentioned James. 'I'm sure you have much better things in Glasgow,' I say, waffling a little.

'Anything that gets them outside is good…' Fiona launches into a diatribe about keeping the boys occupied. It's a perfectly normal conversation between two women of a similar age. I'm glad she's here. I hope I can get to know her better.

Bill comes back inside and goes to check on the others in the kitchen. Fiona turns back to me. 'And your mum?' she says in low voice. 'How's she been?'

'Um, she doesn't want to accept help,' I say, honing in on what really is the least of my worries. 'From me, at least. But she seems… fine. Most of the time.'

Fiona cocks her head. She can obviously see right through to the truth. 'It must have been hard coming back and seeing her after so long. But we're here now. I'm happy to help with her. It takes a village…'

I feel so grateful – that she's acknowledging that it's difficult for me too, even though she doesn't know the whole truth of why I stayed away.

'Thanks,' I say.

'I should warn you, Skye,' she adds. 'Emily's going through an awkward pre-teen stage, as I'm sure you noticed. I hope she doesn't... you know... talk out of turn and upset anyone. She seems very interested in knowing more about Ginny.'

'She did mention her.' In a way, I'm glad that Fiona's acknowledged the elephant in the room.

'Right... um... sorry.'

'It's fine. I'm happy to talk about anything she likes.' I lean in towards her. 'It's just kind of weird that my bedroom is the same after all these years.'

Fiona nods. Clearly, she knows what I'm talking about.

'There's an extra bed in the cottage if you want to stay with us,' Fiona says.

'Thanks,' I say. 'But I think it's best if I stay put for now. I don't want to upset the apple cart.'

'What's that?' Bill comes back into the room.

Fiona gives him a look. 'We were talking about Skye's room,' she says, her voice still lowered.

'Oh... that.' He sucks a breath in through his teeth.

'I was thinking that I might clear some things out,' I say. 'Doing up the rest of the house seems to have done Mum a world of good.'

'Maybe...' Bill sounds unconvinced. I understand that he's worried about Mum's mental state, but clearly he must see that enough is enough.

'Anyway,' I say. 'We'll see.'

The boys run out of the kitchen with chocolate smeared on their faces. Mum follows behind them, surprisingly quick with her cane. Emily lags behind. Clearly 'family time' is already taking its toll on her.

'I thought I might take the boys to the beach,' Bill says to me. 'Do you want to come along?'

'Yes,' I say. 'Sounds good.' I'm not sure I'm up to the walk, but I need to get Bill on his own. For once, I feel like he's the one who has the explaining and apologising to do.

'Come on, Emily,' Fiona says. 'Let's go find the jigsaw puzzle. We can set it up here.'

'And we can decorate the tree later,' Mum says. She looks a little lost, like she's not quite sure why everyone is leaving when they just arrived. Fiona notices it too.

'We'll be right back, Mary.'

'Yes…' Mum leans against the sofa, her hand quivering on the handle of her cane. 'Yes, please come home.'

Fiona exchanges a look with Bill. 'Why don't you get the jigsaw?' she says to Emily. 'I… might stay here.'

I liked Fiona before. Now, I feel like hugging her.

'Come on,' I say to my two rowdy nephews. 'Let's get going.'

CHAPTER 20

Walking is harder than I expected. My chest is tight and my lungs feel like they're still weighted down by water. The boys run on ahead. I ask Bill a few questions about the kids and his work, while I consider how to broach meatier topics. When we pass Skybird, I think of the enigmatic Nick Hamilton, my 'rescuer'. But there's no sign of him or Kafka and the car is gone.

We begin the steep climb up to the lochan. I decide it's best just to cut to the chase. 'You lied to me, Bill,' I say. 'Mum didn't ask for me. She doesn't even seem to want me here.'

'I didn't lie… exactly.' Bill sighs. 'She did ask for you – in a roundabout way. I came up to see her immediately after the fall when she was still in hospital. She asked when you were coming home.' He takes a breath. 'You… and Ginny.'

'Christ,' I say. If I hadn't seen it myself, I wouldn't have believed it. 'How long has she been like this?'

Bill slows up. He kicks a large stone from the path.

'About six months. That's when they think she had the stroke.'

'The… stroke?'

'I didn't want to tell you by email or over the phone,' he says. 'I just needed you to be here.'

'What stroke?' I say icily.

'Apparently it was very mild. More like a seizure. She doesn't have the usual symptoms of slurred speech or facial paralysis. But she does have coordination problems. And the occasional break with reality.'

'God.' I put my hands over my face. Six months – around the same time that she heard the rumours that the 'rogue wave' story was a fabrication. It's all too much to take in. I feel so… terrible. For Mum, and for all those years that we've lost.

'She might get better over time,' Bill says. 'The brain does have a remarkable capacity for healing itself. But long-term it could get worse again. It's "complicated" – that's the word the doctor used.' He stops walking and turns to me. 'The main thing we can do is help her stay calm. Keep her blood pressure under control and avoid upsetting her.'

I give a weak laugh. 'And you thought me being here would help?'

'Well, at least you can be another hand on deck.'

'Great,' I say, thinking how useless I've been so far.

He gives me a sideways glance. 'I mean, don't you think it's about time you – what is it they say in America? – stepped up to the plate?'

I keep my anger in check. Bill doesn't know the reason I left, or why I stayed away. I'll tell him – at some point – but having just heard about Mum, it's obviously not the right time.

'I guess it is,' I say.

He nods, and I'm glad that he seems content to leave it there.

When we reach the cove, there's no trace whatsoever of my 'incident' from the previous day. The sun is peeking out from the clouds and casting an orange sheen on the dark grey water. The sea is much calmer today, almost placid, the waves lapping against the rocks like playful puppies. The two boys run ahead, pushing each other and getting their trainers wet trying to outrun the foaming water at the tideline. Bill joins in the race. I try to take in what he's said about Mum – actually it explains a lot. But out here, the tension I feel when I'm in the house seems remote and distant. When the race is over and Bill returns, I tell him that for Mum's sake, I hope we can make some new memories – good ones – now that we're all here together. I mean it in a positive way, but it doesn't quite come out as I intend.

'It must be hard for you being back,' he says. 'Reliving everything after so long.'

'Yes,' I admit. 'Pretty much everything reminds me of *her*.'

'I'm sure,' Bill says. 'I guess my memories of Ginny are a lot different than yours. Mine are mostly good. Like her running down the beach trying to fly.'

Maybe it's the breeze whipping my hair, or just the cold, but a tear streams from my eyes. 'My memories are mostly good too,' I say. 'Why wouldn't they be?'

'I don't know.' Bill hesitates. 'It's just that you were twins, and sort of... I don't know... rivals for everything. That's how it is with Robbie and Jamie. They're so close, and yet, they're trying so hard to be individuals. Sometimes, I think they must have duffed each other up in the womb. I'm surprised they both came out.'

'Do you think I was jealous of her?' I say. 'Because I don't remember that. I mean sure, occasionally. I was jealous when she was the Queen of the Fleet, and I guess I wished I had her voice. But I loved her so much. She was half of who I was. The better half.'

'I was going to say more the other way around,' Bill says, after a pause. 'I think she was jealous of you.'

'No. I don't think so...'

I frown. Between what Byron said, and now Bill, I'm beginning to realise that not everyone has the same shiny memories that I do of my sister. Is that because they don't want to hurt me by reminding me of the good times that can never be again? Or because I've chosen to block out the negatives? Perhaps it's me who's keeping a shrine to her in my mind, just like Mum has in our room.

Robbie pushes Jamie into the surf and he falls down. Bill walks quickly down the beach in their direction. Jamie starts to cry; he's soaking wet. Bill herds them off to practice skipping stones.

I'll have to tell Bill about the pub gossip and the suspicions that have been growing in Mum's mind. Maybe he knows already, but if not, it will be good to have him on side so that together we can put her mind at rest. But when eventually the boys get tired and we start walking back, I can't quite bring myself to do it. Mum's words continue to echo in my head. *People lied about that night. I don't know anything… not any more.* Ugly words that I want to forget, banish them from lurking in the shadows of my mind. Words that aren't true.

They just can't be.

CHAPTER 21

It's almost dark by the time we get back. Bill takes the boys to their cottage, and I return to Mum's house. Everyone is in the kitchen: Mum and Fiona are sitting at the table chopping vegetables, and Emily is flipping through a magazine with her headphones on. I eat a mince pie that's fresh out of the oven and go up to have a bath. It's a relief to sink into the warm water, but once again my mind strays: Mum's book, her suspicions, her *stroke*. I know Bill said not to upset her – and I agree – but is keeping silent about Ginny the answer? Maybe if we talked about the happy memories, then that would help put her mind at rest. Accept that her daughter's death was a terrible accident, and move on.

I get out of the bath, dry off, and get dressed. When I'm back in the room, I pace back and forth, determined to use Ginny's 'presence' there to conjure up some good memories. Ginny dancing around the room in her dress before the Queen of the Fleet ceremony. Ginny lying on the floor laughing as two of the barn cat's calico kittens licked her face. Ginny playing her harp, singing 'She Moved Through the Fair' at a fundraiser for a local care home. My shining sister – a happy girl, an extrovert. A girl who never in a million years would have taken her own life.

A tear trickles down my cheek, blindsiding me. Maybe Bill is right after all. Maybe it's best not to try and remember. Maybe I'm lucky that I'll never know for sure what happened that night.

When I woke up in hospital after the accident, I had no idea how I'd got there. I'd been in my room… I'd rowed with Ginny. She'd left. Mum had asked me to bring her home. And then, there was nothing. I was scared and in pain. I'd asked for Mum, was told that she'd been to see me and gone home to wait for news. Of my sister. I was given the barest of details. There'd been an incident out at the lighthouse. I was told to expect the worst. That was when I'd felt it. The strange, horrible emptiness; the sensation of a glowing electrical thread inside of me that had been snuffed out. Half of myself... gone.

I remained there under observation for three days, groggy on painkillers. When I was lucid, I wanted to crawl out of my skin. The anguish was unbearable. As was the gaping hole where the memories should have been. The doctors said that I had a concussion and head trauma. A brain injury – another thing I now have in common with Mum. And just like with her and her stroke, the prognosis for my recovery was 'complicated'. I was told that, most likely, the brain connections that held my memories of that night had ceased to function, the memories snuffed out, just like the part of me that was linked to Ginny. However, it was also possible that under the right stimulus, some or all of the memories might return. Over the years I've had occasional 'flashes': faces in the firelight, the sickly taste of whiskey and Coke. Something thrown at my face. A flashing light. To me the so-called memory flashes are a jumble and I don't know if they're real or not.

I sit down on my bed and close my eyes for a moment listening to the sound of my own breathing. The most powerful 'flash' of memory I've had of that night isn't even a memory at all. I imagine that I see my sister out on the rocks. Arms outstretched, her hair lashed by the wind. And with the vision comes an overriding feeling of fear. Because I know I'm going to have to go out and rescue her, pull her to safety. 'Protect her' because that's what Mum asked me to do.

The reality is that I didn't see Ginny that night out at the lighthouse. The witnesses all said the same thing. I arrived at the party and Ginny wasn't there. People were coming and going all night long, and when I arrived she'd gone off with James. I'd been annoyed, angry that she wasn't there. I had a few drinks. I was tired and cold, I wanted to go home. I thought that James could be relied on to take her home. He was her boyfriend, after all.

I left the party. A mile or so down the treacherous single-track road, I hit a huge boulder. The road zigged, I zagged. I woke up, my memories gone.

And Mum… she has no first-hand knowledge of what happened, because she wasn't there. Maybe to her it makes more sense that Ginny chose her own destiny, rather than having been the victim of a terrible accident. I don't know. But is not talking about it really the right answer—?

'Aunt Skye?'

There's a knock at the door. 'Can I come in?'

'Sure,' I say, grateful for the distraction.

When Emily walks into the room, it's almost like I've gone back in time. To a world where my sister is alive and we both had our lives and dreams ahead of us. I know that it's not the truth, and in fact, while there is a resemblance between Emily and Ginny, it's not as strong as I initially thought. Emily is taller and more substantial, built more like a volleyball player than a ballerina. Her jaw is squarer, her eyes set closer together. She has Fiona's nose. But most of all, her eyes lack that ethereal light.

'Hi,' I say. My throat is parched and my voice sounds raspy. 'You OK?'

'It's time for supper.' Emily glances around her, obviously curious about this room.

She goes over to the Celtic harp in the corner and runs her fingers over the strings. The sound makes me shiver.

'Is this yours?' she says.

'No,' I say. 'It was my sister's. Someone was getting rid of it, and Ginny asked if she could have it. She learned to play a little bit.'

'What was she like?' Emily asks. 'Ginny.'

I don't answer right away. Whatever I tell her won't be the whole truth, or even close to it. How do you explain what a person was 'like'? To me, Ginny was a living, breathing person made of light, shadows, memories and emotions. She may be dead, but she's with me always. But I feel an obligation to Ginny – and Emily – to find an answer to the question.

'My sister was unlike anyone else,' I say. 'She was funny, and beautiful, and full of energy. She had a very special voice. Everyone loved her – me most of all.'

I hone in on the good memories. 'When we were kids, we used to snuggle in one bed on the coldest nights. We'd burrow under the covers with a torch smuggled in from Dad's shed. We'd read, or else just talk for hours. About total rubbish.' I give a little laugh. 'What man we were going to marry, how many kids we'd have. What we wanted to be when we grew up. Ginny wanted to be Princess Leia. I wanted to be the lead singer from Abba. The blonde one, not the brunette.'

I swallow hard and turn back. Emily's picking at her nail polish: purple with silver sparkles. 'Do you miss her?' she says.

If Bill knew she was asking me these questions, he'd probably put a stop to it. But Emily is twelve years old. She's never experienced death and I hope that it's a long, long time before she does. It's natural that she's curious.

'Of course I do,' I say. 'She was my twin.'

'Yeah,' Emily says disdainfully. 'I'm sure it's a lot harder with a twin.'

I go over to the small window between the beds and stare out at the grey sky above the trees. 'There's a book I read once about a captain of a whaling ship,' I say. 'He becomes obsessed with hunting down the white whale that bit off his leg.'

'I don't think whales eat people's legs,' Emily says.

'This one did. And when the captain lay awake at night, he could feel his leg. A kind of phantom pain. That's what it's like to lose a limb.' I sigh. 'And a twin.'

Emily frowns. 'It's like she's there but not there?' she says.

'Exactly,' I say. 'It's as if she might walk into the room at any moment. And if she did, I know that we would hug each other and talk, and probably fight, and get angry. And then make up again. Because that's what people do who love each other.' I feel the familiar ache inside. 'But that's not going to happen, so I feel pain. Does that make sense?'

'I guess so,' she says.

Maybe it does make sense to her on some level. A twelve-year-old girl is less likely to filter her emotions through a grid of orderly thoughts. Stages of grief, and all that. I've been through the stages of grief. But I still feel pain.

'Anyway…' I force myself to look at her and smile. 'Let's talk about something more pleasant. Like supper. I'm starving. Let's go downstairs.'

'Yeah, OK.' She goes back over to the harp, looking at it wistfully.

'You can have the harp if you want,' I say. 'I'll tune it for you.'

'Really?'

'Ask your mum if it's OK, but it's fine with me.'

'Gosh, thanks.' Emily brushes the strings with her fingers. She glances down at Ginny's bed where I've put my suitcase and Dad's guitar case.

'Will you play for us after supper?' she says, pointing to the guitar. 'Nan wants to decorate the tree. But the boys can do that.' She glances at the floor, looking a little shy. 'Maybe we could sing together.'

'Sounds good.' I take out Dad's guitar and begin tuning it. It's been almost twenty years since it's been played, and it is out of tune, but the pegs move easily and the strings all seem sturdy. I strum a few chords, then move on to arpeggios and riffs. The sound is dark and pure and the instrument feels almost warm in my hands. Dad is dead, but his guitar is alive once again. He would have appreciated that.

In the end I do take the guitar with me when Emily and I go downstairs. Dinner is a loud affair, with the boys laughing and squabbling, Bill talking with Mum about the cottages, and Fiona and me talking about the best time of year to go to L.A. Emily sits mostly in silence, pushing the vegetables around on her plate and picking at the salmon. I find her attitude a bit irritating.

When dinner is over, we all move into the sitting room. Mum sits in the wing chair near the fireplace, her cane propped against the arm. Bill appoints himself to put the lights on the tree like Dad used to, which makes me smile. The boys tear into the ornament boxes and even Emily gets up off the sofa and starts unwrapping ornaments and baubles.

'Are you going to play for us?' she says. She unwraps a snow globe with the New York skyline that I sent Mum one year after I'd played a gig upstate. As she shakes the globe, sparkles float upwards and the top of the Chrysler Building lights up. It's tacky, just like the gifts I've brought with me this time.

'Yes, please do, Skye,' Fiona says. 'We'd love that.'

Robbie steals the snow globe away from Emily. It falls to the floor and the boys scramble for it under the sofa. I sigh. Snow globes, oven gloves, sunglasses and beach towels. There's only one real gift that I have left to give.

'OK.' I take Dad's guitar out of the case and sit on the sofa. Emily sits next to me.

'How about some Christmas songs?' I say to her. 'You can sing along.'

I launch into some songs for the kids. 'Jingle Bells', 'Frosty the Snowman', 'Winter Wonderland'. Bill finishes the lights and Fiona supervises the boys putting the baubles and other ornaments on the tree.

Emily watches me play but doesn't really sing. I try to encourage her to join in, but she shakes her head. I keep strumming and singing, occasionally glancing over at Mum. On nights like this of old, she would have joined in singing carols, her voice high and slightly flat, like a church soprano. Now, though, her lips are clamped shut and she's staring at the wall. I can't tell if she's enjoying the music, or if the memories are too painful.

'Can you play "Warrior Woman"?' Emily says, taking me by surprise. 'I like that one.'

'Um…' I glance at Mum, who doesn't react, then at Bill, who nods.

'That's a good one,' he says.

'OK,' I say. It's not the happiest song in the world, but hopefully it won't spoil the mood. Mum's probably never even heard it. I begin playing the opening arpeggios. Actually, I want Mum to hear it, because I'm proud of it. I want her to know that, despite evidence to the contrary, I'm not a complete failure.

I sing the opening verse. Fiona stops to listen. Emily mouths along with the words. From nowhere, a chill seems to seep into the room. I keep playing, but my throat has gone dry. Mum's head snaps in our direction. Emily has begun to sing:

'I've played the joker,
I've played the ace.
I've seen the love dying on your face.
But I'll rise up from your cold embrace
'cause I'm a Warrior Woman.'

She doesn't have Ginny's special voice. Still, her manner and bearing, the way her blonde hair shines in the twinkling lights – it all just feels uncanny.

Mum opens her mouth and closes it again. Her eyes are glassy and too bright. Emily hasn't noticed and keeps singing. I try to catch Bill's attention, but he's busy with the boys, who are looking at something on his phone. My neck is tense, my fingers tingly and strange. But I keep playing to the end.

When I finish the final riff, I put the guitar down and begin clapping. Fiona joins in too. 'That was great, Emily,' I say. 'The song really suits you. Take a bow.'

Emily's face is flushed a perfect shade of rose. She takes a mock bow, and Bill joins in clapping too. She straightens up, beaming—

The cane thunks to the floor. The chair creaks. Mum grips the arms of the chair and heaves herself to her feet. Bill stops clapping, exchanges a worried look with Fiona. They both take a step towards Mum, but she picks up the cane and waves it to fend them off.

I feel once again like I'm underwater and can't breathe. Mum hobbles over to Emily. No one else moves.

Mum goes up to Emily, and places a thin, veined hand on her cheek. Emily flinches.

'That was lovely, darling,' Mum says. 'I wanted to hear you sing again. It's been so many years.'

Emily's face becomes a frozen grimace. I feel like I – or someone – should intervene...

Mum drops her hand. She hobbles to the stairs. Then, she turns back.

'Why did you do it, Ginny?' She wags a finger at Emily. 'How could you have done that to me?'

CHAPTER 22

It's hard to see a way back from this. Mum goes up the stairs, Emily looks stunned, her eyes shiny with tears. Fiona goes to comfort her, and after a few minutes, she and the children leave to go back to the cottage. Bill lingers at the bottom of the stairs as if he's unsure what to do. I stare at the Christmas tree, so beautiful and sparkly. Right now, it seems like a joke.

'I'm sorry,' I say when the others are gone.

'Yeah,' Bill says, grimacing. Upstairs, Mum's door closes. The footsteps fade away.

'You have to talk to Emily,' I say. 'Tell her that it isn't her fault. That none of it is her fault.'

'Yes,' he says. 'I will. But I think we're best not mentioning or talking about Ginny around Mum, don't you?'

I know he's probably right, but still I feel torn. I think of the conversations I've had with Mum, skirting closer and closer to her feelings. I'd thought that we were making some positive strides forwards, towards clearing the air. I thought that with Bill's help, we could *agree* that Ginny's death wasn't deliberate; and put Mum's fears on that account to rest.

'I don't know…' I say.

'Come on, Skye,' Bill says. 'You saw how Emily reacted – which was perfectly understandable. At least let Mum get used to her a little. Let them get used to each other.'

'OK.' I sigh. 'If you think it will help.'

'I do,' he says. 'I'll tell Fiona and the others. No more rocking the boat.' He puts on his coat to leave. 'You OK here? You could sleep at ours if you want.'

'No, thanks,' I say. 'Someone needs to be here, especially now. I'll check on Mum before I go to bed.'

'Good,' he says. 'Tomorrow – new day.' He gives me a wave and goes out the door.

No more rocking the boat. I run my fingers over the smooth wood of Dad's guitar and put it in the case. I feel sad, because other than Mum's outburst, I was enjoying myself. I'd forgotten how much fun it is to play music without expectation or pressure. The simple joy of singing songs with my family. Now, though, it seems that Dad's guitar will need to stay in its case, and the memories – good and bad – will need to stay under the carpet.

I tidy up the sitting room and kitchen, and make a cup of tea for Mum. When I take it upstairs, her door is slightly ajar and the room is dark. She's asleep – or pretending to be. I take the tea to my room and drink it. I frown over at Ginny's empty bed. Mum's words come back into my head like a vinyl record with a tick. *'Why did you do it?'*

As I get in bed, I think of my vision of Ginny on the rocks; the torn up coach ticket; the empty grave… I lie awake for a long time and go to sleep with the light on.

*

The next morning when I wake up, rain is hammering on the roof and the shutter is banging again in the wind. On the plus side, my breathing is easier and I can no longer taste salt water. On the minus side… just about everything else after last night. I get out of bed and dress in jeans and a black long-sleeved jumper. Then I brave going downstairs.

From the kitchen there's the sound of a wooden spoon battering the edge of a bowl. My heart speeds up as I go in the door.

'Mum,' I say. 'Hi. Are you OK?'

She stops mixing and looks up at me from the table. For a second her face flickers with something like shame.

'I've made coffee,' she says.

'Thanks.' I go over and pour myself a cup. How am I supposed to act? What on earth do I say?

'Lorna's coming over this morning,' she says. 'To help out with the baking. It's going to take a lot of effort to keep everyone in mince pies and biscuits.'

Biscuits is a conversation I can usually handle – but not this morning. I know I promised Bill I wouldn't upset her or mention Ginny, but this morning she seems lucid. It seems a good opportunity to find out how deeply her separation from reality goes, before closing the subject down for good.

'Mum, do you remember last night? Emily sang. You… had a bit of an outburst.'

'Emily?' The confused look is back. *Don't rock the boat.*

'Your granddaughter.'

'Yes. Yes, such a lovely girl. But too thin, if you ask me.'

'Do you remember, Mum? You thought that she was Ginny. She does look a bit like her… I guess.'

'Ginny? No, don't be ridiculous.' The cold, hard shell snaps firmly back in place. 'Ginny is dead.'

'Yes, Mum,' I say. 'But last night Emily kind of… freaked out because of what happened.'

'Well… I don't know.' The lines in her brow narrow into a frown. 'Do you like your shortbread with chocolate on top, or plain?'

'Plain, Mum.'

'Yes,' she says. 'Plain. Perhaps with a dusting of sugar.'

I debate whether or not I should continue the conversation. But as the oven timer beeps with the first batch of mince pies ready to come out, I decide to leave it there. Bill and Fiona will have to do their bit to clear the air, for Emily's sake. I'm glad, however, that in the light of day, Mum is aware that Ginny is dead, and Emily is her granddaughter. That's something, at least.

Mum looks towards the oven and starts to get up. 'I'll get them,' I say. 'Even I can manage that.' I keep my tone light, indicating a truce.

'Thank you,' Mum says, short and clipped. 'My back is a little stiff today. It must be this awful weather. I think it's supposed to clear later, though.'

'Hard to believe,' I say.

'Yes, well, you know what they say. Don't like the weather in Scotland…'

'Wait five minutes,' we say together.

I smile at Mum, grateful for even the smallest kernel of solidarity. I take the tray of mince pies out of the oven and set them on a wire rack.

'I hope it does clear,' I say. 'Because those little boys are going to be climbing the walls if they don't get out. Speaking of which…' I take a breath. 'Do you think I might take a few of those mince pies over to Skybird? I want to thank Mr Hamilton for helping me the other day.'

Mum stops mixing and looks up. She seems fully back to her senses now, and it feels like she's appraising me. I ignore the little stab of annoyance I feel.

'Of course,' she says. 'Take what you like. There are some ginger biscuits left too.'

'I think a few mince pies will do,' I say.

'Yes,' she says. 'You're probably right. He can be a bit touchy about visitors.'

'So he's not having family come round for Christmas?'

Mum's put on a good act of knowing nothing about him, but I'm sure she knows more than she's letting on.

'He hasn't mentioned it.'

'That's a shame.'

'Well,' she says, sprinkling some flour on the mixing. 'It's not the most pleasant thing to spend Christmas alone, but you get through it. It's just another day that passes. You know?'

'I know, Mum. Spot on.' Maybe it's a deserved little dig, but I choose to take it as something else we have in common.

I put some of the mince pies on a plate and cover them with cling film. As I'm doing so, Mum's friend Lorna pulls up in her car outside. Perfect timing.

Mum insists on getting up and hobbling to the door. I don't stop her. I'm not in the mood for a long chat with Lorna, so I bundle up in a borrowed raincoat and leave by the back door. I clutch the plate and hurry down the lane, bowed against the wind and rain. I pass The Stables and even over the sound of the storm, I hear shrieks and voices. I'm glad I have something to do other than brave the chaos and any lingering effects of last night's episode. Any excuse to escape from the house and clear my head is welcome right now.

When I get to the smaller cottage, however, and see the silver Vauxhall parked in front, I experience a flutter of nerves. Which is just stupid. This will take five minutes at most.

Up close, I can see how much work must have gone into converting the old stone building into a habitable cottage. The rocks and gorse have been cleared, the trees and rhododendron cut back, and the sagging walls reconstructed and repointed. The cottage has been whitewashed with the door painted dark green. On either side of the porch is a conical-shaped topiary in a clay pot. A ceramic plaque next to the bell says 'Skybird' in cursive writing, with a line drawing of two seagulls and a sunset.

The porch roof is so small that I end up standing in a drip getting wet. I ring the bell and also knock firmly.

I wait: long enough to rethink this. I could leave the mince pies on the doorstep and leave. If he's in the middle of something, then I'm disturbing him, which isn't my intention. I'm just about to go when I hear a bark from inside. Kafka. A moment later, the door opens.

God, I *have* disturbed him, but not at his painting. He's standing before me, his head wet, wearing nothing but a towel around his waist. One of us is clearly at a disadvantage and I have the feeling it might be me.

'Yes?' he says tersely. He rakes his wet hair back from his face. Kafka comes out to give me a sniff and a wag of his tail. I bend down to pat him.

'Um, hi,' I say straightening. 'Sorry. I… came to thank you. For… rescuing me.' I keep my eyes focused on his face. OK, that's a lie. He's obviously quite fit to have carried me up from the beach and he looks it. He has a scar on the left side of his stomach, like maybe he's had an appendix removed. Not that I'm looking at his body. Because, really, that would not be called for in this situation.

'I brought you some mince pies.' I thrust the plate towards him. 'And, um, it's wet out here. Can I come in? Just for a second?'

He sighs, the frown on his face unwavering. 'Move, Kafka,' he says. 'Let her in. I'm going to get dressed.' He seems to be speaking only to the dog.

I step inside. I don't look at the back of him as he walks to the narrow staircase that leads to the bedrooms above. I see him, of course, but I'm not *appraising* him.

He gets high marks.

Kafka nuzzles my hand, his tail still wagging. At least one of them is welcoming. The dog goes over to the rug by the fireplace and lies down, panting. The hearth is black and cold without a fire in it, though one has been laid in the grate, with newspaper balled at the bottom, a layer of twigs, and then logs on top. Clearly, Nick Hamilton is skilled at making fires. As I look around the room, my eye snags on the tartan rug draped on the back of the sofa. Only two days ago, I was lying under that blanket. Naked.

I can't stop my mind from going *there*. He must have lain me down and unwrapped my coat from around me. And then he would have removed my wet clothing: my top, my bra, my pants. Then he would have towel-dried me, or else just put the blanket over me. But either way, in no logical scenario would he have put the blanket over me first to preserve my modesty and then taken my clothing off.

I'm sure it all happened very quickly. I'm sure his only thought was to get me warm so I didn't get hypothermia…

Jesus Christ.

I should have left the mince pies on the porch.

Too late. He comes back downstairs wearing jeans and a navy hoodie that brings out the blue in his storm-coloured eyes. It's then I note that his face is only half-shaved. That must have been what he was doing when I knocked. I feel a little better. How silly to have a half-shaved face.

'Sorry…' I say again, and then catch myself. 'Sorry' is about the most useless word in the English language. I recover with: 'Do you like mince pies?'

He gives a little half-smile. 'I haven't had a mince pie in two years,' he says.

'Really?'

'Really.'

I hold out the plate and he takes it. My hands are quivering. Stupid…

'I didn't make them,' I say. 'My mum and sister-in-law did. They're good at baking and… things like that. You've probably seen that the other cottage is occupied. My brother and his family are staying until New Year's. They've got three kids. I hope they don't bother you.'

'*They* haven't bothered me so far.' He looks bemused, the meaning clear. I'm the only one who's disturbed his solitude.

'Yes, well. Fair warning.'

'Fair warning.'

He turns and takes the plate of mince pies into the kitchen. I don't know what else to do, so I follow him. This strong, silent shit is starting to annoy me. If he wants me to leave, he should say. If not…

'I guess I should offer you a cup of tea,' he says.

'That would be nice.' I throw caution to the wind. 'Given that you've undressed me and breathed into my mouth. I've had less intimate experiences with people I've had sex with.'

He laughs, and I feel a little undercurrent between us. He knows that I know. There's no point in pretending that it was blanket first then clothing off.

'Is that so?' he says.

I shrug. 'I'm sure it was all purely professional on your part. I heard the paramedic. She called you DCI Hamilton.'

The laughter fades from his face. He turns away and puts the kettle on.

'Are you a DCI?' I press. 'Because everyone around here seems to think you're an artist.'

He doesn't answer for a long moment. Just because he rescued me doesn't give me the right to be asking him personal questions.

'I *was* a DCI,' he says, his back to me. 'Once. Not any more. But in that particular situation when I called for the paramedics, I thought it would help focus their minds on getting here more quickly. Which seems to have been the case.'

'Right.' It makes sense. I've certainly dropped the odd name in my time to get tickets to a show or a table at some swish restaurant. And if it works for getting medical attention for a woman who almost drowned on a freezing beach, then good on him, I guess.

He doesn't say anything else as the kettle boils. He takes two mugs out of the cupboard, opens a cannister helpfully marked 'tea', and plops a teabag into each mug.

'Milk and sugar?' he says.

'Black with one sugar.'

He makes my tea and then his own. A splash of milk, no sugar, I note, like I'm the investigator on the scene. My mind flashes with different openers to break the silence. But I decide that I've asked enough questions. If he chooses to speak, then fine. If not, this will be a very awkward cup of tea.

It feels like a victory when he speaks. 'Mince pie?'

A very small victory.

'No, thanks,' I say. 'They're for you.'

He unwraps the cling film and takes a mince pie off the plate. Then he leads the way back to the sitting room. He gestures with his head for me to sit down on the sofa. He sits in a wing chair on the other side of the fireplace. Kafka is lying on the rug, snoring softly; his tail gives a thump in his sleep.

'So, are you staying long?' he says.

This seems to be the neutral question that people are asking in lieu of talking about the weather.

'I don't know,' I say. 'I'm playing it by ear.'

He gives a little laugh like I've made a joke. 'Well said. I guess as a musician you do that a lot.'

I don't smile back. Clearly there is some sort of point scoring going on here. I've got out of him that he was once a DCI. He's made it clear that he knows who I am. 'I suppose I do,' I say.

'Right,' he says. He bites into the mince pie. 'This is delicious, by the way.'

'I'll tell Mum you think so.'

'And is she doing better now?'

'Better?' I sip the tea, letting it burn my throat. Mum's made it seem like she knows very little about her tenant, but he clearly knows something about her. Another point scored. 'In what way?'

He sits back in his chair, cupping his hands around the mug of tea. 'I don't know your Mum well, obviously,' he says. 'So I may be talking out of turn. She came to clean one day – a month or so ago – before she had the fall. I liked her. She was straight and no-nonsense. Not… chatty.'

'That's Mum,' I say, unexpectedly proud. 'She used to teach maths. There's no nonsense about that.'

'True.' He traces the woodgrain on the arm of the chair. His fingers are long, like a pianist's… or an artist's.

'And then, I went to see her about a week ago. After the fall. Brought her some biscuits and a newspaper, as you do.'

I raise an eyebrow. I didn't have him down as the neighbourly type.

'She seemed totally different. You were all she could talk about. You and your sister. How you were stars in America. How inconvenient it was that she hurt her leg because you were coming home and she needed to get everything ready.'

I sit very still, feeling the pit open up in the bottom of my stomach.

'My sister died fifteen years ago,' I say.

He lets out a low whistle. 'Right. That explains the gossip I overheard in the village. I did wonder.'

'Yes, well…' I stand up. I've had enough of this. 'Thanks for the tea. I'm sorry if I disturbed you.' I give him a tight smile and go to take my mug back to the kitchen.

'It sounds like quite a difficult situation to come back to,' he says. 'So, I won't beat about the bush. When you went into the water the other day, were you hoping to drown?'

That stops me. Clear and to the point. Whether I just went for a swim or went in the water with the intent not to come out again – I'm beginning to see how it *does* make all the difference.

'No.' I take my mug to the sink. 'No, I wasn't.'

He comes up and stands next to me looking out of the window. The sea is hazy and grey and raindrops are racing down the glass. It's a good place to be lonely, though if he is, there's little sign of it.

'I love this place,' he says. 'On a clear day, you can see the Small Isles. Just about. It's an idyllic spot.'

'Yes, that's one word for it.' I wash the mug and put it to the side.

'Look, Skye, I'm sorry if I offended you,' he says. 'I guess on some level I'm still a policeman. What is it they say in America? "To protect and serve?" I've seen a lot of…' he hesitates '… things. And what they do to the people left behind. I'm just making sure Kafka doesn't need to practice his doggy paddle again.'

I sigh. 'He doesn't. Not on my account.'

'Good.'

He's standing between me and the door. I'll have to go around him, which will be awkward. 'So why did you stop being a policeman?' I say.

He doesn't answer right away, and I begin to wonder if he's going to. He rinses out his mug and puts it to the side. I go around him to the door.

'Well, if you have a minute, I'll show you.'

'OK…' I say, a little wary.

He goes past me and up the narrow stairs. I follow him to the door of what I imagine is the larger of the two bedrooms. I stand beside him and look inside.

The room is filled with a forest of easels and canvases. The bed has been pushed to the far corner of the room and the floor has been covered with canvas drop cloths. There's a strong smell of turpentine and oil paint.

I go into the room, feeling a spark of excitement at the artwork. Each painting is a study in grey, blue, and silver: sea and skyscapes mostly, though there are some views of boats and the village as well. But as I look more closely, I see that each one actually contains a kaleidoscope of colours: a pop of orange or violet, a shimmer of gold or a streak of magenta. They're stormy and complex, with a strong sense of movement: wind on water, ripples on sand, clouds moving across sky. There's a slightly chilling quality about them that evokes the power of nature and people at its mercy.

My eye is drawn to a larger canvas near the window. It's well over a metre long and almost as high. It's clearly a work in progress and, from the tray of paints next to it, maybe the last thing he was working on. The sky is painted in moody shades of grey and mauve, with a streak of pink on the horizon. I recognise the view: the beach below the cliff, with the huge boulders framing the scene. What arrests my attention, however, is that this is the only painting that contains a figure, pencilled in and unfinished. A woman sitting on a rock, her back to the viewer. She seems to be naked from the waist up, and from the waist down, the sketch gives the impression of a slick, dark body like a seal. The Selkie. I shiver.

Nick comes into the room and stands just behind me, studying the painting. 'It's just a rough idea,' he says. 'I'm… experimenting.'

I stare at the girl, the lines of her body strong, and yet her pose giving her a fragility, a vulnerability. I move on to look at another picture near the window: of a small boat being tossed against a sky of seemingly endless depth. 'These paintings,' I say, '… they're wonderful.'

He shrugs. 'Some of them are getting there. It would be nice to have a little more space. I'd like to work on a larger scale. I'm hoping to get enough work together for a show in the spring. But one thing at a time.'

I recognise the evasiveness. An artist who is desperate for his work to be seen and appreciated, but doesn't want to get his hopes up. I've been that way before, when I'm in the zone of writing my own songs, creating things that are fresh and different, poetry and melodies that I'm proud of. For me, it's been a while. But Nick Hamilton is clearly in the zone with these paintings. 'You have a right to be proud of them,' I say, as if he's been following my train of thought.

'For me it's about the process,' he says. 'If it's going well, then I try not to worry too much about the result.'

I understand that one too. 'They say that art is the act of making the infinite finite,' I say. 'Committing your imagination to a medium and a moment in time.'

'Yes.' He looks a little surprised that I could come up with something like that.

'For me, when I'm writing songs, it's narrowing down all the possibilities of words and emotions, and creating a melody that "fits".'

'It sounds similar. Is that what you're doing while you're here?'

I turn back to the painting of the Selkie. The movement of her hair in the wind gives her a sense of freedom. But the figure seems transfixed by the horizon. Is she waiting for someone to come home? Or longing for escape? 'I guess you could say that I'm open to inspiration,' I reply. 'Focusing on the process, not the result.'

'That's all we can do, isn't it?'

He moves close enough so that his arm is almost touching mine. I can feel the pull of him, like he's his own source of gravity. I move away.

'So to answer your question,' he says, 'I'm no longer a policeman because I'm having a go at this.'

He picks up a pencil from the paint tray, frowns at the canvas, and bends down, correcting a single line. Then he stands back, considering. His face is a mask of concentration. There's clearly more to the story than he's letting on.

'I'll leave you to it,' I say quietly. I move towards the door but it's almost as if he's forgotten that I'm there. 'Thank you for showing me.'

I'm almost out the door when he stops me.

'Skye,' he says.

I turn. His grey eyes hold mine.

'Good luck. With your songs. And… your mum.'

CHAPTER 23

The rain has let up as I walk home. I can't quite chase the enigmatic Nick Hamilton from my mind. On the one hand, he's a bit of a cold fish. Condescending, unfriendly, trying to score points, not volunteering anything about himself. I did, however, appreciate him showing me the paintings. I don't know much about art and what is and isn't 'good'. But I know what I like. Nick's art was powerful and beautiful.

Either way, it's irrelevant. I'm not going to let myself be attracted to him. We're both here temporarily. He owes me nothing, and I've paid back my debt with… mince pies.

The lights are off when I pass The Stables and Bill's car is gone. Maybe Emily threw a strop, refused to go to 'Nan's house' so they went to the village instead. In truth, I can hardly blame her. I think of what Nick said about Mum: how quickly she went from normal to 'losing the plot'. Bill's got his family to deal with – I've got nothing. It's down to me now to look after her. While Emily is here, I'll stick to my agreement with Bill and not raise the subject of Ginny. But if I am going to be staying, I need to do something about my room. After seeing Nick's art, I almost feel inspired to try writing my songs again, and I'll need a place to work. But most of all, keeping the room as a tomb of memories can't be good for Mum's mental state – or mine. I need to make a start.

Today. Now.

When I get back to the cottage, Mum and Lorna are in the kitchen, and a new rack of mince pies is cooling on the worktop.

I say hi to Lorna and we chat for a few minutes. I'm grateful that she's been such a support to Mum over the years, and vice versa – Lorna being a widow too. Mum doesn't join in the conversation, and there's no sign that she's told Lorna about what happened last night. I go to the cupboard under the sink, grab a roll of bin bags, and make my exit.

I go upstairs to my room and shut the door. I look around at the familiar things – the posters, the two beds, the view out of the window – and feel an overwhelming sense of sadness. So many memories – most of them good ones. But I have to stick to my guns. I *know* that what I'm doing is for the best.

The first thing I do is take down the posters. I remove Noel Gallagher and the concert calendars that are now years out of date. I consider taking down Bob Dylan and Joan Baez, but eventually, when all the other walls are bare, I decide they can stay for now. The knotty pine looks very dated, the room would look so much brighter if it was painted white. Another job to add to my list. I roll up the posters so they can go in the attic if Mum doesn't want them binned.

Next, I brave the chest of drawers. I'm relieved to see that Mum's cleared out the clothing and is using it to store extra bedding, gift wrap, and files of papers. I check my old wardrobe and find that she's also using that to store her old things. That's all very positive. But when I go over to Ginny's wardrobe and fling open the doors, I recognise her things immediately: the dress she wore when she was Queen of the Fleet, a jumper that our grandma knitted for her in moss green wool (mine was navy blue), a blue cowboy shirt with mother of pearl snaps and red stitching on the breast pockets. I run my finger over the stitching, feeling a deep ache of loss. I can remember Ginny wearing this shirt when we performed once at the Highland Games in the village. I wore my matching shirt: white with blue stitching. They were our lucky shirts. We were going to wear them to the audition. I don't know what happened to mine.

I go through her clothing, allowing each memory to rise and then float away like an autumn leaf. I'm beginning to see how difficult it must have been for Mum to get rid of anything. But it needs to be done. I put the dress, the jumper, and the cowboy shirt in a bag to take to the attic. The rest I put in another bag for the charity shop.

It's only when the hanging items are gone that I notice a wad of clothing balled up and shoved at the back. Immediately I recognise my cowboy shirt. There's also a few T-shirts and a pair of jeans with rhinestone swooshes on the pockets that were mine. I'd wondered what had happened to those jeans…

I put the cowboy shirt in the 'keep' bag and toss the jeans onto my bed to see if I can still fit into them. I spot something else shoved at the very back where the wooden shelf is coming away from the boards. A notebook with a blue cover that looks like a school composition book. Ginny's other journals had pretty covers of mountains or unicorns or goddesses – whatever she was into at the time – never a plain notebook like this one. I take it out and as I'm opening it, something falls onto the floor. A ticket. I pick it up.

It's a coach ticket. Eilean Shiel to Glasgow via Fort William. The same journey we were supposed to be taking together for the audition. The same journey that was on the ticket Ginny ripped up. I turn the ticket over feeling a twisting in my stomach. Ginny tore up the ticket that I'd bought for her. This one I've never seen before. There's a date on it.

It's for the day she died.

CHAPTER 24

I try to make sense of what I'm holding in my hand. A ticket to Glasgow. I shake the notebook to see if anything else comes out, like a return ticket. But no… I already know from the chill I feel inside of me. It was one way. Ginny was leaving – without me.

No. I don't believe it. She wouldn't do that to me.

Would she?

I stare at the empty spaces on the wall, the pine slightly darker where the posters were hung. My head hurts as I try to recall those last few months when I was working hard to secure our future. We had our usual rows over who got to use the car, who got the shower first, and whose turn it was to do the washing-up. She'd spent time away from the house with James and other friends, but that wasn't unusual. I don't remember the morning of the party very clearly – just the row we had that night. Had she seemed quieter than usual? More withdrawn? Not that I can recall. She'd been a little unwell the week before. A stomach bug. Other than that… nothing.

I stand up and pace back and forth. If she'd gone so far as to buy her own ticket, then why didn't she get on the coach? And what was she planning to do once she got there? The audition was still six weeks away. Was she going to get a job? Where was she going to stay?

I rub at the lines on my forehead and sit back down on the bed. None of it makes sense. Is there some sort of innocent explanation that I'm overlooking? Maybe Ginny found the ticket? Maybe it wasn't even hers…?

Or maybe she was going with someone else. The thought is like a smack in the face. Her boyfriend, James. Of course. His family had money: they could have stayed in a nice hotel, seen the sights... Not like the awful hostel I stayed in, the rough café where I worked double shifts before I went to America.

I throw the ticket aside and open up the notebook. It's mostly blank, but on the fourth page there's something written in small neat handwriting: Ellen McCree. 12 Cranach Terrace. The writing isn't Ginny's: hers was loopy and flowing and took up a lot of space on the page. I've never heard of an Ellen McCree.

I flip through the rest of the book. On random pages in the middle, I find some of Ginny's writing. A few notes of dates and reminders, a few words dashed here and there. Snippets of thoughts and songs. No outpouring of emotions and recounting of events as was her usual practice.

I close the notebook and toss it onto Ginny's bed. My skin feels crawly and dirty. I go over to the harp in the corner and grab the strings in a fist. I feel like yanking them off. They gouge into my skin. Damn it.

It's *bloody* nothing.

But is it nothing? If Ginny was supposed to be on a coach to Glasgow the day she died, then she wouldn't have been going to the party. She wouldn't have... died. I lean against the wall and put my hands over my face. What does it all mean—?

'Aunt Skye?'

Jesus.

'Just a second.' I shove the ticket inside the notebook and put it under my suitcase. When I open the door and see Emily's innocent blue-green eyes that so resemble Ginny's, I feel angry – at myself. My sister was keeping secrets from me, and I didn't even have the slightest clue.

'Hi,' I say, raking back my hair. My brow is clammy with sweat. I stand aside to let her into the room. I don't want to talk to anyone right now, but equally, I don't want Emily to think that something is wrong.

'There's a man downstairs. Brian or something…'

'Byron.'

'Yeah, that was it,' Emily says. She looks around at the empty walls and the bin bags. 'What are you doing?'

'Having a clear out,' I say.

'Oh.' Emily sits down on Ginny's bed. Seeing her there is unsettling. 'Do I really look like she did?' she says, as if she's read my thoughts. 'Dad says that's why Nan freaked out last night.'

'There's a slight resemblance.' I downplay my own reaction. 'Your hair, the colour of your eyes, and your height. But I'm sorry about what happened. Mum – your nan – shouldn't have done that.'

Emily shrugs. 'Nan's just old,' she says. 'Maybe she's got dementia or something.'

I frown but let the comment pass. Mum's only in her late sixties. Though I have to admit, between the cane and the breaks with reality, she does seem older than that.

'I think she's probably just a little overwhelmed having everyone here,' I say.

'Yeah, whatever.' Emily looks down at her hands and begins picking at her nail polish. I get the sense that 'the incident' – while disconcerting, and even a little frightening at the time – has now become a bore. 'Anyway, should I tell the man that you'll be down?'

'Yeah,' I say. 'I'll only be a minute.'

Emily leaves the room. I close the door and sink against it. I stare at my sister's bed, breathing hard. 'I'm going to find out what the hell you were up to,' I whisper to nothing and no one.

CHAPTER 25

I put the bin bags in the wardrobe and shove the blue notebook underneath Ginny's mattress. I don't want Emily snooping around and finding it – or Mum, if she comes into the room. I check my reflection in the mirror, brush my hair and put on lip gloss. It's not that I care whether or not I look good for Byron, but I don't want to look as shaken as I feel.

I go downstairs to the sitting room. Between Byron and the Christmas tree, the room seems to have shrunk. Mum's sitting at a foldout table where a jigsaw has been set up. It's a thousand pieces and still has the 50p sticker on it from the charity shop. It's a picture of stockings hung by the fire and presents under a Christmas tree: someone's ideal vision of Christmas. Lorna is standing by the fireplace doing most of the talking as usual. Emily is standing by the kitchen door just out of Mum's sight line. The others don't seem to be around.

'Hi there,' I say.

'Skye.' Byron comes up and gives me a kiss that's more lips than cheek. 'You're looking well. And I love the tree.'

'Thanks.' I frown over at Emily who's not even bothering to hide her obvious interest in my relationship with this man. 'Would you like a cup of tea?'

'I can't stay, I'm afraid.' Byron looks apologetically at the two older women. 'I'm on my way to Fort William to pick up Kyle. Thought I'd save the little blighter the coach ride. He gets car sick, or coach sick, whatever you want to call it.'

'That's a bother,' Lorna chimes in.

'I don't mind the drive,' Byron says. 'Gives me a chance to clear my head.' He looks back at me. 'I just came by for a quick word. It's stopped raining now.'

'OK,' I say. 'Let's go outside.'

Byron goes out onto the porch. I put on my coat and follow him outside. In truth it's a relief to get away from Mum. Did she know about the coach ticket? Surely not. Although… Ginny and Mum were always close. I think of the conversation Mum was having with Alice Thomson: *I never told her.* It's probably unrelated, but right now my worldview is completely off-kilter. If Ginny wasn't confiding in me in the months before she died, does Mum know something? Something concrete that's made her question whether or not Ginny's death was an accident?

'You OK? You seem a little preoccupied.'

Byron's comment distracts me from my thoughts.

'Sorry,' I say. 'It's just that there's a lot going on at the house. It's all pretty chaotic.'

'It's that time of year,' he says jovially. We go around to the back of the house. On one side there's an old swing set. Byron and I used to sit out here sometimes. The chains are rusty and the seats are wet but I sit down anyway. Byron sits on the other swing.

He clears his throat like he's planning to address a weighty issue. 'Sorry to be a bother,' he says, 'but I just wanted to ask again about the festival. See if you've changed your mind. One of the band member's mum is having her hip done. Been on the waiting list for months. They really could use you—'

Ignoring his question, I make a snap decision. Byron is a little like Annie MacClellan – in fact, they're distantly related. He has a lot of friends, and he knows just about everything that's going on in the village. Maybe he's heard something over the years that might explain what Ginny was thinking. It's worth a try.

'I found something in Ginny's wardrobe,' I say. 'A coach ticket to Glasgow. And a name: Ellen McCree.'

He glances at me warily. 'What are you talking about?'

'I just wondered if the name rang any bells. Or if there was any gossip at the time that I might not have known about. Like about her leaving… with someone.'

'Well, yeah, she was leaving with you. For that audition.'

'No.' I shake my head. 'The ticket I found was for the day she died.'

'The day she…' He lets out a low whistle.

'It's odd, isn't it?'

'Yes. But I've no idea. I guess you'd need to ask someone who knew her better than I did.'

'I thought *I* knew her.'

I'm expecting him to agree, but instead, he turns and stares at me, his eyes strangely cold. 'I thought you didn't want to dredge all that up again.'

'I don't… but…'

I think of Mum and that glassy, haunted look she gets in her eyes when she loses her grip on reality. Has not talking about Ginny over all these years helped her? Or has the uncertainty made the wound fester beneath the surface. I think of how unsettled I've felt in my old room, living among the memories, but with the most important memory – of that night – being nothing more than a gaping hole.

'If she was supposed to be on a coach to Glasgow,' I speak my thoughts aloud, 'then that means she wasn't supposed to be at the party. So why did she change her mind?'

'Well, she was like that, wasn't she?' He sounds annoyed now. 'On a coach, at a party. It was all the same to her.'

I shake my head. Once again I'm surprised at how negative he sounds. 'I have no memory of that night,' I say. 'Nothing but flashes. I want to fill in the details of what happened. Then, maybe, I can put it behind me.'

'To be honest, Skye, I think you should stop picking at old scabs. What happened was terrible – a tragedy. But frankly, all of us in the village have tried to move on. Get past it.'

'By lying, you mean?' I turn and stare at him. 'By telling a nice "story"? Is that what Jimmy and Mackie did? Because they didn't see anything at all, did they? There was no "rogue wave". The whole thing is complete and utter bollocks.'

He looks stunned. 'Why… would you think that?'

'Because Mum heard a rumour about it,' I say. 'People drink, and people talk.' I repeat her words. 'People lied about that night.'

'Your mum heard that?' He clenches his fists tightly around the chain of the swing.

'It was pub gossip, apparently. Your *cousins*… shooting off their mouths. What exactly did they say? Were they boasting about it – how nicely it wrapped everything up? Or about how they got away with fooling the police?'

'It wasn't like that,' Byron says tightly.

'So what was it *like*, Byron?' I'm not going to let him get away with dodging my questions. 'Because your finger is on the pulse, isn't it? You were there that night.'

'I wasn't there,' he bristles. 'Not for most of the time. I was off to get the keg. Remember?'

'I don't remember. I only know what I've been told.'

'Yeah, so there you have it, then. You had a few drinks at the campfire, and then you left without her.' He sits back in the swing staring straight ahead. 'It was a good thing that Donald McVee was on the case. He was the officer in charge. Otherwise, you might have got done for drink-driving.'

'Donald McVee?' I frown. The weeks following my accident and Ginny's death are little more than a desperate haze of grief and confusion. I recall a big policeman coming to the house and asking me questions I couldn't answer. Mum intervening: telling him I was in no fit state. The name is familiar, but not because he was a policeman. 'Isn't he your… I don't know… something?'

'Godfather,' Byron clarifies. 'You met him once, at my cousin Meg's wedding. Sadly, he's passed on now. He was on duty that night. And believe me, that was a good thing. Your family had been through enough with Ginny dead.'

Oh God. My head is starting to pound.

'You were a complete mess when I found you that night. Blathering on about lights and bracelets and getting help. I couldn't make heads or tails of it. Then you passed out. It was clear that you were badly injured and I didn't want to move you. I went back up to the lighthouse to use the emergency phone. That's when I realised Ginny wasn't at the campfire. No one could remember when they last saw her.' He clenches his teeth. 'The whole fucking thing was chaos. The boys helped me search. When we found her scarf and her jumper, I just felt a hole open up inside me.' He shakes his head. 'I mean, we weren't supposed to be out there. We were trespassing, and we had… stuff. Without Donald on the case to pull some strings, heads might have rolled. It made sense for everyone to get their stories straight. Jimmy and Mackie had seen her earlier, out on the rocks. They may not have seen a wave take her, but it was pretty clear what had happened.'

'So no one saw her go into the water? They don't know if she was swept away or if she…' I can't say the word.

'That's exactly the point.' He turns on me suddenly. I can only remember Byron being angry once or twice – always with his mates, never with me. But now I recognise the look in his eye. The same one as before he broke Jimmy's nose for cheating him out of a twenty quid bet at the pool table.

'You know how Ginny was. She did something stupid – like the shite she was always getting up to. She went out onto the rocks.

She was taken by a rogue wave, but people might have thought she fucking jumped.'

I sit back, stunned.

'They did it for you.' He sounds almost desperate now. 'Don't you see that? For you, and your mum.'

'*They* barely even know us.' I stare at him, challenging him. 'But they're *your* cousins.'

He lets out a long sigh. 'OK. *We* did it. And I would do it again. Your mum wouldn't be half the woman she is now if she'd thought even for a second that her daughter jumped. An accident isn't great – obviously – but you can sleep at night. So I suggest…' he glares hard at me '… that you just leave it alone. Tell your mum that Jimmy and Mackie were just mouthing off that night at the pub, and nothing's changed. Quit rocking the boat.'

Quit rocking the boat.

The swing creaks as he stands up, his face flushed and stormy. I stand up too. And burst into tears.

'Hey,' he says. 'Look, I'm sorry.' He reaches for me. He takes my arms, and gently draws me near. I stiffen and he lets go. 'I know how painful it is. But you have to let it go, Skye. Really, it's for the best.'

'How can I let it go?' I say. 'The whole thing has Mum in an awful state. And now, I'm starting to question everything too. I feel so… helpless.'

He laughs grimly. 'I know how that feels. I mean, I hated my old man. He was a complete bastard. But when I think of him, strung up on the boat, I just wish that things had been different, you know? Especially now that I've got Kyle. I just don't understand how he could have done… that.'

'Do you think that's what Ginny did?' I stare out at the grey haze. 'Did she decide to end her own life?'

'No, I don't think that,' he says emphatically. 'It was an accident. A terrible accident. And everyone else thinks that too. Why wouldn't they? Ginny was happy.' He smiles grimly. 'I can picture her out there on those rocks. Singing her head off. She just got a little too close to the edge.'

I nod slowly. I'm beginning to understand. Fifteen minutes ago, my sister's death was open and shut. A 'rogue wave'. Everyone believed it and everyone got past it. And now... it's all a lie. The black pit of unanswered questions has yawned wider, doubling in size. I wish it was possible to wind back the clock. I wish it was possible to un-know. Jimmy and Mackie have a lot to answer for, and not for making up a story on the night...

'Now... shit.' He checks his watch. 'I'm late.'

'Go then,' I say. 'Thank you for telling me the truth.'

Our eyes meet and for a moment, he brightens. This time, when he moves closer to me and puts his hands on my arms, I don't pull away.

'When Kyle's here,' he says, 'I'd love it if you would meet him. I'm going to be taking some time off from the pub to spend with him. Maybe we could all go for a pizza. I mean... only if you want to.'

'I... OK. I guess so.'

He smiles. 'Good.' He lifts a finger and traces a line lightly down my cheek. 'I remember us from back then. We were good together. And I'd like to get to know you again. As you are now.'

I keep my expression neutral. 'We'll see,' I say. I just want him to leave.

'Good,' he says, like it's settled. I walk with him to the Landy and he gets inside. 'Thought I'd get in and ask you before Lachie does. He always had a thing for you, you know.' He rolls down the window and starts the engine.

'No,' I say. 'I don't.'

'Aw, come on.' He winks at me. 'Now you're lying.'

My smile is a wince. 'I guess that makes all of us then.'

CHAPTER 26

I feel shaken to the core. Angry, desperate. I want to go back to the way I was only days ago when I arrived. I'd felt regret and guilt, but those were feelings I'd lived with for years: negative, but comfortable.

Now, though, I feel like fifteen years, and any perspective I've gained during that time, have been erased in one fell swoop. I'm angry at Byron and all the others – for knowing much more than I do about the most important night of my life and reducing it to a 'nice' story, supposedly out of concern for Mum and me. I'm angry at Ginny and the things I found in her room that have upset my long-held version of her memory.

And, most of all, I'm angry with myself. For my lack of memory, for the decision I made to run away from what happened leaving Mum to face everything alone. For refusing to acknowledge that there were obviously cracks in my relationship with my sister that I chose to plaster over, both at the time and in my memories. If I hadn't done so, would things be different now?

I can't go back inside and face Lorna's chitchat, Mum's tense silence, and Emily's curious looks, so instead I walk to the beach. Everything that Byron said and didn't say plays in my head like an infinite loop. His godfather part of the investigation, deciding to look the other way over my accident. People getting their stories straight – lying to the police. Could that possibly be true?

I know it could. Byron was right. The 'rogue wave' story tied everything up neatly and simply. And part of the story involves me. Now that I know that part of the story is a lie, how can I believe the rest of it?

I rub hard at my temples willing the mists to clear but the fog is as dense as ever. More than one person gave a statement that I arrived at the party, came to the campfire and had a couple of drinks. Whiskey and Coke. Even now the half-remembered taste makes me nauseous. Ginny wasn't there, and I was told she was off somewhere with James. It was cold out, I was upset at Ginny and I wanted to go home.

But would I realistically have sat there at the fire, socialised for a while, and then just left? The problem with the 'story', that I've never wanted to acknowledge, is that that just isn't *me*. I would have gone to look for her. Maybe even had another row with her. Told her that Mum sent me to bring her home, so could she please get ready to leave? And maybe she would have laughed at me, and maybe then I would have told her to get a ride with someone else. At least I would have been able to tell Mum that I'd tried and failed – Ginny chose not to come home with me.

Which leaves my 'vision' of Ginny on the rocks. My head hurts as I conjure it up in my head as I walk up the steep path. Ginny on the rocks, her arms outstretched. Daring me to rescue her. When Ginny engaged in one of her attention-seeking escapades, there was always an audience. Usually me. Ginny was happy as long as everyone loved her and was fawning over her. It was only when she felt angry, or slighted that she had to do something daft. There were very few or no incidents when I wasn't close by.

Is it possible that that my 'vision' is a real memory? That people lied about my going directly to the car and leaving without her? What other lies were told about that night that I believed?

I have absolutely no idea. I'm breathing heavily as I reach the pass between the hills and begin the descent down to the beach. Before I get all the way down, however, I stop. Nick is down there, walking slowly along the tideline. Kafka is streaking back and forth retrieving a ball.

I stand for a few minutes watching them, imagining what it would be like to have a peaceful, happy moment like they seem to be doing. Of course I know nothing about Nick and his situation but it strikes me that whatever he's been through, he hasn't ended up too badly. He's in a beautiful place, with inspiration for his art and a dog for company. Watching them takes me out of my own troubles, until he looks up and spots me.

He waves and I wave back. And then I leave and walk back up the hill. I don't want to speak to him, and have the moment spoiled by words, or silence, small talk, or even the attraction that I feel for him. Right now, I have nothing to offer to him or anyone. Not until I find out the truth.

CHAPTER 27

The next morning, I'm not feeling any better. I stay in my room until everyone else has had breakfast. I eat a piece of toast and then go outside to the garden and drink my coffee on the patio. A boat is making its way slowly out of the harbour, trawling a path through the inky grey water. Everything is grey here. The sea, the sky, my memories. But in the light of day, I know what I need to do. I need to speak to Lachlan – he seemed willing enough to talk about 'what really happened that night' when I arrived, and yet I didn't want to hear what he had to say. And James… If Ginny was going away to Glasgow, then she was likely going with James. I'll need to talk to him too.

There's a commotion as the two little boys run around the side of the house. Bill follows them, throwing a football down onto the wet grass for a kick about. Fiona comes out to watch them. She smiles at me, friendly and genuine, and I feel an intense sadness. I had so hoped that we could all have a happy Christmas: together for the first time in so long. But right now everything seems spoiled.

'Skye,' Fiona says. 'Are you OK?'

'Yes, thanks.' I make an effort to smile.

'We were thinking of going out to the beach,' she says. 'The boys are sick of being cooped up, and it looks like the weather will be clear for most of the afternoon.'

I have a sudden idea how to kill two birds with one stone. 'Why don't I take them to MacDougall's Farm?' I say. 'It would give you and Bill a break. We can go after lunch.'

'That would be brilliant.' Fiona looks relieved. 'I mean, are you sure you want to? The boys can be a handful.'

'Oh, we'll be fine,' I say, not very sure at all. 'It will be fun.'

'Fantastic, then it's settled. Bill…' she calls out. 'Skye's going to take the troops to the farm.'

One of the little boys kicks the ball hard at Bill. It hits him in the stomach and he gasps as the wind is knocked out of him. The ball ricochets right over the fence at the end of the garden.

'Game over,' I say as the boys and Bill go off to determine the fate of the ball. Fiona shakes her head. 'I need more coffee,' she says.

As I go back inside, I debate whether or not I should call ahead and try to arrange to speak to James, or just turn up. I decide on the latter. I'm beginning to see that it's best not to give anyone time to 'get their stories straight'.

In the kitchen, Fiona's making coffee and Emily is buttering a piece of toast. Mum's sitting at the table mixing bread dough. Her eyes look dark and puffy like she didn't sleep well. 'Are you OK?' I say as I rinse out my coffee mug.

'Yes,' she says. 'Fine.' She seems very flat.

'Skye's going to take the boys to the farm park,' Fiona says. 'MacDougall's. Isn't that nice? Emily, do you want to go too?'

Before Emily can answer, Mum swivels around and glares first at Fiona, then at me. 'You shouldn't go there.'

'Oh, the boys will love it,' Fiona says. 'They love animals. It will be perfect—'

Mum's face changes almost instantly. That look in her eyes: shiny, wild. 'James is two-timing you,' she says, looking straight at Emily. 'And that's not right. That Katie. She's such a little… tramp.' There's venom in her voice as she pounds at the dough in the bowl. I can feel the pent-up emotion escaping like a cork popping out of a bottle. 'You have to talk to him. He'll see reason. I promise you, he will.'

Emily narrows her eyes as understanding dawns. Fiona moves in front of her, a human shield.

'Mum?' I try to put my hand on her shoulder but she presses a flour-covered hand to my hip and pushes me away with such surprising force that I almost lose my balance.

'I'm going to get Bill,' I say to Fiona.

'Bill…?' Mum says. The mention of my brother's name brings her back to her senses but her eyes are still confused. I want to comfort her, but I'm too shaken. I'm best getting Emily off the scene as soon as possible.

'I'm taking the kids to the farm park, Mum,' I say. 'Come on, Emily.' I don't wait for a response. But as I'm going out, I hear Mum's cane clatter to the floor followed by swearing. I'm frightened by this version of Mum that I don't recognise. I hurry outside to find Bill. 'They lost the ball,' he says, with a shrug. 'I said that would happen if—'

'Mum's in a state,' I say. 'I'm taking the kids now.'

My brother's face drains of colour. 'Fine, I'll see to her.' I can't tell if he's angry at her or at me. He spots Emily who's followed me out.

'Dad?' she says, her voice high like a little girl's.

'Everything's going to be fine, love,' he says. 'You go and have a good time.' He digs in his pocket and tosses his keys to me. 'Best if you take the Audi.'

'Thanks,' I say. 'Come on, boys.' I turn to my nephews. 'Let's go ride the train and have some fun.'

'Yay!' they scream.

I give Emily the keys and instruct her to get her brothers inside. As they go off, I follow Bill back up to the house to get my coat and handbag.

In the kitchen, Mum's crying. I feel awful that I ever mentioned the farm park to Fiona without telling her that it might upset Mum, and cause another incident with Emily. Awful that my presence here seems to be rocking the boat no matter what I do. I hear Fiona and Bill both speaking softly to her, trying to calm her down. I make a swift exit. This time, running away seems like absolutely the right thing to do.

CHAPTER 28

It's a relief to be out of the house. Bill's Audi Q5 is big, but easy to drive. Before we leave, Emily runs to the cottage to get the boys' iPads and some snacks. I let her sit in front with me, something she's probably not allowed to do ordinarily. I glance over at her as I pull out of the yard. It's a little unnerving: like this could just be one more time driving with my sister. I did most of the driving back then, which left her free to pick the music and sing along. Maybe that's why I developed my passenger seat phobia: I don't like not being the one in control. Right now, I don't feel like I'm in control of anything.

When the house is behind us, Emily seems to relax a little. She asks if she can put on a CD, and I agree immediately, hoping she'll choose something I like that will enable me to get out of my own head. I'm a little disappointed when, instead, she chooses a disk of candyfloss Euro-pop music, with a pounding beat that sets my teeth on edge. Since riding in the car with Lachlan, I've had a hankering to hear some traditional music, like the songs I used to write. I haven't completely given up on that part of my old dream. I remember the conversation I had with Nick Hamilton about the creative process and feel a flash of excitement. If he can live his dream of being an artist, maybe there's hope for me…

'Who wants crisps?' Emily asks. She's got her rucksack on her lap and has fished out some bags of Mini Cheddars.

'Me!' Both of the boys call out at once from the back.

Emily tosses them each a bag. 'Do you want some crisps, Aunt Skye?'

I focus on the road where an oncoming lorry is a little bit over the line. 'Sure,' I say.

'Here, catch…'

It all happens in an instant. A loud rushing noise as the lorry passes us. The orange bag tossed towards me, a little too high, glimpsed in my peripheral vision. The bag hits my shoulder. I jam on the brakes, swerve off the road onto the hard shoulder, and into loose gravel. The car fishtails. I brake harder. In the back someone yells and an iPad hits the floor. We come to a stop inches from a ditch aside the road. My hands are clammy on the wheel.

'Jesus,' I yell, putting my hand to my temple. 'Why did you do that?'

'I'm sorry!' Emily says.

But when I look at her, it takes me a few seconds to realise who she is, where I am. My head is pounding. Ginny. Throwing something at me. It hit me. It hurt.

I have no context for the thought. And yet I'm sure it happened. It's the same as the other flashes I've had over the years. But this one couldn't be real. Or if it was, it couldn't have happened the night she died because we weren't in the car together. I want to tear the thoughts from my head and the emotions that go with the memory. Hurt, loss. Disbelief. They can't be real either.

'Aunt Skye?'

I look over at Emily. Her lower lip is quivering like she's about to cry. I feel terrible for lashing out at her.

'It's OK,' I say, trying to calm my breathing. 'Sorry about that. It startled me, that's all.'

'Sorry,' she says again.

'That was cool,' Jamie yells out from the back. 'Can we do it again?'

I laugh – it seems the right thing to do. I pull back onto the road and we continue onwards. But despite the boys going back to their video and Emily turning the volume up on the music, the incident has upset me. I feel like turning around and going home. But I can't let the kids down, and besides, going back to Mum in a state is hardly appealing. Most of all, though, I need to speak to James.

The car park at MacDougall's is more crowded than last time now that school's out for the holidays. As soon as we're out of the car, Jamie runs behind a reversing Jeep. My heart is in my mouth as I take his hand and tell him to be more careful.

'I need a wee,' Robbie yells, running on ahead.

I roll my eyes at Emily. She gives me a smug little smirk in return. It seems that the earlier incident is forgiven.

The shop is busy with people stocking up on Christmas gifts and food, and there's a queue of children waiting for the train to see 'Santa's reindeer'. I send the boys off to the loos. Emily and I join the queue for hot chocolate and I look around to see if there's some kind of office where James might be. The boys return and then run off again to look at the toys and jigsaws in the shop. I'm feeling on edge and the queue is taking forever, and—

'Skye? Is that you?'

I turn around. The man standing behind me is shorter and smaller than I remember, and his once impressive head of wavy blonde hair is thinning. He's wearing glasses too. But the moment he smiles, it's like the sun coming out from behind a cloud.

'James!' I say. 'Hey there!' We lock in a warm embrace.

'I heard you were back,' he says as we come apart. 'And you look amazing! Your mum must be over the moon that you're home.'

I'm aware of Emily watching us. Her face is a mixture of admiration and disgust, like she's wondering if I've shagged every man of a certain age within a fifty-mile radius. Her brothers return, running up to us.

'Are they yours?' James asks, ruffling the hair of the two little boys.

'God no,' I say. 'They're Bill's.'

'Aye, wee Bill,' he says, exaggerating his accent and giving Emily a wink. 'Your dad is a good sort, you know?'

Emily gives him her 'whatever' look.

'Do you have time for a coffee?' I say to James. 'I'd love to…' I hesitate, 'catch up.'

'That'd be great,' he says. 'Let me just go check that the assistant manager is back from break.' He steps up and has a word with the coffee cart girl, then waves us to the front of the queue. 'Whatever they like,' he directs, 'on the house.'

I do the obligatory protest and he insists, which is just so like James. Mum may have her grievances, but I could never hold a grudge against him. He's so uncomplicated… so guileless. He pops off to have a word with a man at the tills and returns as we're collecting our food and drinks.

'All sorted,' he says. 'Shall we find a big table?'

'Actually,' I say, taking a breath, 'I was wondering if we might be able to have a quick word. Alone. Emily can watch her brothers.'

James's sunny face flickers for a second like he's sussed something's up. 'How about they go see the animals?' he suggests. 'My boys are with Clemmie, their nanny. If your three get on the train, they can meet up at the other end.'

'Perfect,' I say.

James takes a walkie-talkie off his belt and sorts everything out. Emily doesn't want to go, but I promise to buy her a notebook in the shop later if she looks after her brothers now. She gives me her devastating look, and agrees.

When the kids are on the train, I go with James to a covered area at the back of the barn with picnic tables. We sit down and watch the train trundle up the glen. James tells me some of his grand plans: for Scotland's longest zip line, and the Hogwarts-themed soft play that's under construction in the large barn.

As he talks, I consider how to broach the subject of *that night*. So far James has been just about the only person I've seen since I've been back who hasn't looked at me and seemed immediately to think of my dead sister. Which is great – or it would be. Except now, I need to talk about her. Finally he seems to realise that he's been doing all the talking. He asks me how I'm settling in, and I take the plunge.

'It's been difficult,' I say. 'Mum's not in a good state after her fall. And for me, everything is a reminder of Ginny. As you can imagine.'

His face seems to close up. 'I'm sorry we never had a chance to talk about what happened,' he says. 'I thought I'd see you, but then you left. I'm sure it was devastating. You two were so close.'

'Well, I thought so,' I say. 'But now I'm not so sure.' I take a breath and dive in the deep end. 'James, were you planning on going away with her? To Glasgow. Was she going to the audition… without me?'

He stares at me, his eyes narrowing. 'What?'

'She ripped up the coach ticket I bought for her,' I say. 'But she had another for the day she died. Which she didn't use, obviously. So can you just tell me the truth, so I can… put it to bed?'

'Hold on a minute…' He puts his hand on my arm. 'Slow down, Skye. I really have no idea what you're talking about. I certainly wasn't going away with her. She dumped me. Back in August. Three months before she died. But you knew that, right?'

'No.' I stare at him, stunned. 'She didn't. I mean… you and she were so… tight. You were so good for her.'

'I don't know if I was good for her or not, but she definitely wasn't good for me. She messed with my head,' he says.

'I'm starting to think that she messed with mine too,' I say.

'When she dumped me, I felt like my world had fallen apart,' he says. 'I started drinking a lot. Taking drugs. It was me who brought the stuff that night.'

'You?' I look at him, surprised. No one admitted bringing the drugs that night, though later on, an Irishman who'd dropped in at the party was arrested on charges of supplying.

'Yeah, me. Not that O'Rourke bloke.'

I feel sick to my stomach. It seems that the police got this wrong too. Or was it another example of everyone 'getting their stories straight'? I can believe that Byron and his mates lied. But James?

He stares down at his hands. 'Those three months were the worst time of my life. But Katie saved me. She was there, helping me through it. Which was why…' he rubs his hands through his hair '… I felt so conflicted.'

'About what?'

'When Ginny got to the party, she took me aside. I was already drunk, and Katie was there. But I went with her.' He shakes his head. 'She said that she loved me. That she'd made a mistake. She didn't want to leave home, and she wanted to get back together.'

'OK…?'

'But I'd been so hurt by her. I'd realised by then how she toyed with people. She put on that vulnerable little girl act and had people falling at her feet. People like me. I'd convinced myself that I hated her.'

Hearing the words – and everything he's just said – I feel a little shocked.

'I got upset. I accused her of cheating on me.'

'No – she would never do that.'

He gives me a long look. 'That's what she said. And then she laughed at me. Acted like I was turning her on. She wanted to have sex. And I hated the fact that I wanted to, even though I didn't… if that makes sense. But I told her that we were over. That I'd moved on.' He looks stricken. 'She started to cry. I wanted to comfort her. But I played the hard man. I walked away.'

'You left her there – on the rocks?'

'No, we weren't on the rocks. We were in my car, up near the lighthouse. I didn't see her go near the rocks.' He frowns. 'If I had, I wouldn't have left her there. Obviously.'

'Obviously,' I say.

'I went back to the fire. Drank some more. And from there it gets vague. Maybe Katie remembers more. I don't—'

'Maybe Katie remembers what?' A lilting female voice comes from behind us. We both startle a little and turn around.

'My…' she says, 'have I interrupted a wake—' She cuts off. 'Skye!' Her face colours as recognition dawns. 'I'm sorry. I—'

'Katie. Hi.' I stand up and come around the bench to hug her. 'You're looking well.'

She is looking well, but then she always had one of those open, friendly faces with a mouth that turns up into a natural smile. She was a year behind us at school, so we weren't exactly friends, but she always seemed nice. Her blonde hair is pulled back into a ponytail, and her cheeks are rosy from the cold. She's dressed in an expensive-looking padded jacket with a fur collar and a matching scarf and gloves. It strikes me that Ginny would have hated having anything to do with a place like this. But Katie looks perfectly in her element.

'So do you, Skye.' She beams at me. 'You've inspired us to plan a trip to America. Maybe next summer. You must give us some tips.'

'Sure. I'd be happy to.'

'Everyone OK?' James asks her.

'Yes, all fine.' She turns to me. 'The kids are feeding the alpacas.'

'Good,' I say. It's nice to see Katie, but I'm not here to learn about alpacas. As I'm trying to think of a way to steer the conversation back on track, James intervenes. 'We were just having a word about what happened… before.' He looks apologetically at his wife. 'Skye is trying to fill in the blanks in her memory. I've told her about the row I had with Ginny.'

Katie tuts. 'It was such a terrible thing, and we're all so sorry, Skye,' she says. She takes James's hand protectively, making it clear that they are a united front. 'I know it was years ago, but it still must be hard for you. Every time we go to the seaside, I think of her…' She trails off, as if she's misspoken.

'Yes,' I say. 'It has been hard. Everything triggers a memory, but not the ones about that night. After the car accident, all my memories are blank. But I'm hoping to put the pieces together, get it out in the open, and then, hopefully, close it again. I don't want things to be awkward. You know?'

Katie's face is guarded. 'Your mum seems to think it was all James's fault. Because he didn't "take care of her". But she wasn't his responsibility. They weren't even together.'

'I know,' I say. 'I guess Mum just needed to blame someone. She certainly blames me. I should have collected Ginny that night and brought her home.'

'She wasn't a child,' Katie counters.

'I know but I still feel responsible.'

'Yeah, sure,' she says. 'I understand. But I'm not sure I can help. To be honest, I've tried to forget, not remember.'

'I tried that too,' I say.

Katie nods. 'OK, well, James and I started getting close after she dumped him. His heart was broken, but for the first time I was in with a chance. She was leaving… going off to that audition. Everyone knew that.'

I glance at James. He's staring down at their laced fingers.

'So I wasn't very happy when she turned up at the party and took James away. I was jealous.'

I nod.

'I went to find them. I was pretty off my face. And when I did…' she winces '… it wasn't pretty. James was happy to get back with her.'

'No…' James tries to protest. Katie gives him a look. It's pointless.

'I started calling her names,' Katie says. 'I said a few things that I shouldn't have.'

'Katie…' James warns.

'It's OK,' she says. 'I want her to know. She's right, we need to get it out in the open.'

'I know,' James says, 'but—'

'I told her she should bugger off and not come back.' Katie gives a long sigh. 'She just laughed in my face. Said "you wish". I was really angry.' She takes a breath. 'I would have hit her, but James held me back.'

'Katie!' James stands up, as if to shield her from me.

I look from one to the other. 'You didn't mention that,' I say to James.

'He's protecting me,' Katie says. She takes James's hand again and they have eyes only for each other. 'I didn't ask him to, but that's the way he is.'

I ignore the display of affection. 'So what happened next?'

'James told Ginny that he was really sorry, but it was over. He'd moved on.' There's a hint of smugness in her voice. 'I went back to the fire. He stayed with her to make sure she was OK.'

'We sat in the car for a while,' James says, 'and then I went outside and smoked a couple of cigarettes. I said she should come back with me and join the others. She said no, she wanted some time by herself. So eventually I left to go find Katie. Ginny was still there in the car. I didn't see her go down to the jetty. Besides, there were other people there, coming and going. Lachlan – he was trying to get with Maggie, I think. Byron, and others. It wasn't like she was alone.'

'Byron? I thought he left to get more alcohol.'

They exchange a look. 'Yes,' Katie says. 'At some point. I don't remember the timing of all of it. But when I got back to the campfire, you were there.'

'Me…?' I try desperately to remember. Faces flickering in the firelight… the taste of whiskey and Coke. And nothing else.

'I don't remember you arriving,' she says. 'You must have got there when James was in the car with her. You seemed annoyed – that you drove all the way out and she wasn't there. You had a few drinks. Kept going on about a ripped up ticket?'

'So what did I do?' My brain is desperately trying to put all the pieces together.

'You said you were going to find her and take her home. You walked back up towards the car park. That's all I know.'

'I said that? I went to look for her?' In every other account, people have said that I just got fed up and left.

'Yes, I think so,' she says, frowning.

'But did I find her? Did I speak to her?' I'm desperate, terrified to know.

'I don't know, Skye.' James shakes his head. 'I'm not too clear on the timing of any of it. All I know was that sometime later, Byron came and said you'd been in an accident. He wanted to find Ginny to tell her, but no one had seen her. Some of us went to search and ran into Jimmy and Mackie. That's when we heard.' James puts his hand on mine. 'That wave… I didn't see it, but I can picture her out on the rocks. There one moment, and the next just… gone.'

'It's all just so tragic,' Katie says.

I stare up at the barren hills, the shadows shifting across them as clouds cross the winter sun. Everything I've heard just seems *wrong*. People seeing things, not seeing things, coming and going. People lying. How can I ever find out the truth? The sound of a steam whistle pulls me back to the here and now. The train is pulling into the little depot. Emily gets off the train, yanking Robbie by the hand. Jamie sees me and runs over. In a way, I'm grateful that they're back. I couldn't stand another minute of this awful conversation.

I give Emily a ten-pound note and send her and the boys to buy a notebook and some sweets. I stand up, feeling dizzy and unsettled.

'I'm sorry, Skye,' James says. 'Sorry that I… that we…' he indicates his wife '… didn't tell you all this before. We weren't the last people to see her alive. But that's not an excuse. We helped with the search. I told the police I'd spoken with Ginny in the car park. But I didn't see her die.' He chokes back a sob.

I nod slowly. James might not have told the whole truth at the time, but I believe that he's come clean now. I decide not to tell him that the 'rogue wave' was most likely a complete fabrication of Byron and his mates. James and Katie clearly feel guilt over what happened that night. As they should. If James hadn't rejected her, if Katie hadn't come upon them during their 'reunion' there almost certainly would have been a different outcome. Just like there would have been if I'd found Ginny and brought her home. But, in the end, it was Ginny herself who chose to go out onto those rocks, and maybe… I have to consider the possibility now… chose to die.

I muster a smile. 'We all wish that night would have ended differently. I appreciate your help. Sorry to dredge up all those painful memories.'

'Sure.' James steps forward and gives me a hug. 'And don't be a stranger, OK? Come back and let's talk of happier times.'

'I will,' I say. 'I promise.'

I round up the children and wave to James and Katie as we go out of the farm shop to the car park. I feel a little closer to Mum, knowing that I will *never* be setting foot back here again.

*

At dinner, the boys give an enthusiastic account of the farm, the animals, James's kids, and the sweets I bought them. At first I'm worried that the mention of MacDougall's might send Mum round the bend again, but she seems entirely back to normal. I manage a quick word with Fiona as we're doing the washing-up. Apparently Mum cried for a while when we left, had a cup of tea, and then got on with making the bread, kneading out her aggressions in the dough.

'Bill doesn't necessarily agree, but I think it's a good thing that she has these little bouts of grief,' Fiona says. 'Like a volcano blowing off steam. Better to do it a little at a time than to have a full-blown eruption.'

'Grief is one thing,' I say. 'But her breaks with reality are very unsettling. Especially for Emily.'

'She'll be fine,' Fiona says, sounding not entirely convinced.

'I hope so.'

As I go upstairs to my room, I wonder how Mum would react under Fiona's 'volcano theory' to what I learned from James and Katie. Ginny must have been in a bad state after the encounter with her ex and his would-be new girlfriend. I wouldn't have known that when I went to look for her. Did I call out to Ginny, telling her that I'd come to take her home? Did she answer that she didn't want go with me, or just keep quiet and I didn't see her in the dark? My vision of her on the cliffs – it's looking more and more like it could be a real memory. But how can I find out?

Before going to bed, I tune the harp for Emily. I wish I could move it out to the hallway, but then Mum would definitely know that I'm clearing out the room. I don't want to cause another one of her 'mini-eruptions'.

I move the harp back into the corner and take out Dad's guitar. I spend an hour or so experimenting with chords and notes, trying to bring my own ideas to the surface. Just melodies, not words. I'm not ready for words. Eventually I put the guitar away and lie awake staring up at the ceiling in the circle of lamplight. The knots of the pine take the shape of sinister faces and accusing eyes. If I did find Ginny and speak to her that night, what passed between us? If she was upset, did I comfort her, tell her that everything was going to be fine? That it wasn't too late – we'd both go to the audition like we'd planned? Or did I get angry with her? Say the wrong thing, intentionally or unintentionally, exaggerating the hurt she was already feeling? For fifteen years, I've believed that my sister's death was a tragic accident. But if that isn't true, then what else might have happened? When I saw the book about suicide in Mum's room, I'd dismissed the possibility – absolutely certain that I knew my sister. Now, I realise that I didn't know my sister at all.

CHAPTER 29

It's almost dawn before I fall into a restless sleep. When I wake up, bright sun is shining through the window. The temperature has dropped and there are frost florets on the glass. In the morning light, my fears from the night before seem ludicrous. Ginny never would have taken her own life – not when she had so much to live for.

I stare up at the knots on the ceiling, but now they just look like knots. If Ginny had lived, we would have spent nights in motel rooms all over the world, staring up at different ceilings. It would have been such an adventure! I just wish that she'd confided in me: told me that she was feeling a little bit homesick, a little bit guilty for breaking up with James, maybe still a lot in love with him. I could have helped her deal with his rejection, and we would have gone to the audition together. There was no way her nostalgia for a local boy would have held her back once she escaped the misty veils of Eilean Shiel.

When I go downstairs Lorna is with Mum – they're getting ready to go out to a WI event. The others are going to the village. Emily asks if I'll go with them, but I decline. There's something else I want to do. Emily seems a bit sulky at my response. 'Are you seeing your boyfriend?' she asks. 'The man who was here the other day?'

I frown at her as my mind slips back in time. Ginny in our room, sulky. *Are you seeing Byron again?'*

'He's not my boyfriend,' I say.

'No?' she teases. 'Seemed like maybe he wants to be.'

'I don't think so.' I leave it at that.

When she and the others are finally gone, I take the car keys from the peg. Maybe I should have asked Mum if I could borrow the car, but in the spirit of 'not rocking the boat' I've decided just to do it.

Outside, the cold is shocking. My breath curls and rises in the air as I start the car and use a credit card to scrape the ice from the window. The road will be icy and treacherous. Where I'm going, I'll need my wits about me.

I drive past the village of Eilean Shiel, heading south. The road undulates up and down, twisting and rising through frost-covered hills and windswept dunes. The sea is hazy and blue, and the mist-shrouded islands shimmer like magical, drowned worlds. Eventually I reach the turn off to the single-track road that leads to the Shiel Peninsula, and the lighthouse where my sister died.

For the first few miles, the road winds along the shore of a narrow sea loch. I pass through ancient woodlands of oak and rhododendron, the moss-covered branches of the trees forming a tunnel over the road. Further west the landscape turns almost lunar as the road snakes through a barren land of bog and boulders with tiny arctic plants clinging to life in the waterlogged soil, and the odd sheep poking its head out of the bracken. In the spring, the land will be a kaleidoscope of colour: the yellow broom, the bright greens of grass and fern, and in summer when the heather blooms, the hills will be carpeted with dark purple. But now, the landscape is soft browns and greys with a light dusting of frost like icing sugar.

After driving for almost an hour, I reach a crossroads. The north road goes off to a settlement of caravans. I continue going west. The last few miles of track going up to the lighthouse are twisty and treacherous, with the verge dropping off sharply in places to a rocky, boggy wilderness cut deep with ravines. I pull into a passing place in the shadow of a huge rock face with a frozen waterfall snaking down a fracture in the rock. From here, I can see the tip of the lighthouse on the cliffs, the road zigzagging below.

I get out of the car and walk along the road. I don't know exactly where I had the accident, just that the car went off the road on a bend into a rock, and ended up teetering at the edge of a steep gully.

A car comes around the bend and I jump out of the way. Even though it's daytime, it has its headlamps on and flashes me. Headlamps? A flashing light. Did I see flashing headlamps that night? Was there another car oncoming? Is that why I swerved and went off the road?

'Damn it,' I say aloud as the car goes by. It's hopeless trying to remember. I stop walking and turn back. Having gone only a short distance, I can no longer see the top of the lighthouse. Another one of Dad's sayings comes into my mind. 'The road of life is full of twists and turns. Best, love, always to go in a straight line.'

A straight line. I get back in the car, feeling that the truth of that night is more twisted than ever. The flashing lights… is that a real memory? How can I ever be sure?

I drive on to Shiel Lighthouse, perched at the top of the headland. I remember learning on a long-ago school trip that the lighthouse is built in the 'Egyptian' style – like the lighthouse at Alexandria. There's a legend that any sailor who successfully navigated the treacherous seas around the point would earn a sprig of lucky white heather to nail to the mast of his ship. I drive past a small museum, closed this time of year, to the parking area below the lighthouse.

I park the car near the remains of a toppled wind turbine, felled like a soldier in battle. There are a few other vehicles parked next to a row of rusty fuel tanks. The wind practically takes the door off when I open it, and I have to wrestle it closed. I imagine Mum arriving here, tired after the long drive, and yet determined to 'find' my sister.

I pull my scarf over my mouth and bow my head against the freezing wind. To the left of the car park is a trail down to a small cove: just a fringe of sand dotted with lichen-covered rocks. The cove was where the party was that night. I guess some genius chose it because of its remoteness, and the fact that there would be no caravaners out at that time of year to disturb the fun.

I take the path down to the cove. That night, I would have seen the campfire from above and gone there, expecting my sister to be with the others. I find a rock to sit on that's sheltered from the wind. The force of the waves vibrates through the rocks, and the air shimmers with spray.

I close my eyes and focus on the flickering light of memory. Faces around the fire. Are the memories real? Or am I projecting what my conscious mind 'knows' from the police report and other people's accounts?

The party was for the 18th birthday of a girl called Maggie, who was a classmate of Katie's. Ginny and I were almost twenty and Byron and Lachlan were already twenty. We were gatecrashers, really. Along with Maggie and Katie, there were several other girls from their year and a few of James's mates from the rugby team. Byron's cousins, Jimmy and Mackie, came late to the party. All in all, there were about fifteen people, excluding me, who saw, or said they didn't see, Ginny.

Mum was relying on me to bring Ginny home safely. I didn't do that. But what did I do? I kick at the sand in frustration. Faces in the firelight. Katie's face? She said she heard me say I was going to look for Ginny. Once again, it's a memory filled in by someone else.

I go back up to the lighthouse and take another path to the right of the car park, a dirt track that zigzags down to a small picnic area and the remains of an old jetty used for getting in supplies. Near the bottom, the path is cut into the rocks, and I can hear the shriek of sea birds and the pounding of the surf below.

The ruined jetty is a small rectangular platform with a rusty metal ring stuck in the concrete. My heart is in my throat as I peer out over the edge. With each wave that breaks against the rocks, long tendrils of kelp move in the water like mermaid hair. Hypnotic and chilling. The Selkie… No. Selkies aren't real. If Ginny went out on the rocks it wouldn't have been because of some supernatural call – or a moment of happiness and freedom. James had rejected her, he had 'moved on'. She would have been upset. Devastated.

At the edge of the platform there's a rusty barrier, and beyond that, the black, barnacle-studded rocks. I step beyond the barrier and instantly I know this place. It's the same as in my 'vision'. I close my eyes as the water booms beyond the furthest rocks. Ginny, her arms outstretched, a strange fire in her eyes. The light from the lighthouse pulsating above. Her bracelet glinting in the darkness as she unfurls her scarf and it catches in the wind and flies away.

And then… nothing. I open my eyes. My head is pounding in time with my heart. I retrace my steps, stumbling up the path. Above me, the shadow of the lighthouse is a long, thin arrow pointing out to sea. I go back up to the car park and slow down to catch my breath. What happened after the 'memory' ends? Maybe she slipped and fell from the rocks. Maybe a wave took her. Or maybe she really did jump… right in front of me. I was hoping that being here where it happened might trigger something else, but so far it hasn't done so. How can I complete the memory?

I walk closer to the lighthouse and its outbuildings, which are enclosed by a waist-high stone wall. I peer over the wall at the sheer black cliffs and fissures in the rocks pounded by the relentless waves. If Jimmy and Mackie had seen my sister die, it would have been from up here.

A walkway leads down to the old foghorn building and a series of small viewing platforms for seabird aficionados. As I near the steps, a dog begins to whimper excitedly. A dark shape streaks towards me. I know that dog…

Nick Hamilton is about the last person I want to see. He's set up his easel on the viewing platform nearest the top, his back to me. I pat Kafka and then go quickly down the steps past his owner. I stand on the lowest platform with my back to him. I feel angry that he's come here; set up his easel to paint a pretty picture of the view so near to where my sister met her death. It seems so *wrong*… though the rational part of me knows that he's probably unaware of it.

The wind is as sharp and cold as any I've ever felt, and my hair lashes against my skin. The sea below is a seething abyss of white water as the waves crash against the rocks. Further out, the water is ice blue, turning to silver at the horizon, and the islands are covered with wisps of pink clouds. A lone gull swoops lazily on the wind, landing on the rocks nearby.

'Skye.' Though I was expecting it, the voice startles me.

I don't look at him, but continue staring out to sea.

He moves over to the far side of the platform, resting his elbows on the railing.

'It's a beautiful spot,' he says after a minute or two. 'I come here quite often.'

'My sister died here.'

'I know.'

There's a plank for sitting at the back of the platform. He goes to it and sits down. I hear a clacking sound, then liquid pouring into a cup.

'Coffee?' he says.

I ignore him. 'Mum thinks she went in deliberately. That she… took her own life.' I don't know why I'm saying this, confiding in him. I stare down at the broiling sea, about twenty metres below. More birds are swooping now, and out beyond the breakers, I can make out a tiny dark spot in the water. A seal, bobbing up and down on the waves.

'Is that what you think too?'

'No.' I swallow back a sob. 'She just… wouldn't. She wouldn't have been that cruel.'

I turn back, defeated. I don't know anything any more. I go to the plank and sit down, as far away from Nick Hamilton as possible. Even so, I'm drawn to him. I remember watching him on the beach. The feeling that I didn't want to acknowledge. That I wished I'd been there with him, laughing as the dog ran down the beach. Happy; at peace.

'Here.' He hands me a steaming cup of black coffee.

'Thanks.' I take a sip. It burns my throat.

'You're shivering,' he says.

He stands up and walks away. I don't look to see where he's going. He returns a few minutes later with a blanket. Without asking my permission, he drapes it over my shoulders. It's a tartan rug similar to Byron's – I guess every red-blooded Scotsman must have one squirreled away in their car. I pull it around me. It smells vaguely of dog and paint.

'That coat is not going to get you through a winter here,' he says. 'You should get a warmer one. If you're staying for a while.'

'I don't know how long I'm staying,' I say. 'It's… complicated. Mum's not well, as you know. And I'm trying to find some answers.'

I glance over at his profile outlined against the sky. His chin is covered with dark stubble, and his cheekbones are as sharp and craggy as the cliffs. He belongs here. This place… he may not be from here, but somehow, he's become part of it.

'And have you found any answers?' he says.

'Just that people lied.' I pull the blanket around me but nothing can keep out the chill of those words. 'Everyone lied about that night. They lied to protect me… and Mum… And themselves. And I…' I shake my head '… I can't remember a damn thing.'

My anger sparks when I hear him laugh.

'First rule of policing,' he says. 'No one wants to talk and everyone lies.'

'I want to talk,' I say. 'I want to know the truth. My sister was keeping secrets from me. That much I know for sure. I was angry with her. But I loved her so much. Her death has torn all of us apart. I don't know if it's possible to ever put it to rest. But if I know the truth about what happened that night, then maybe I can face it and move on. Help Mum move on too. I don't know. It's just...'

'Yes?' he says, after a pause.

'What if I don't like what I find out?'

He pours a second cup of coffee. I'm on the verge of refusing – if he's going to be out all day he'll need the coffee to keep warm. He takes a sip from the cup and hands it to me. His fingers brush mine and I feel a jolt of electricity. It feels strangely intimate as I put the cup to my lips. I don't want to trust him. I don't want to feel a connection. But maybe it was my near drowning, or the rescue, or his paintings. I can't deny that there's some sort of unfortunate attraction between us. I drink the coffee and set down the cup. Then, I begin to talk.

I give him the official account of what happened. Then I tell him about the 'new evidence' I've uncovered. Ginny breaking up with James and then wanting to get back together. The coach ticket in the wardrobe. I tell him about James and Katie lying, and what Byron said about people 'getting their stories straight', supposedly to protect my family from the heartbreak of suicide. Finally, I tell him about my memory flash of Ginny on the rocks, and how I'm becoming more and more certain that I saw her that night.

He listens in silence. I like that he's a good listener. Several times I falter and have second thoughts. Why am I telling him this? Just because he was once a cop doesn't mean he'll be able to help – or be on my side. He tells me to 'go on' in a quiet voice. I do so. And when I get to the end, my thoughts are no less muddled, but I feel better for having told someone.

'So what happens now?' he says. 'How are you going to find out more?'

'I don't know,' I say. 'I wish could get a copy of the police file. Piece together what people said at the time, see if it sparks anything. But it's probably pointless.' I sigh.

'Maybe, maybe not.' He frowns, considering. 'I hadn't heard the whole story. Just bits and pieces in the village after your Mum's fall.'

'Yes. I'm sure it was common knowledge. There are no secrets in a place like this.'

'Yes.' He frowns out at the view. The pink clouds have gone, replaced with dark grey ones on the horizon like an approaching army.

'And we're all on eggshells around Mum right now. She's not well. Bill says we should just leave things be. Try not to talk about Ginny. He won't like the fact that I'm "rocking the boat".'

Nick lets out a long sigh. 'In my experience, most people benefit from facing up to the truth, even if it's unpleasant. I can't say that you're doing the right thing, but if it's any help, I'd be looking for answers too if I was in your situation.'

I nod. Actually, it feels like a big help.

'I also know how terrible it is to lose someone so young. Someone with their life ahead of them. I can see why it's affected you and your family all these years.'

'She was my twin,' I say. 'Half of who I was. So I thought, anyway.' I shake my head. 'I wanted to think it. It somehow made things easier. My successes were because of her. And my failures.'

'Don't sell yourself short,' he says. His eyes meet mine, and I feel something awaken inside me. 'For either your successes or your failures.'

Before I can even think of how to respond, he gets up. I take the cup and Thermos and follow him back to the upper level.

Kafka is lying on the ground near the easel, chewing on an old bone. I pour the last of the coffee into the cup and lean against the railing, staring out to sea. I'm aware of Nick picking up a brush and dabbing it in some paint on his pallet. Then he stands back, staring out at the view. He steps forward, makes a single mark on the canvas and steps back again.

I turn back towards the sea, finishing the coffee. I spot the dark blob in the water again: the seal. There's two of them now, flipping and diving. I give up wondering about Nick and let my own thoughts come into my head. One of the seals comes back up to the surface but the other has stayed beneath the water for several minutes. Maybe I should write another song about the Selkie, a different song about two playful seals. A song about happily ever after.

Eventually, the seals disappear, and I reckon that they've come ashore somewhere on the rocks below. I walk back over to Nick and screw the cup onto the Thermos. Kafka's tail gives a thump and then he goes back to his bone.

'Thanks for the coffee,' I say. 'Sorry, but I don't think there's any left.'

He gives me a bemused smile that almost, but not quite, turns his eyes from grey to blue. 'That's OK. It was worth it.'

'What…? Oh—'

I break off as I see what he's painted on the canvas. The background is a shimmering silver sea, the islands veiled with pink wisps of cloud. But he's roughed in the railing in pencil and he's also sketched… me.

It's only lines, but he's somehow managed to capture depth and movement. The wind whipping my hair, my hands gripping the cup.

'It's…' I begin.

'Unfinished,' he says. 'And I don't like unfinished.'

'It looks pretty good to me.'

He stands back from the canvas, crosses his arms, and frowns. Then, he looks at me.

'I'd like to paint you,' he says.

I laugh awkwardly. 'You mean, like paint my portrait?'

His eyes lock with mine. Grey now, no trace of blue. 'No, Skye. Not like your portrait.'

'Oh,' I say. As his meaning sinks in, I feel another shiver wrack through my body, and this one is not from the cold. 'Oh.'

'Think about it.' He turns back to the painting, his face a laser beam of focus. 'You know where to find me.'

I toss the rug down on his camping stool and begin making my way up the steps. 'Yes. I do.'

CHAPTER 30

No new memories are triggered as I walk along the cliff path back to the car. The view has changed again, and the islands have all but disappeared into the mist. In many ways the sea is a perfect resting place for my sister, who was so changeable, her emotions so large. If only she was at rest. Instead, the secrets around her death are unsettling everything.

I don't feel closer to the truth having come here, but in a way it has been cathartic: like I've faced something and come out the other side. Maybe Mum experienced something similar before she slipped and hurt her leg. Or maybe in her mind she was some other place entirely: a world where my sister is still out there somewhere, and she's trying to call her home. I shudder at the thought.

In any case, I do feel better for having talked to Nick. An outsider, detached from what happened; someone who listened, and on some level, I felt that he understood. Maybe he's lost someone too.

When I arrive back at Mum's house, the others are still out. I call the taxi company and try to reach Lachlan, but I get his voicemail and don't leave a message. I eat a sandwich and then go upstairs to run a bath. As I slip into the steaming hot water, I think of the two seals and my earlier idea for a song. My skin in the water feels slippery and smooth. I run my hands over my body luxuriantly, and then go under the water to wet my hair. I have to stop myself thinking about Nick, his eyes memorising every shadow, curve and plane of my body... his lips that once breathed life into mine… No, I can't allow my mind to wander. Yes, there's an attraction between us, but that's as far as it goes. There's nothing right about any of this: not the time, nor the place, nor the person. I'll take my kit off for him if he wants to paint me. After all, it's nothing he hasn't seen before…

There's a commotion downstairs. Bill's family back from the village. I get out of the bath, get dressed, and blow-dry my hair. As I'm finishing up, there's a loud thunk outside the door. I coil the cord around the dryer, hearing footsteps, and then, someone yells: 'Fucking bastard!' For a moment, I'm transported back in time.

'Dad!' A girl giggles.

I open the bathroom door, afraid of seeing some kind of ghostly apparition of my dad and myself as a girl. Instead, Bill is up the ladder to the attic, having just hit his head on the hidden beam. Emily is below, peering upwards.

'Hi, Emily,' I say warily. 'What are you up to?'

'Dad says your old vinyl albums are up there.' She points to the hatch, as Bill heaves himself into the attic and his legs disappear. 'I saw some records in the village shop but Dad wouldn't let me buy them. He said there were plenty at home.'

'Yes, they must be up there somewhere,' I say, a little irritated.

Emily begins climbing up the ladder. Dust rains down and I feel a sneeze coming on. 'But there's lots of stuff and we don't want it all down,' I say. 'Someone will have to put it back up when you leave.'

'I knoooow…' Bill's voice sounds like he's in an echo chamber. 'That's what I said.'

'And remember,' I say to Emily's disappearing feet. 'You can have the harp…'

She's gone. Up to the wonderful world of someone else's attic. I can't blame her. When we used to visit my gran I loved poking around in cupboards and wardrobes, rifling through old clothing, photos and books. A treasure trove for a kid. It's just my gran didn't have anything so sordid as a dead sister—

'Look! What's this box? Ouch!'

I'm not proud to admit that I feel a little satisfied that Emily fares no better than anyone else when it comes to the hidden beam.

'It's old journals. Diaries, I think.'

'Leave those…' I plead.

'I've found the record player.' Bill's voice is muffled. 'Here, hand it down to Skye.'

'OK,' Emily replies. She passes something down to me. But it's not the record player. I stagger under the weight of the box of journals.

'No, Emily…'

'Here's the record player.'

I have no choice but to put the box down and grab the record player and two even heavier boxes of vinyl records. Then Emily wants to take the amps down and Ginny's guitar. I put my foot down.

'Bill, that's enough stuff… please.'

'No, Emily,' I hear him say. 'Leave the guitar up here.'

'But I can play guitar,' Emily says. 'I can even do the F chord and that one's hard.'

'That's good,' I say. 'But that was my sister's guitar. I don't want it down. Or anyone else playing it.'

'You could play it,' Emily says. 'And I could play your one. We could play together. What's it called? A duet. Not here – not around Nan. But at the cottage.'

'No.' I'm on the verge of getting angry. 'Bill?'

'No, Emily. Skye's right. We don't want to upset Nan.'

Emily clops heavily down the ladder, making a cloud of dust fly with each step. When she gets to the bottom, she glares at me and stalks off, leaving all the stuff in a heap on the floor. I've been trying hard to do the friendly aunt thing, but right now, I'm struggling. 'Emily,' I call out. 'Come and take some of this stuff. You can't leave it here.'

She ignores me and strops off down the stairs.

Bill comes down the ladder, blinking from the dust.

'How can you think that this was a good idea?' I say. 'Getting all that stuff down. Talk about "rocking the boat".'

'Sorry,' he says, wiping his face with his hand. 'I shouldn't have mentioned the old records.' He folds up the stairs and closes the hatch.

I sigh. 'She can have them. But can you take them to the cottage? I don't want to hear those records. It's… too creepy. And who knows what hearing them might do to Mum.'

'I know.' Bill glances at the box at my feet and gives me a worried look. 'What's that?' he says.

'Ginny's journals.'

'Oh, God. Sorry. Should I put them back up?'

'No,' I say with a sigh. 'I should have a look through them.'

'Are you sure that's a good idea?' Bill hesitates. 'I thought we agreed—'

'Mum doesn't need to know,' I snap. 'I won't tell her, if you don't. But I've found out some things. For one, the "rogue wave" story was bollocks. And what's more, Mum knows it. She thinks Ginny might have… well… Anyway, I'm trying to figure out what really happened that night.'

Bill's brow creases into a deep frown – not something I've often seen. I'm sure he's going to tell me off, stop me from saying anything else, but instead, he goes down the hall and opens the door to his old room, gesturing for me to follow. I go in and shut the door. His room has the same bed and furniture and a few of his trophies are up on a shelf. I'm relieved to see that his old posters (especially the pin-up from page 3 of *The Sun* and her perky breasts) are gone. It's not a shrine to him, but rather a cosy 'boy' room where his sons might want to sleep someday when they come to visit their gran.

I perch on the desk. 'Look I know you're going to tell me to stop—'

'No, actually, there's something I wanted to ask you,' he says, cutting me off. 'I mean, I didn't want to mention it, but seeing you back here and all, I've just… well… been wondering…' He shifts on his feet, seeming oddly nervous.

'What is it?' I cross my arms.

'I found something…' He looks away, hesitating. 'I didn't tell anyone about it at the time. I was too… squeamish.'

'Squeamish?' Instantly, I send my emotions into lockdown mode. I can't afford to feel right now. Can't afford to wonder how I'll cope if the one person who has been a rock to me for so long – the one person who most certainly was not involved in any of it – might have secrets too. 'What are you talking about?'

'It was a couple of weeks before she died,' Bill says. 'I was throwing something away in the bathroom bin, and I found… it.' He looks out of the window, like the view of grey sky is particularly fascinating. 'A pregnancy kit,' he says.

'What?' I hiss. I grip the edge of the desk.

'Was it yours?' He grimaces. 'Or… *hers?*'

Pieces of the puzzle that I didn't even know were missing slam into place. Ginny breaking up with James, then a few months later declaring her undying love for him. Ginny, bowing out of the audition, ripping up the ticket I bought for her. Throwing away all our hopes and dreams just like that. Ginny who went to the party that night and… died. Ginny who was… *Oh God.*

I feel like I might be sick. I've had it with this whole thing and everyone involved. 'It wasn't mine,' I say, my voice sharp. 'And you should have told me about it. Everyone should have told the truth. Don't you think the police might have been interested to know if she was pregnant? That it might have had an impact on her mental state?'

'I didn't think about that,' Bill says. 'I didn't tell anyone because it was too embarrassing. And besides, I really did think it was yours. I mean, you and Byron—'

'You could have asked…' But even as I say the words, I realise I'm being unfair. Bill was a teenage boy with two loopy sisters that surely he couldn't even begin to comprehend.

'I wasn't even sure what it was,' Bill defends his corner. 'I mean, I had an idea. I was pretty sure it was something that Mum wouldn't be happy to find. So I threw it in the bin out back.'

'And you're sure it was positive?'

'There was a pink cross. I remember that. When Fiona showed me her pink cross a few years later, I knew I'd seen it before.'

I put my hands over my eyes. 'This is all just so… awful.'

Before Bill can respond, there's a commotion out in the hallway. Gripping the wall to steady myself, I follow him out of the room. Emily is there, along with Fiona, who raises a questioning eyebrow when she sees us. Emily has the record player in her arms, the chord trailing along behind her. Fiona is carrying one of the heavy boxes of records.

'Here, let me take that,' Bill says. He gives me a quick glance and I can see how relieved he is to be done with our conversation.

'Sure, be my guest.' She hands him the box.

'I'll take that.' I point to the box of journals.

Emily gives me a black look, but I ignore her.

'I've got a headache from all that dust,' I say. I pick up the box and take it to my room, set it down just inside the door and give it a hard shove with my foot over to Ginny's side. Then I pick up the harp and put it outside the door.

'Can you take this away too?' I say. 'Please.'

'Sure,' Bill says, looking worried.

'I hope you feel better, Skye,' Fiona says.

'Thanks,' I say, pulling the door shut. 'Me too.'

I don't tell her that I couldn't possibly feel worse.

*

I lie on my bed staring at a pinhole in the wall, trying to make sense of this unbearable new dimension to the tragedy. Ginny broke up with James because we were leaving and she wanted to make a clean break. Then she discovered she was pregnant. She bought a coach ticket to Glasgow – but it wasn't because she was going there with James.

Maybe she'd decided to have an abortion: somewhere anonymous, where it wouldn't get back to Mum through the grapevine. I don't know for sure, but it does make sense. Then, at the last minute, she had second thoughts. She decided to keep the baby, tell James, get back together. But James rejected her. She was upset, everything seemed hopeless. Did she make a snap decision to end the pain once and for all?

Again I don't know, but what I really don't understand is why she didn't confide in me? I loved her, I would have helped her. If she wanted an abortion, I would have stood by her – and made sure that James paid for a coach ticket for both of us.

Or, she could have had the baby. Mum disapproves of abortion, and I'm sure she would happily have raised it. I would have made sure that James damn well paid child support.

It would have been an awkward and upsetting time, but we would have got through it. We were a family. It was only Ginny's action that destroyed that.

I hear a car outside. And voices. Mum: home from her WI do. My suspicions loom like sinister shadows. *Did Mum know?*

I think of her antipathy for James, the farm park, and Katie. Then there was the conversation I overheard between her and Lorna: *'I never told her.'* It could have been about any of the secrets she was keeping – the stroke, the made-up story, her suspicions of suicide – anything. But could it have been about my sister being pregnant?

The more I think about it, the more certain I am that Mum must have known. It explains why she was so worried the night of the party. Begging me to collect Ginny and bring her home. Wanting me to protect not only my sister but also her unborn child—

I sit up and get to my feet. I don't want to stay in this room a moment longer. Nor do I want to go down and brave the family. The idea of sitting downstairs, interacting with Bill, and Mum – two people that I'd thought were just as perplexed as I was about what happened all those years ago – seems impossible. They too were keeping secrets… they too were *lying* all this time.

I glance over at the box with Ginny's journals. In truth, I don't *want* to change my view of my sister. I don't want to taint the good memories or think of her as scared and depressed, her heart broken by a boy who wouldn't stick by her. A girl who might decide that her life was hopeless and not worth living. I don't want to know the truth.

But it's too late now.

I kneel down and take out the books one by one. I flip through the pages, trying to dull the pain of seeing her loopy, rambling handwriting. The first page of each journal has a month and year written, along with: 'Property of Virginia Turner – Keep Out!!!'

For the most part, I did keep out. Ginny read me snippets from time to time, but I never tried to read her journals or steal them. Why would I? I knew everything about her. I didn't need to know her secrets because she didn't keep any from me.

I toss a few of the journals into an old rucksack. They only seem to go up until the time she was eighteen, so there must be at least one that's missing. I take the rucksack downstairs. I'm not going to read them here.

Mum's in the kitchen with Fiona, and the others don't seem to be around. Both of them look surprised to see me. Fiona offers me a cup of tea.

'No, thanks,' I say. I don't look at Mum or try and make small talk. All the secrets… all the years… 'I'm going out,' I say. 'I won't be back for supper.'

CHAPTER 31

The light is fading as I reach the village. I pass the coach stop, and it seems like years instead of days since I arrived, worried about coming home and seeing Mum, but hoping for the best. It also seems a lot longer than mere hours ago when I drove back from the lighthouse feeling better for having gone out there. Now, all I can feel is an icy chill inside of me.

I drive through the village and pull into the car park of the little stone church, nestled in a copse of trees. It's eerily quiet as I get out of the car, taking the rucksack with me, and go around the back to the graveyard. An elderly woman is standing before one of the graves near the church, her head bowed. I turn up the first aisle and walk to the far end, where there's a gnarled oak tree, and the graves of my family.

I've been here many times after the Sunday service we used to attend as kids. Before going on to tea and biscuits in the church hall, we'd come here and say hello to Grandma and Granddad Stewart – Mum's parents – who died when we were little, and Grandpa Turner, whom Dad said we had to forgive for being half English and giving us our surname. Our great grandma Millie fell in love with a man from the wrong side of the border, but they'd met while serving in Passchendaele, so her indiscretion could be overlooked. Next to Grandpa Turner is his wife, Mary-Annie. She was a champion open water swimmer, and it was a shock when she died, when I was about twelve.

Dad's grave is just past his parents'. It's marked with a shiny granite headstone with a cherub playing a harp. It was the closest to a musical theme that we could find in the standard repertoire of headstones. Dad's funeral was one of Ginny's greatest performances. She sang 'Green Grow the Rashes O' while I strummed along on the guitar. Her voice had never sounded so pure, so bell-like, especially when it began to break with emotion. I can still see her standing just beyond the tree, tall and slender, her long hair straight down her back. In her black dress with lace sleeves she looked like a dark angel, otherworldly and untouchable. At one with death and yet immune from it. Her voice was one that was destined to live on for years, touching the hearts of millions. Ginny was her family's darling and soon she would be the world's darling. It had seemed inevitable.

Now, her headstone is next to Dad's. Black granite with blue metallic sparkles, luminous like her eyes. But Ginny isn't there. She chose her own grave. A grave of wind and rock and crashing waves. A grave for her and… her child.

Tears sting my eyes, but I didn't come here to be sad. I sit down on one of the Stewart graves and take out one of Ginny's diaries. I open it to a page at random.

Grandma finished her Brussels sprouts and then she let out a huge fart. I looked at Mum. She was staring down at her plate and then she started choking. I looked at Skye like 'should we help her?' Then Mum snorts – seriously – and she's laughing. Grannie lets another one go… I swear, I laughed myself sick…

There's much more of the same. Some parts are funny, some are mundane descriptions of her day-to-day life. I enjoy reliving some of Ginny's good memories, especially of family Christmases.

For the most part, they mirror my own. Laughter, jokes, music, food. So much to live for.

But towards the end of that journal, there are a few references that give me pause:

> *S is like five minutes older than me. But she acts like I'm a silly, stupid little girl. It's driving me crazy.*

Or one from the beginning of the next, when we were both seventeen.

> *She didn't know I saw her. He totally had his hand up her shirt and his tongue down her throat. She didn't see me. But he did. And the look he gave me... I hate her.*

I stare at the words on the page, feeling hurt and a little betrayed. OK, so I probably was a bit smug when I was with Byron. But surely that's understandable given how most people fussed over Ginny, not me. I skip on to the entry when she first started going out with James:

> *It's finally my turn to get what she has. J's so nice, and he makes me laugh. I feel like a princess. If I were staying here, I could do worse. And better...*

So James didn't exactly sweep her off her feet. That doesn't surprise me. I am surprised by the thinly veiled references to her being jealous of me.

I read one of the last entries in the diary from that year. She goes on and on about being Queen of the Fleet, the dresses, and the 'maidens' in her court. But towards the end, another line snags my eyes:

S thinks that she knows everything about me. She thinks we want the same things, and that she's got it all figured out. So I just play along. There's only one thing that she has that I want.

What did I have that she wanted?
There's only one thing I can think of. One thing we didn't share.
One person.

CHAPTER 32

It's dark when I stuff the journals back into the rucksack and leave the graveyard. I feel more alone than I ever have in my life, even the moment when I found out Ginny was dead. At that time I was in denial – my sister, it seems, was not only a talented singer, but a very good actress. But I can't deny her own words. She resented me. She was jealous of me and Byron. Could that really be true?

I drive back to the centre of the village and park the car. I'm chilled from sitting outside, but I have to try and speak to Lachlan. If anyone was lurking about in the shadows: if anyone saw 'what really happened' – not just that night, but in the months leading up to it – then surely it would be him.

I walk down to the harbour. The boats are bobbing up and down, the streetlamps casting jagged golden shapes on the water. The door to the Fisherman's Arms is open, a yellow parallelogram of light spilling onto the dark paving outside. I can hear music: traditional fiddle and flute music. For a second, my pulse quickens. Live music? No – after a few seconds I recognise a track from a CD. When I first arrived, I didn't think I'd ever want to join in another session. Now, though, the uncomplicated joy of making music, laughing, catching up with old friends and making new ones seems like a dream I could relish. If I were staying here long term, then maybe I'd start one. One where everyone felt welcome, especially young people who were just starting out. But I won't be staying. Not after what I've discovered.

The pub seems more Christmassy than last time. The tree Byron bought has been put up next to the fireplace and trimmed with red baubles and white lights. I'm not sure what it means: did his son Kyle not come after all? He'd told me that he'd be taking some time off from the pub to spend with him. I'd been hoping that I wouldn't have to see him tonight.

The tables in the pub are about half full, with some people eating and others just drinking. Then, there's a loud cheer from upstairs where, according to a banner above the door to the toilets, a pool tournament is going on.

I make my way over to the bar looking for Lachlan on the stools but instead I see that he's behind the bar serving drinks.

'Hi, Skye.' Lachlan looks up from the pint he's pulling. 'You well?' He puts the pint on the counter in front of an old man on one of the stools, and checks his watch. 'If you're here for the tournament, then you're too late. The women have just finished.'

'I'm not here for that,' I say. 'I was hoping to have a word with you.'

'OK…' He eyes me warily.

'It won't take long.'

'Why don't you go upstairs and watch the tourney? I'll join you in a few minutes.'

'Watch?'

Lachlan gives me an appraising glance. 'Well, if you fancy playing the men, I could have a word with Richie.'

'I'll think about it,' I say. One of the things that Lachlan was better than 'almost' at was pool. He and me both.

'Fine. I won't be a minute. You want a drink?'

'Just a ginger ale, please.'

He makes the drink and I take it with me upstairs to the pool room. I'm surprised to see that the two old pool tables and racks of warped cues are gone. In the centre of the room is a genuine, fourteen-foot long snooker table.

'Do you like it? It's my pride and joy?'

I turn, startled. Byron has come up behind me carrying a keg of beer. I notice another bar along the back wall that wasn't there before. Seeing him brings back the anger I felt the other day when I discovered that he orchestrated the lie about my sister's death. But what else did he lie about?

'Um yeah,' I say. 'Nice.'

'I thought it was time for an upgrade,' he says.

'Did you?' I say, my voice laced with sarcasm. Someone calls him over to the bar.

'I'll catch up with you later?' he says. 'You OK for a drink?'

'Yes. I'm fine.' As he walks to the bar, I roll back the years to our then-relationship. The rational part of me says that I'm making something out of nothing. So what if my sister wrote in her journals that she was jealous? That doesn't mean anything happened between them. I can't recall Byron ever treating Ginny as anything other than my younger sibling, usually rolling his eyes at some of her antics. He was a grounded person and so was I. We were good together. And Ginny? She was happy with James. Until she broke up with him…

I'm not sure of anything any more.

There are a few women sitting around the tables drinking beer and about twenty men. Some people I recognise, others not. I spot Byron chatting to a bald man with a dark tattoo down his neck – Danny Morrison, one of Byron's tougher mates from back in the day. He breaks off and points at me. The man nods. Maybe I'm just being paranoid, but I sense an undercurrent of hostility. In the old days, I used to be part of this crowd, but now I feel like a stranger, an outsider. Being here is definitely a bad idea.

As I'm standing there, Lachlan comes up the stairs. I'm about to tell him that I don't want to play in the tournament, but before I can do so, he calls out to a fat, balding man who's holding a clipboard and asks if I can sign up. The fat man, Richie, eyes me, tits first, then face. 'It's men only,' he says.

'Come on, Richie,' Lachlan says. 'It'll be nicer seeing her arse around the table than yours.'

Everyone is looking now. I can't back down, and now that I'm being challenged, I want to prove myself. I channel the performer in me, the cute little country and western singer who's in her element on stage in denim hot pants and sequin halter tops, boots and a Stetson. I take a cue from the rack. There are some balls scattered on the table, a few reds, and all the colours. I drop down and aim for a red near the cushion. It rattles the jaw of the pocket, and there's a collective holding of breath as it drops. I pot the black ball and straighten up.

'So what do I need to show?' I say. 'A dick, or a minimum level of competency?'

Richie looks blank. Lachlan snorts with laughter. Byron comes over from the bar and gives Richie a clap on the back. 'Come on, mate,' he says. 'It will be like old times.'

Richie punches him in the arm and goes to speak to another man. While they're debating, I pot some more balls. I've only played on a real snooker table a few times in my life, and it's a lot bigger than a pool table. I'm definitely out of practice, but it's a welcome distraction, and the basic shots come back to me like riding a bike.

Richie relents, saying that I can play a qualifying match. I put down the cue and wait for my turn to play. Lachlan comes up again holding pints of beer. He hands me one of them.

'Thanks for backing me.' I take a swig of the beer for some Dutch courage.

'No problem.' He shrugs. 'Obviously, I'd rather watch you play than these louts.'

'Obviously.' Awkward bugger.

He stares into my eyes for a second too long. I remember what Byron said about him having a crush on me—

'Byron said you two are going to dinner,' Lachlan says. 'Does that mean you're back together?'

'*What?*' I look at him, startled.

'You and Byron.' He makes it sound like it's obvious. 'It's been a long time, but now you're both here. Both single. Right?'

I take a step back. 'He asked if I wanted to meet his son. That's it.' I don't know why I'm feeling so defensive.

'Sounds serious then.' He raises a wry eyebrow.

I turn on him. 'Do you really think I'd get back with the man who got everyone to lie to the police about my sister's death? I know the "rogue wave" was complete bollocks. That's what you were trying to tell me the night I arrived, wasn't it?'

Lachlan doesn't answer right away. He swirls the beer around in his glass. 'He told us at the time that we were doing it for you.'

'So you're admitting that it was all a complete lie? That Jimmy and Mackie saw nothing, just like everyone else?'

Lachlan pulls me to the side. 'Keep your voice down,' he says. 'You're right that most people saw fuck-all. Everyone was shit-faced.'

'Yeah, what else is new?' I take a step closer, getting in his face. 'But what about you, Lachlan? Were you shit-faced too? Or did you *see* something? Something that you didn't tell the police?'

'The police…' He gives a grim laugh. 'Inspector McVee. He wanted to keep things simple as much as anyone else. Better for the deceased's family, better for the community. Open and shut. It certainly was convenient, you losing your memory like that.'

I clench my fists by my sides. It won't do any good to get angry now. 'It wasn't convenient,' I say. 'I suffered head trauma. You can choose to believe what you like, but it's the truth.'

He leans in and whispers in my ear. 'So you don't remember being there on the jetty with her?'

'No,' I say, standing my ground like this doesn't faze me. 'I was told at the time that I never left the campfire. But Katie said that I went to look for Ginny.'

He snorts. 'Katie certainly used the situation to her advantage.'

'I have to agree,' I say. 'But then again, James was a free agent. Ginny had broken up with him. She and James had a row that night.' I shake my head. 'And I knew nothing.'

'The twa sisters, twa bonny swans,' he intones. 'One fair and one dark, one good and one bad.'

I stare at him.

'But which one was which? That's the question? Did you know you were sharing everything?'

'Stop being a dick,' I hiss, as I picture Ginny… her lovely golden hair spread around her as she lies back on Byron's tartan rug. Teasing him, laughing as she pulls him down over her…

No. She wouldn't do that to me. And neither would—

'You OK?'

I've clearly summoned the devil. Byron comes up. He puts his hand protectively on the curve of my back, then moves it lower in a gesture of possession.

'I don't blame you Skye, for turning your back on her,' Lachlan says. 'I don't blame you at all.'

He turns away and goes down the stairs.

'What the hell is up with him?' Byron says.

I move away from Byron's hand, swivelling to face him. My heart is hammering, my head feels like it might burst. But I force myself to act normal. 'I think Lachlan's a little jealous,' I say breezily. 'Seems as though you get all the girls, Byron.'

He gives me a pained look. 'What are you on about?'

'I think he's implying that there was a *wee* something going on between you and my sister.' My throat tightens uncomfortably. 'Now, why would he say a thing like that?'

Byron shrugs. 'Because he's trying to drive a *wee* wedge between us.'

Now that I've allowed the suspicions to take root, I can't stop them growing to a monstrous size. 'He said I had a right to be angry. What do you think that means? That I found out that my sister was sleeping with you? I left her there and she went into the sea? And then, conveniently, got in a car accident and lost my memory?'

Byron's face closes down. 'That's bullshit.'

'Which part?' I glare at him.

'All of it,' he growls. His voice is loud and people are starting to look. The crowd has expanded. Byron's tattooed mate moves in closer, as if sensing that his ringleader is under threat. I glare at him. I see Aunt Annie arrive, spreading her ample backside onto a tall stool.

'Well, that's good to know,' I say. 'Because it looks like Ginny might have been pregnant when she died.' I study his face while that sinks in.

'Who the fuck is feeding you this shit?' Byron lowers his voice. 'She was leaving. Going to that audition. Even she wouldn't have been that stupid.'

'Not so "stupid" as to keep the baby, maybe. Did you know that she'd broken up with James? And then tried to get back with him that night?'

Byron laughs. His face is starting to look sick and ugly. I'm struggling to see how I ever could have felt anything for him. Loved him even...

'James,' he repeats. 'God, what she ever saw in that dickhead. His Preciousness was all too happy to lie to the police. If it wasn't for me he would have been bending over in a jail cell somewhere for dealing drugs. And I don't think your mum would have liked that, would she?'

'You've been a real patron saint to my family, Byron.'

'You're fucking right about that—'

'Skye Turner. You're up. You play Finlay.' Fat Richie makes a tick on his clipboard.

The previous match has finished. I'm angry and upset, and the last thing I want to do is play snooker. But everyone is watching. If I back down now, then there'll be no coming back from it.

My hands feel clammy and weak as I pick up the cue. My opponent, Finlay, is an elderly man with a wicked blue-eyed smile. He's probably been playing snooker since I was in nappies. As I watch him break off, reds splaying everywhere, I almost miss Aunt Annie, talking to a man on the stool next to her.

'She thinks she's so much better than the rest of us. Always has, the daft cow. Her sister was worth ten of her. That poor lass. Topped herself out on the cliffs.'

A tremor of rage travels through my body. I have no idea what she has against me, and I want to find out… and I will.

'Your go, lass,' Finlay says. I've got no choice but to continue. I pot two reds and a blue, but miss the next colour. Finlay takes his turn, but he misses an easy red, and I get the idea that the poor chap needs glasses. He cocks his head like he can't quite believe he's missed. 'Thar ya go, lass,' he says graciously. 'Left you in amongst 'em'.

I take my turn, potting balls one after the other until someone puts their hand on my arse and I miss. 'Foul!' I yell.

There's a line of four men, any one of which could be the culprit, but no one owns up. Richie tells us to play on. I stand on the sidelines, fuming. We play on until, eventually, Finlay's bad eyesight gets the better of him. I sink the last red and then start on the colours, which I pot in the required sequence: yellow, green, brown, blue, pink, black. More people have come to watch the tournament. One person in particular.

Nick Hamilton.

I miss the blue but it doesn't matter. Finlay shakes my hand and I offer to buy him a pint. 'Aye, lass,' he says. 'If you insist.'

I go to the bar taking care not to glance in Nick's direction. I feel a little irritated to see him here. Maybe it's because I'd heard that he kept to himself and didn't come here. I liked the fact that he wasn't trying to fight the uphill battle of acceptance. Unlike me.

Byron is behind the bar along with a blonde curly-haired woman that I don't recognise. I order Finlay's drink from the woman.

'Can I get a drink for her too?' I point to Aunt Annie. 'Whatever she's having.'

Byron gives me a hard look. For a second, I think he wants to continue our earlier argument. 'Whiskey and Coke,' he says. 'That's her drink *too*.' He turns away from me.

I pay for both drinks and hand Finlay his pint. I take the whiskey over to Annie. As a peace offering, or a gauntlet thrown down before battle – I'm not sure which. I can feel people watching as I approach. Annie is talking to the man next to her. He seems entirely focused on her wrinkled cleavage rather than her scintillating conversation.

'Here, Annie.' I hold out the drink. 'I may be a daft cow and nowhere near as good as my sister, who topped herself. But my money's as good as anyone's.'

She looks at me in surprise, and then realises that I overheard her nasty little comment.

'Sorry,' she says, 'I didn't mean—'

'Yes you did,' I say.

I sense, rather than see, Nick coming up on my right.

'The point is, Annie,' I say, 'I'm back now. If you have a problem with me, then say it to my face. Stop whispering behind my back.'

'I've got no problem with you,' she says.

'Good,' I say. 'Enjoy the drink.'

There's whispering as I walk away, and one of the 'hand on arse' candidates sniggers: 'Can I slag you off too, lass, if you're buying?'

I pretend to laugh and then perch on an empty bar stool. Lachlan plays next and wins his match easily. Nick goes over and has a word with Richie, then goes to the bar. I begin to feel annoyed – which is stupid given that I'm the one avoiding him.

Nick leaves the bar carrying two half-pints of beer. For a horrible moment, I think he's headed in the direction of a red-haired woman in a tight T-shirt. At the last second, he diverts and comes over to where I'm sitting.

'Good one back there.' He indicates with his head towards Annie. 'But if you want to leave, just say. Otherwise…' He hands me one of the half-pints.

'Who says I want to leave with you?' I'm not sure why I'm being so awkward.

'Your brother. Your mum's worried about you. I went over to return her plate. They thought you might have come here.'

'Is she worried about me – or the car?' I take a long swig of the beer.

'Come on Skye, you're better than that.'

'Am I?' I snap. It's like a dam has broken inside me and I can't stop these words from coming out of my mouth.

'Nick Hamilton?' Richie calls out.

I cock my head. 'Did you sign up?'

'Yes, I did.' He gives me a bemused smile. 'So if we're not leaving, then it's my go.'

He sets down his glass and walks over to the table. Richie glowers and hands him a cue.

Nick's opponent is the man who's been sitting next to Aunt Annie; Mum mentioned a husband, Greg, so maybe it's him. She gives me a toothy smile and raises the empty glass of whiskey like we're two old friends having a toast. Aunt Annie's man is good, but Nick is better. He gets in amongst the balls, moving around the table with rhythm and focus. Aunt Annie's smile quickly turns umbrella-shaped. I feel a rush of nervous adrenalin with each ball that Nick pots. He misses a blue off the spot and swears under his breath. When he stands back to let his opponent take his turn, his eyes fix only on me. I stare back with a slow smile. Nick's opponent misses and Nick clears up easily. There's a long silence as the last ball drops.

The other man admits defeat with an over-egged bow and there are whistles and cheers. When Richie proclaims Nick the winner, there's nothing. That angers me, so I stand up and cheer and whistle. A few people join in clapping, but there's an undercurrent of animosity in the room that seems to be rippling from the direction of Aunt Annie and the friends surrounding her.

'That was impressive,' I say to Nick as he returns to my side and takes a sip of his beer.

He shrugs like it's nothing. 'Thanks.'

'You're clearly a man of many talents.'

He gives me a smouldering look like we're the only two people in the room. I wish we were. He hands me his drink and I take a sip.

'I don't feel welcome here,' he says. 'Do you really want to stay for the next round?'

'I'm happy to leave.' I set down the glass. 'Maybe we could come back another time and play our own tournament.'

That sounds like a bad pick-up line if I've ever heard one. I blush and look away. My eyes fall on Aunt Annie. She's whispering something to her companion, and pointing at me.

I tense up.

'Come on, let's go,' Nick says.

'You sure you don't want to play your match? Be the conquering hero?'

'No. I'm here to collect you. Getting to watch you play...' his face softens just for a second '... was a bonus.'

'Oh,' I quip, 'were you thinking about painting me? At the snooker table.'

'No, Skye.' He lowers his voice. 'Watching you play, I wasn't thinking about painting you.'

He leaves that hanging between us and walks off towards the stairs. I go to follow him, aware of people watching us. The gossips will have a field day with this. Skye Turner, the girl who's too good for everyone. Going off with the city bloke who's too good to hang with the locals. Petty, small-town bullshit. I *am* better than this.

'Skye.' Byron waylays me at the top of the stairs. 'About earlier...'

'I don't want to talk about it,' I say. 'My ride is leaving.'

'I can bring you home.'

'No,' I say. 'You're working. And then, there's Kyle... If he even exists.'

Anger twists his face. 'He bloody exists,' he says. 'He's with Annie's daughter and her kids. I don't have to justify him to you, or anyone.'

'No, Byron, you're right. You don't have to justify your son to me. It was over between us long before Ginny died. I just didn't want to admit it. So whether you had a thing with her or not, well, it's been fifteen years. It doesn't matter any more.'

'Then stop acting like it does. Stop raking all this up. There's no point.'

I peer at him closely. 'I think you forgot to deny it,' I say.

'What?' He looks confused as well as angry.

I laugh in his face and move around him to the stairs. For a tense second, I think he's going to try and stop me. Then, he hangs his head, looking as broken as I've ever seen him. 'Go to hell, Skye,' he says.

I go down the stairs and when I get to the bottom, I turn back. 'Where do you think I've been all these years?'

CHAPTER 33

Nick is chatting to the female bartender when I re-enter the downstairs bar. I feel stupidly jealous until I realise that he's only ordering food: takeaway fish and chips.

'I thought you probably hadn't eaten,' he says. Before I can protest, he takes out his card and zaps it on the reader. 'If you have, then I guess I'm in for a second supper.'

'I haven't,' I admit.

He leans one elbow against the bar and appraises me openly, without saying anything. It's damned disconcerting, which I'm sure he intends.

'So where did you learn to play snooker?' I say.

He shrugs. 'There was a hall near the police station. I spent about an equal amount of time potting balls and busting people there.'

I laugh. 'I bet you were popular.'

'Something like that.'

I want to keep him talking, glad to have something to focus on other than my sister – her life, and her death. Besides, I'm genuinely curious about him. 'And what about your family?' I say.

He stares at the twinkling lights of the Christmas tree, his face hardening again. 'What about them?'

'Do you have family? Parents? You never talk about them.'

He sighs like I've disappointed him. 'I have family,' he says. 'We're not in contact.'

'Why not?' I have no right to pry, but on the other hand, he knows all my secrets.

He stays silent until I'm almost certain that he's not going to answer. 'My dad was a policeman,' he says. 'So was his dad and so is my older brother. You can imagine, I'm sure, how it went down when I told them that I was going to art school.'

'Yes, I suppose I can.'

'I did two years at the Slade in London.'

I raise an eyebrow, impressed. Even I know that that's a top school.

'In my second year,' he continues, 'I had a disastrous relationship with another student. When she and I split up, I decided that art school wasn't for me.' He shrugs. 'So I tried the police. If I couldn't please myself, at least my dad would be happy. But that didn't work out either.'

The bartender returns with my food. Unlike my childhood memories of fish and chips wrapped in newspaper, they're now in a Styrofoam container. I add salt and vinegar.

'Any more questions?' Nick sounds like a police commissioner conducting a press conference.

'Yes,' I say. 'Loads. But I'm sensing that you don't want to answer them.'

He laughs. 'Maybe you should have been in the police. Though it's not hard to spot a reluctant witness. Or suspect.'

We go outside and sit on a bench. I open the Styrofoam container, lamenting the good old days of newspaper.

'Yeah, I guess it's health and safety this and that these days,' Nick says. I offer him a chip.

As we eat, I stare out at the boats bobbing up and down on the incoming tide. 'I've found out something,' I say. 'About Ginny. I think she might have been pregnant.'

I'm half-expecting a drumroll or at least an exclamation of surprise. Instead, Nick just nods. 'Yes,' he says. 'That's why she broke up with her boyfriend and then, later on, was desperate to get back with him.' He takes another chip.

'Well good for you for working that one out,' I say, a bit put out. 'But did you also know that it's looking like she stole my boyfriend? Byron – the big bloke back there.' I indicate with my head. 'I don't have any proof, but I'm going to keep looking. He was the one who came up with the whole "rogue wave" story.'

Nick frowns. 'You think he had more to do with it than that?'

'No, not really,' I say. 'He was gone for much of the time when I was at the party. Getting more alcohol from the caravans nearby. He found me and came back to the lighthouse to use the emergency phone. I was told that he wanted to find Ginny – to tell her what had happened. No one had seen her, so he went off to search with his cousins and a few of his mates. Not long after, Jimmy and Mackie came back, telling everyone what they'd seen.'

'So you're saying that they made up the story to keep questions to a minimum?'

'Well, it wouldn't look good if people found out that he'd rejected her too, as well as James, if that's what happened. And then she went out onto the rocks and threw herself into the sea.'

Nick lets out a low whistle. 'You should have been a cop,' he says.

'No.' I sigh. 'It seems like everyone else knew something except me.'

'Exactly,' he says wryly.

We sit in silence for a minute. The whole conversation – and everything, really – is making me feel sick. Or maybe it's the fish and chips. They are delicious, but greasier than I remember.

'Here,' I say. 'Have the rest.'

'No, thanks.' He stands up and takes the empty container to a nearby bin. I stand up too. I sense that Nick Hamilton has quite a few additional thoughts that he's not sharing. That annoys me.

'So should we go, then?' I say tetchily. 'I can drive my own car. I've barely had anything to drink.'

He frowns. 'You've had beer.'

'So have you.'

'Less than half a pint.'

I shrug. 'You're the cop. You decide.'

'I have.' His voice is firm. 'You're coming with me. We can sort your car out tomorrow.'

'It's damned inconvenient for everyone.'

'Inconvenience is better than regret.'

I've got nothing to say to that as we walk to the car park. Nick opens the door of his Vauxhall for me and I get inside. The car smells of paint, and the back seat is full of Nick's easels and equipment.

I put on my seat belt, forcing myself to breathe, but I can feel my pulse quickening. My hands grow clammy; the fish and chips are heavy in my stomach...

He glances at me as we leave the car park. 'I know you're upset,' he says, 'but maybe you need to get away from all this for a while. How would you feel about coming round tomorrow? I could make a start sketching you. I'll cook you breakfast.'

I experience a fizzy surge of adrenalin, like a shaken up can of Coke. 'I'll have to see what the family is up to,' I say, not wanting to seem too eager. 'And how Mum's doing.'

'Of course,' he says.

As we drive towards the main road, a group of teenagers is huddled near the bus stop. A car comes towards us, and one of the kids tries to kick a bottle under it. Another one runs across the path of the car to get the bottle before it reaches the opposite kerb. Nick has to slam on the brakes. 'Fucking kids!' he yells.

But I'm not paying attention. My hand clenches on the door handle, as somewhere in the damaged part of my brain, a spark ignites. Headlamps... a figure rushing across. A flashing light. I let out a little cry as the images vanish.

'Are you OK? What is it?' Nick pulls up at the side of the road.

'I ... I just remembered something.'

The words come out garbled as I try to recreate in my mind that drive down the single-track road after I left the party. A person...

running in front of the car headlights. Did I swerve? Did I hit them? No. The steering wheel... where was the steering wheel? Why does everything about the memory seem wrong?

'Who was it? Do you know?'

'I... I think it was Ginny.'

My head hurts and I want to claw at my skull and rip away the veil and release the memories. The right memories, not these flashes that don't make sense. Ginny was up at the lighthouse, not anywhere near the road. The idea that this new memory – a new precious glimpse into what happened that night – might be false, is just too much. A sob escapes my throat. But I can't allow myself to cry... I just can't.

Nick doesn't say anything at first. We sit at the side of the road, and I can tell that he's worried about me.

'This can't go on,' he says, his voice unusually gentle. 'It's tearing you apart.' He takes a long breath. 'I think I should get the police file. Like you mentioned before. All this needs looking into. Properly. Do you agree?'

'Yes, I mean... I think so.'

'These flashes: you've had them before?'

'I've had nightmares. A "vision" of Ginny on the rocks, that I now think might be real. I also have panic attacks. I get them when I'm in a car and someone else is driving. But this one is new. The headlamps and the... girl.'

'There are a lot of misconceptions to do with memory loss caused by head trauma,' he says. 'In films, the memories all come back at once in a rush. And sometimes that does happen. But in the majority of cases, when there is nerve damage, the complete picture may never return.'

'That's what I was told.' I sigh. 'But how can I know if these flashes are real?'

'You can't,' Nick says. 'Not with a brain injury. That said, the mind works in mysterious ways. Sometimes with the right stimulus, memories can return. The flashes might be a piece of the puzzle, but they're not conclusive. You'd need other evidence to back them up, if that makes sense. Then, we might be able to see the whole picture.'

My mind sticks on the word he used. *We.*

He goes back onto the road, driving towards home. I stare straight ahead as we leave the village. It's foggy and the twin beams of the headlamps barely penetrate the inky blackness. When we pull into the cottage yard, the rectangle of light in the kitchen window is a welcome sight.

'Thank you,' I say to Nick, my voice heavy. 'For rescuing me again.'

'Don't thank me yet,' he says. In the dim light, his eyes are a luminous, twilit blue. 'I'll get my mate to drop the file around tomorrow.'

'Thanks. I just want to know the truth… that's all.'

His eyes hold mine, and I want much more than that. I feel an electric charge arc between us, like the crackling in the air before a storm. He reaches up and brushes away a strand of hair from my face. My skin glitters at his touch.

'Good night, Skye,' he says, his voice low and deep. 'I'll see you tomorrow.'

I get out of the car. 'Good night.'

CHAPTER 34

When I go inside, Bill is in the kitchen. He tells me that Mum
has been agitated all evening because I wasn't there. I feel bad for
causing her stress, and glad that she's settled now, and has apparently gone to bed. He perches against the sink. 'Look, Skye,' he
says, 'I'm sorry about Emily getting the diaries down, and about
not telling you about the… other thing.'

'It's OK,' I say. 'I don't think knowing would have made it
any easier.'

'Do you think it explains anything?' he says, looking worried.
'Ginny's state of mind or… her hormones? Do you think it would
have helped the investigation if I'd told the truth?'

'I honestly don't know,' I say. 'But if it makes you feel any
better, I think Mum knew about the pregnancy too.' I tell him
my suspicions about the second coach ticket and Mum talking
Ginny out of the abortion. 'It's looking like she didn't tell the
police about the pregnancy either.'

'Mum lied?' He looks as shocked by hearing this as I do by
saying it.

'Yes, I think so,' I say. 'When I heard that the "rogue wave"
story was made up, I told her that that didn't matter. That Ginny
would never have committed suicide. But now, I see that Mum
knew more than she was letting on. She knew that Ginny went
out to the lighthouse to get back with James.' I decide to keep my
suspicions about Ginny and Byron to myself for now. 'As soon as
he rejected her,' I continue, 'she had a motive to throw herself into

the sea. When Mum heard that no one saw the accident, she knew that it was at least possible that Ginny might have killed herself – and her unborn child. It's no wonder she's coming unravelled now. That must be the worst thing for a parent.'

'Yeah,' Bill says. He paces back and forth. 'It would be.'

'And there's one other thing you should know,' I say, taking a breath. 'I've asked Nick – my friend in the cottage – to look into the case. He used to be a DCI.'

Bill frowns. 'Is that wise?' he says. 'What do you think he'll find?'

'Maybe nothing. But I think it needs to be done.'

'What about Mum?' he asks the perennial question.

'I'm doing it for Mum,' I say with force. 'And all of us. It's the secrets and the uncertainty that have kept us apart for so many years. Nick may not find any new answers.' I get ready to go upstairs. 'But I hope he does.'

CHAPTER 35

I don't sleep well. My mind is full of strange flashing lights: will-'o-the-wisps luring me into a deep, impenetrable bog... Images of my sister out on the rocks like a terrible dark angel. A sting on my cheek, a bone-shattering jolt. Blackness. A voice. A running figure. *Help, I'll go and get help...*

I wake up with a start, the dream dissolving to nothingness. Who was speaking, what was happening? I yank at my hair like I can somehow dislodge the memories, make the dream return. *If* I was dreaming...

I sit up. I'm in my bed. Outside the window there's only swirling white. Snow is falling!

I get out of bed and dress quickly. I can already hear the high, excited voices of the children outside in the garden. Though it's dark and cold here in the winter, because we're right on the coast we don't get much snow. I understand why the kids are excited.

When I go downstairs, Mum is in the kitchen, staring dreamily out at her grandchildren. The boys are hurtling themselves around in circles like whirling dervishes, trying to catch the flakes on their tongue. Emily is on the swing, staring absently at the flurry of dancing white. 'It's so beautiful,' Mum says.

'It is.' I smile. Right now, I don't even feel angry with her.

I put on my coat and boots and walk over to Skybird. Nerves flutter inside me. This time, they have nothing to do with my sister or that night. My hair is covered with snow as I stand on the porch and knock. A minute later, the dog barks and the door opens.

Nick is wearing jeans and a blue jumper. His hair looks freshly washed, and I can smell his aftershave and an undernote of masculinity. I remember the brief touch from last night and feel a little dizzy.

'Skye.' He gives me that smug, bemused look. 'You're late.'

'Sorry. I... didn't have a great night.'

'No problem.' For a second he frowns. 'Do you want to... no. Actually, stay right there.'

I stand there on his doorstep as he disappears back inside. Kafka runs out and begins sniffing everywhere, like he's been transported to a new world. I go off the porch and join him, holding out my hands and twirling slowly like the boys were doing. Kafka clearly thinks I'm off my rocker and starts to bark at me and chases his tail. Clever dog.

I stop twirling. Nick is standing on the porch with his sketchbook. He looks up from the paper. 'Don't stop,' he says.

I laugh as the dog jumps up and tackles me. I fall on the layer of snow in the grass, and Kafka licks my face and I give him a big hug. I've forgotten what it's like to have a dog, and it seems like even my laugh is rusty. The snow continues to fall, and eventually I gather enough snow to make a big snowball. Nick is so intent on what he's drawing on the paper that he doesn't even notice before I throw it at him and it splats him in the chest.

'Hey!' he says. He sets his sketchbook down and pelts me with snow. I try (not too hard) to run away, but he grabs me, and the next thing I know, I'm pressed against him. His eyes are soft as he looks at me, and his hands brush the snow from my hair. But then he lets me go. He walks back to the porch and picks up his sketchbook.

'Come inside,' he says to me. 'Kafka,' he commands. 'Go to the kitchen.'

'Is he going to make the tea?' I joke. As I go inside the cottage, my earlier nerves return in force.

Nick laughs. 'I'll do that. Have you eaten?'

'No,' I say, 'but if you're going to sketch me, then I'd like to get on with it. Before I…' *chicken out*, I want to say '… change my mind.'

'Fine.' His eyes don't leave mine. 'I'm going to light the fire.'

The fire has been neatly laid just like before. He takes a box of matches from the mantelpiece, crouches down, and lights the paper at the bottom. There's a rushing sound as the kindling goes up in a pyramid of flames.

I take off my coat and put it over the edge of the sofa. I'm unsure what's meant to happen next.

He stays down for a minute, watching the flames. Then, he straightens up and turns back to me. 'I'd like to draw you here, by the fire. You'll be warm. You can get changed in the bathroom.'

'Into what?' I've got a pretty good idea that the answer is nothing, but I want to hear him say it.

'There's a robe there,' he says. 'I can make you a cup of tea.'

I take a breath. 'I've never seen much point to that "change behind the screen and put on a robe" thing,' I say. And before I can second-guess myself, I take my top over my head. I'm wearing a black lace bra, the nicest that I have. I unhook it, never taking my eyes off his face.

'You can stay like that.' The catch in his voice is the only thing that gives him away. He takes a step back from me. 'Turn and stand facing the fire. A little to the left.' I oblige him. 'Your hair…' He comes up to me and loosens my hair from its bobble, arranging it down my back and over my shoulder without ever touching my skin. I shiver, every cell in my body aware of him.

He steps back. 'Are you cold?'

'No.'

'Good. Now, just relax.'

'Yeah, right,' I say with a sarcastic edge.

But actually, I do manage to relax, my mind free of the stress I've been under with my family. I stare down at the fire, which is mesmerising in its motion. He positions himself on the edge of the sofa with his sketchbook, and I can hear the sound of his pencil making lines on the paper. I'd been worried beforehand that I'd be bored or twitchy, unable to hold the pose. As it is, I'm hardly aware of time passing. I feel I could stand here forever, basking in the heat of the crackling flames, knowing that he's watching me.

'Am I allowed to talk?' I ask.

'If you like,' he says.

I don't point out that I never did get that cup of tea.

'Am I doing OK?'

'Perfect.'

I weigh up the word and how he says it, my mind wandering as to where this might lead. After another ten minutes, he comes closer to me.

'Now, lie down,' he says.

The way he says those words… I move my hair back so that my breasts are fully bared. His eyes follow the motion, but already I feel that he's seeing all of me at once, whether he's staring at my face or my body.

He brings me a cushion to prop against. I stare directly at him, daring him to show even the slightest bit of arousal.

'So did you enjoy undressing me last time,' I say conversationally. 'When you rescued me from the sea?'

He picks up his pencil and sketches intently. 'I needed to get you out of your wet clothes and get you warm. That was all I was thinking about.'

'All?'

He stops sketching. The flickering light of the fire is reflected in his eyes. He responds only with the slightest of laughs. I like him looking at me. I like the possibilities crackling between us.

I put a teabag into a mug. 'It can be hard to let go of the good times,' I say. I mean it to be comforting, but it comes out sounding trite.

'No.' He looks up, like he's just remembered that I'm here. 'Not the good times. It's just…' He breaks off. 'Sorry, you didn't come here to be bothered with my shit.'

The kettle switches off and I pour water into his mug.

'Tell me.' I set the mug on the table. 'God knows, I've told you everything.'

He shakes his head. I feel that it's important that he confides in me, and whether he does or not will determine how things lie between us. Just when I'm certain that he's not going to, he speaks.

'Liz was with me in the police. We worked in the same office, but in different divisions. We dated for two years and then got married. Our schedules were such that we didn't see a lot of each other, but that kind of worked. She was ambitious, and I was ambitious. I got promoted. She didn't.'

I nod.

'That was the first strain on our relationship, but there were others. We both wanted kids, but it wasn't happening. Then four years ago, it finally did. She got pregnant. I was over the moon. I thought that having a baby would solve everything, plaster over the cracks in the relationship.'

Is that what Ginny thought too? That keeping the baby would plaster over the cracks, or in her case, cement her relationship with James. Or Byron? I sit rigid, wishing I'd made myself a cuppa too. As if he's reading my mind, he gets up and puts the kettle on again.

'So who knows if we would have survived in the end? She was working on an operation involving a gang of traffickers. I pressured her to take a desk job, take it easy. She resented it and didn't want to derail her career.'

The kettle boils, and he drops a teabag haphazardly into a cup. 'We had a row in front of everyone, and it was all very unprofessional. I learned later that she hadn't bothered to tell her boss about the pregnancy.'

He slams the mug down in front of me. 'To make a long story short, Liz continued on with the operation. She went to investigate a tip off and ended up getting shot. She... lost the baby.'

I grip the mug so tightly that the heat stings my hand.

'So that was it – for my marriage and my career.' He shrugs. 'I walked out pretty much then and there. I guess I was a bastard not to have been more supportive. But I was just so angry. And three weeks later, she was back at work. She finally got that promotion.'

The agony on his face tears me in two. I reach out and take his hand. I don't say 'sorry' or any other meaningless words of comfort. Because when it comes to a deep, heart-wrenching loss like he's suffered, there are no words to be said.

In only a few seconds, the hard shell of Nicholas Hamilton begins to crack. His eyes fill with tears. I grip his hand more tightly and look away so he can be unashamed in his grief. For the loss of his baby, another innocent life.

'Nick,' I whisper softly. I trace the line of a tear down his cheek.

'Sorry.' He shakes his head. 'I don't know why I'm telling you...' He stops speaking. His eyes say it all. 'Yes, I do...'

He pulls me gently onto his lap. He studies my face and I know he's seeing straight through me. He kisses me, with such a tender sweetness, and I curl up onto his lap as the warmth flares to heat between us, and tangle my fingers in his hair pulling him harder to my mouth. I gasp as he reaches up under my shirt and his hand caresses my breast. I want him, all of him. I want to give him all of myself. There's no past and no pain, nothing but the promise of the moment. His hands move to undo my jeans and I'm about to take my shirt over my head... The dog barks from the utility room, and there's a crunch of gravel outside. Nick groans and closes his eyes, severing the connection between us.

'Talk about bad timing,' he says.

I slide off his lap, straightening my clothes. 'That's for sure. Are you expecting someone?'

Nick stands up from the chair and puts the kettle back on. This time, I know it's not for me.

'My mate from Fort William,' he says. 'I called him late last night. He's brought me your sister's file.'

CHAPTER 36

The snow has turned to rain as I make my way back home. I feel like a horse that's run a race and is still in a lather. The alternative reality takes shape in my head. Lying by the fire with Nick, my hair splayed out on the rug. Rising above the pain of the past and stealing a moment, a future, even. And later on, when he finished what he started, he would show me the sketches: beautiful and skilful, but somehow unfinished. Only by making love to me would he truly be able to know the woman on the page.

Before I left Skybird, Nick's mate had come inside and they'd given each other a blokey, back-clapping embrace, complete with a few choice swear words on how long it had been since they'd last caught up. Nick had introduced us briefly. DS Alain Paterson's eyebrows had lifted when Nick gave my name.

'I was just leaving,' I'd said, trying not to look at the thick file in his hand. I was in that file. So were all of my friends and the people I'd grown up with. And Mum. And my sister. What was Nick going to find when he started reading? Part of me had wanted to stick around. Observe him as he read witness accounts and officer reports. Take note of any reaction, exclamation of surprise, or frown at an unanswered question.

Instead, I'd tried to look grateful and non-plussed. 'It's very kind of you both to help me out,' I'd said. And then I'd left. It was better for all concerned. Let Nick catch up with his friend. Let him go through the file and draw his own conclusions.

He'd given me a brief kiss on the cheek as I left. That kiss had said it all, but it was something that I'd known already. That as long as Nick has that file, as long as he's looking into my sister's death, then anything between us will need to be put on hold.

I feel an ache of regret as I go back through the gate to Mum's yard. At the side of the lawn, there's a small, misshapen attempt at a snowman. I remove my boots by the porch and go inside. The twins are wrestling on the floor of the living room, and Fiona is shouting at them to settle down. Emily is picking up some pieces of the jigsaw that must have been knocked off the table in the melee. Mum and Bill are in the kitchen.

'Where have you been?' Emily asks me, straightening up. A bracelet jangles on her wrist.

My mouth opens, but I can't answer. The breath leaves my body, my head pounding like it might explode. I run forward and grab her wrist.

'Ouch,' she says.

'Where did you get this?' I hiss. I run my fingers over the smoothed edges of the glass and the tiny iridescent seashells. The golden heart charm. The bracelet I made for my sister. That she was wearing the night she died.

Emily's eyes grow wide with fright like they did the night Mum had her outburst. My hands are shaking hard as I try to unknot the cord.

'Here.' Emily does it for me. 'Take it. I'm sorry.'

'Skye? What's going on?' Fiona comes up, clearly concerned that I'm giving Emily a hard time.

'Where did you get it?' I shout at Emily, ignoring Fiona. I take the bracelet, feeling the weight of it in my hands. The weight of all my hopes and dreams when I made it for my sister. All the love I'd felt for her, sealing our unbreakable bond.

I'm half aware of Bill coming to the door of the kitchen, along with Mum, teetering on her cane.

'I… found it,' Emily says. 'In the jewellery box in your mum's room.' Her eyes fill with tears. 'I know I shouldn't have taken it, but it was just so pretty, and—'

'Emily, you didn't!' Fiona looks shocked, but she clearly doesn't know the significance of it.

'I'm sorry,' Emily sobs.

I feel like shaking her.

'Where did you get this?' I turn on Mum, my voice raised.

'Hey, calm down.' Bill steps forward between us. 'Don't upset her.'

'Mum…' I say, ignoring him, 'where did you get this?'

'I…' Mum's voice shakes, 'don't know. Exactly.'

'I know where she got it.' Bill's voice is tense and icy. 'It was found under the passenger seat when the police examined the car.'

'The car? What car?'

'The car you crashed,' Bill shouts. 'It was in the things they returned. Your coat, rucksack, water bottle. All the old rubbish from under the seat. Some stuff of Ginny's. I don't know what all of it was. Not that you were *around* to help take care of the logistics – they couldn't even find the damn car keys after the fact. But the car was sold anyway. Dismantled for parts. I put most of the stuff in the attic. Mum wanted to keep the bracelet.'

'But how did it get in the car?'

'I have no idea.' Bill steps forward getting in my face. 'She probably lost it under the seat days before she died. Who knows? What does it matter?'

'No…' I shake my head. 'She was wearing it that night.'

'I thought you don't remember anything about that night,' Bill throws back at me.

'No…' My head is still pounding. I feel like screaming. 'Is the stuff still up in the attic?

'I've no idea…'

'Nan…?' Emily speaks. 'Are you…?'

Emily moves in a blur over to Mum. Bill moves. I move. But all of us are too late. The cane judders, and then gives way. Mum collapses on the floor.

*

There are going to be consequences, recriminations. That much I know, even as events blur together. Bill makes the calls: the paramedics, Lorna… The rest of us tend to Mum. Fiona, Emily and I help to uncrumple her, and cover her with a blanket. She's out for a few minutes, but then, unexpectedly, she opens her eyes.

'What happened?' she asks.

Fiona explains that she collapsed. 'We've called the paramedics,' she says.

'No… I don't need them.' Mum struggles and manages to sit up. 'I'll be… fine. I must have fainted.'

'That may be,' Bill says. 'But you have to be examined.'

'I'd really rather you didn't make a fuss,' Mum says. 'A cup of tea, and I'll be fine.'

Bill glares at me. 'You need to lie on the sofa,' he says to Mum, taking her arm.

She tries to shrug him off, but she's too weak. Fiona takes her other arm. 'Really, Mary, Bill's right.'

When Mum's settled on the sofa, Bill takes me aside, his eyes ablaze. 'This is your fault,' he says. 'I told you not to upset her.'

'Don't lay this on me,' I hiss. 'You've got plenty to answer for. You should have told me about the things that got returned from the car. I'm surprised you didn't let Emily get them down from the attic and go through them.'

'Go to hell,' he says.

'Fine.' I storm out of the kitchen and up the stairs.

Tears sting in my eyes as I brave the shower of dust and climb back up into the attic. I manage to avoid the beam, but still I want to scream and kick at everything. I want to throw all the boxes down, get rid of everything. Run away, start over, my life a blank canvas.

I find the box over near the old microphone stands. A box without a label, the top not taped shut. Inside, there are several clear plastic bags with police labels. Ginny's jumper found that night, and her scarf. I take them out of the bag and cry, holding them to my face. They smell like nothing, and the wool feels rough and sharp against my skin. Then I look through the other things in the box. There are a few books, a packet of guitar strings, a water bottle, a first aid kit, a small bag of coins, a long-desiccated lip gloss… Nothing. There's nothing here. I throw everything back in and shove the box into a far corner. Nothing to explain how the bracelet got back to us, when she was wearing it on the night she died, and her body wasn't recovered.

I'm still crying as I make my way back down to the hallway and close up the hatch. The door to my room is open. I can hear someone moving about inside.

'Emily?' I say.

She slumps on the floor leaning against Ginny's bed. She looks so young, so beautiful and full of life – so like my sister was. Her anguish tears at my heart.

'Do you hate me?' she says, looking up.

'Oh, Emily.' I close the door and go to her. I sit down beside her and hug her, feeling her solid, living warmth. 'I don't hate you. And I'm sorry for… everything. This must be so terrible for you.'

'No. I mean, yeah, it kind of is. But it's worse for you.'

'I'm a grown-up,' I say. 'Sort of.' I take out the bracelet and hand it to Emily. 'Here,' I say. 'You have it. I made it for Ginny. I gave it to her for her eighteenth birthday, along with a pair of hoop earrings that I put little shells on. I loved her so much…'

'No,' Emily says. She hands the bracelet back to me. 'I don't want it.'

'OK.' Her rejection feels like a painful sting.

'Your sister… she… well… I found something else in the box of vinyl records.'

'What?' I say warily.

'Another journal. I think it's the last one she wrote.'

I get slowly to my feet. 'Show me,' I say.

CHAPTER 37

It's all there. The words written down in the little book hidden away for all these years. I thank Emily for finding it, apologise for shouting at her, and take it to my room to read alone. The silver-tongued betrayal is written down in green biro, Ginny's favourite colour. I sit down on the bed and turn directly to the last entry. Three pages of solid writing, dated the afternoon of the day she died:

A few more weeks and she'll be gone. I can keep the secret until then. I'm glad I didn't go to Glasgow and do something that I would regret forever. Mum says that all life is precious and that she'll stick by me no matter what. She cried when I told her, begged me to think about it one more time. She said that if I made that choice in the end, she would go with me and I didn't have to stay with James's rotten old aunt Ellen. She's so clueless. Of course Ellen isn't James's aunt at all, just like James isn't the father. I'll tell her someday, when S is gone. I can't wait…

I wonder what it will feel like to finally be free of her. Free to live my own dreams. Free to stay, free to love the person I want. The person she didn't love enough. Only a few more weeks. And then it's goodbye and good luck…

I read in stony silence, the words pooling over me, not really sinking in. There's a buzzing sound in my ear, and a deep, stabbing pain in my abdomen.

It's strange, but this little life growing inside of me is like the twin I always wanted and never had. The one who will love me for myself, the real me. S loves the person she wants me to be, not who I really am.

'Bullshit,' I say in a loud, angry voice. 'That is utter and complete bullshit.' My mouth floods with saliva.

Someday she'll understand, and someday, I hope she'll forgive me. I love her so much.

That's the last entry. I slam the book shut and run down the hall to the bathroom. I get down on my knees, lean over the toilet, and am thoroughly, desperately sick.

*

Fiona finds me there, curled up in a ball on the floor. She shuts the door, cradles my head, and I try to gasp out everything. It's garbled and incomprehensible even to me, but she seems unsurprised, or at least, unalarmed by the whole thing.

'Shh, Skye.' She brushes the hair off my face. 'It's going to be fine. Now that it's all out in the open, you'll be able to move on.'

'But I just don't understand! How could she do that to me? Why did she write those things? How could she… feel those things?'

'Let's get you to your room.' She helps me up. I feel like my body has been cut open, stuffed with stones and sewn back up again.

'She…' I gasp '… hated me. Why did she hate me so much?'

'Come now…' Fiona speaks to me like she's comforting a child. 'She was just a young girl. Very confused from the sound of it. Eventually, it would have worked itself out. Not without a lot of brimstone and bother, mind you. And you have a right to feel betrayed. But in the end, what happened that night is still a terrible tragedy.'

That's the long and short of it. No matter what Ginny thought of me, us, and her life in general, she shouldn't have died that night. But how did we get the bracelet? My memories may be damaged but I know one thing with absolute certainty: she was wearing the bracelet when she left the house in Byron's Jeep.

'I'm sorry,' I say finally. 'I've ruined everything by coming back. Bill was right that I shouldn't go digging. And now... Mum... how is Mum—?'

'Fi?' We're interrupted by Bill calling from downstairs. 'The paramedics are here.'

I manage to drag myself downstairs. I'm only half aware of the proceedings: Mum having her blood pressure taken, the paramedics announcing that Mum needs to be taken to hospital for some tests. Bill volunteering to go with her. And then, one of the paramedics comes into the kitchen.

'Skye? Your mum's asking for you.' Somehow, hearing those words, my heart lifts ever so slightly.

Mum has been moved onto a stretcher. I go to her and she grabs my hand. 'Skye,' she says, pulling me down to her with a surprisingly strong grip.

'Oh, Mum,' I say. A tear rolls down my cheek and drips on to her face. She closes her eyes. The paramedics wheel the stretcher away.

CHAPTER 38

In my lowest moments over the past fifteen years, I didn't think it was possible to feel this awful. I can't even find it in me to cry as I take the bracelet and Ginny's last journal over to Skybird. DCI Hamilton will need it to complete the file. I'll drop it with him, and then I'll go back to the house to pack my suitcase. The only thing that had seemed clear to me, as I watched Mum loaded into the ambulance, was that it is better for everyone if I leave, sooner rather than later. And this time, I won't be coming back. Mum is better off without me, I see that now. I will go back to living my life away from here, a tiny boat adrift without an anchor.

DS Paterson's car is gone. It's only been a short time since I was here last, but it seems like another lifetime, when I was a different person. Thanks to Ginny's last words, after all these years, I now see myself for who I truly am.

I knock on the door. It takes several minutes of the dog barking before the door opens.

For a second, I don't recognise Nick. He's wearing small wire-framed glasses that make him look like an Oxford scholar rather than an outdoorsy artist. I almost allow myself to acknowledge how much I want him – or I did… before. But that's not why I'm here.

'I found this,' I say, thrusting the journal towards him. 'Or rather, Emily did. My sister's last diary. And the bracelet she was wearing that night. I don't know how we came to have it back.

Apparently it was in the car after the crash. My brother doesn't think it means anything, but I'm sure it does. I *know* that she was wearing it that night.'

'Come in, won't you?' he says. 'You look… terrible.' He takes off his glasses and tucks them into the pocket of his shirt.

'I got upset at Emily. And then Mum collapsed.'

'Oh, Skye.'

He takes me in his arms. Tenderly, caring. He holds me. Like I'm a human being, a woman who deserves something more than a broken, shattered life. But he's wrong. I push him away.

'No,' I say. 'I can't do this. Not with all this hanging over my head.'

His eyes darken. 'That's fine,' he says. 'But I don't like to see you so upset. I…' he pauses, 'I know that we barely know each other. But I care about you.'

'Why?' I throw the words back at him. 'Why should you? Why care about a control freak who ruined her sister's life. That's what I was – I see that now. There was only one thing that she wanted: for me to go away. So she could have a life with my boyfriend and have his baby. Those were her dreams. And I was too thick – too completely obtuse – to see it.'

I feel like punching him, shouting at him. Seeing him, wanting him… knowing that there is this terrible thing hanging between us… This was how Ginny felt too. 'She was trapped,' I say in a strangled voice. 'Trapped by me, and trapped by her own guilt at what she'd done to me. And Mum… keeping secrets for all these years. Eaten up inside by them. She was right to blame me all those years ago. I see that now.'

'I want to show you something.' His voice is calm and measured. I feel even more like a raving lunatic.

'No. I'm leaving now. It's for the best. I can't stay.'

'It will only take a minute. Then you can go home to your family. You need them, and they need you. Especially now. And I need time to look into all of this properly.'

I have no strength to resist. I step inside, hating myself a little more for being so weak.

The fire has died to glowing embers. When I enter, Kafka licks my hand and I want to grab hold of him, hug him, and put everything else from my mind. Nick directs me to the kitchen. I stand at the threshold staring. The file is nowhere in sight. Instead, the table is covered with Nick's sketches of me.

I go to the table for a closer look. Some are only a few hurried lines, others just an expression in the eyes, or a shaded profile. All of them seem practically to leap off the page with a movement and life of their own.

He picks one up and hands it to me: a close-up of my face with the impression of snow on my hair. I stare at it for a long time. The expression in the eyes, the curve of the mouth. It's like all the details I see in the mirror have been stripped away. Instead of revealing an insipid beauty underneath, he's captured something quite different. An earthly sense of strength, a light in the eyes. Not the woman I am now, but one that I might aspire to be. Recognisable, and yet, unfamiliar.

He studies me as I look at them. 'When I first met you – properly, I mean – you intrigued me,' he says. 'There was something about you. I mean, other than the fact that you're incredibly beautiful, and sexy.'

I laugh. It feels unfamiliar.

'There's a vulnerability about you. The woman on the beach. But there's also this light in your eyes... this inner strength.' He shakes his head. 'I can't describe it in words. But as an artist, I was curious to know more.'

I pick up one of the sketches he did of me standing by the fire, my head just turned in profile. My body soft, languid, and yet, with a few strong lines along the curve of my back.

'And "as an artist", what did you conclude?' That tension has sprung back up between us. I could surrender to this. One glimmer of light, one moment of happiness – and true escape – before I leave this place forever.

It's him who moves away, breaking the connection. He gathers the papers in a stack. He picks up one sketch but doesn't hold it out to me. I see it though, over his shoulder. Me lying by the fire, my knee lolling to the side. In this one, my face isn't showing that duality of strength and vulnerability. My expression is one of sheer, unabashed desire. For him…

'Let's save that one for later, shall we?' There's a catch in his voice. He puts it at the bottom of the stack. 'I'm going to read through the file now.' He presses his lips together. 'Do some real work, as my dad would say.'

'Thank you for showing me.' I feel overcome with emotion.

'I'm not finished.' He comes closer to me. So close, that I can feel his breath on my hair. 'I hope we're only just getting started.'

Heat rises between us as he draws me close, but gives only the lightest brush of his lips on mine. 'Go home, Skye,' he says. 'Let me do this. It may take a few days – I just don't know. But when it's all over… I'll be looking forward to it.'

I nod, a heavy, bittersweet taste in my mouth. I don't tell him that once it's over – once he finds something, or nothing – then I'll be gone.

'Thank you.' My voice shakes, betraying the desperation I feel. His eyes are grey now, closed off. The artist searching for his muse is gone and in his place is the steely, analytical policeman. My earlier anger is gone completely. Now, in its place, I feel… fear.

'I'll be in touch when I have something to report.'

I nod and go to the door, leaving him, another would-be lover, with… my sister. That didn't turn out so well before.

*

In the time it takes me to walk back to Mum's cottage, I make a few decisions. I can't leave until Mum is at least a little better, and until Nick has had a proper look at the file. Christmas is in a few days. I can ruin it by giving in to the anger, regret, and guilt that I feel, or I can look deep within myself and try to find the strong woman, the one that Nick captured, albeit fleetingly, in some of his sketches. One with the courage to put the past behind and try to forge a new future. One who can set her sister free in her mind, and maybe find a new freedom as well. I don't know what Nick will find or what conclusions he will draw. It now seems impossible to salvage this homecoming. But at least I'll have a little time to figure out where I'm going to go next; what I'm going to do with... the rest of my life.

When I come inside, Fiona is in the kitchen making hot chocolate. 'Skye,' she says. 'I was wondering where you went. I was getting worried.'

'I had to clear my head,' I say. 'And I took the journal and the bracelet over to Skybird.'

A slow smile comes over Fiona's face. 'How much clearing of your head are you doing over at that cottage?' she said. 'I've seen Mr Hamilton. He's quite the... artist.'

'You've seen his work?'

'He was nice enough to give Bill and me a little tour. There was one painting in particular... lovely mermaid lass on the beach.'

My cheeks flare, thinking of how his next incarnation of that 'lovely lass' might be wearing rather less clothing. 'Yes...' I say. 'I saw that one too.'

'He seems a decent sort,' Fiona says, 'And he is also rather gorgeous.'

I laugh. 'He is, isn't he?'

'Well then?' Her smile fades a little.

'Unfortunately, I really am trying to get to the bottom of what happened,' I say. 'Especially now. Bill doesn't think the bracelet is significant, but I know that she was wearing it that night. I don't know what Nick might dredge up but I want him to have all the information. People were hiding things. Even… Mum… and Bill.' I pause to let this sink in. 'Whatever the truth is, we can't have any more secrets.'

'Yes,' she says. 'I understand.'

'And when he's had a look at the file, and Mum's back home, then… I'm going to leave.'

'Oh, Skye.' Fiona looks genuinely upset. 'You don't have to do that. It's been so good having you here. Being together – as a family.'

'Fiona, my being here has been nothing short of a disaster.'

'No – that's just not true!' I'm surprised to see her wipe a tear from her eyes. 'It's been good for your mum, even if she doesn't show it. Good for the kids – Emily worships you. And it's been a help for Bill too. And me…' She smiles. 'I never had a sister. It may sound daft, but I, well… when this is all over… I think I could see you that way.'

It's my turn to tear up. Me, who never used to cry, has become like a leaky water fountain since I've been here.

'I already see you as a friend,' I say. 'Part of the family. I'm just so grateful to you for everything.'

She comes over and hugs me. I allow myself to acknowledge the flicker of hope inside that refuses to die.

'Don't go packing your suitcase just yet,' she says when we come apart. 'Let's see how it all plays out. Do you promise?'

'Yes, for now… I promise.'

CHAPTER 39

The next two days are tense and difficult as we wait to hear how Mum's doing. Bill isn't speaking to me, the boys won't stop squabbling, and Emily barely leaves her room at the cottage. I'm tempted to go and see Nick – see if he's found out anything; have a look at the file myself. But having asked him to take a look with his professional eye, I decide that I'm best letting him get on with it. And right now, I don't feel up to any more shocks. I do go to visit Mum in hospital, but she's groggy from the mild sedative she's been given. I sit at her bedside, holding her hand, trying not to cry. I know that it's going to take time for me to come to terms with what I've learned: about Mum, and about Ginny the stranger. But right now, Mum's health is most important.

On my way out I manage to corral one of the doctors. He tells me that she hasn't had another stroke but that her blood pressure is high and she seems to be under a lot of stress. I feel awful that a lot of that stress is down to me.

On the third day, Mum comes home. She's feisty and irritable but seems perfectly lucid. I even dare to hope that the stay in hospital might have done her some good. Getting away from the house, away from the memories. It makes me even more determined to finish clearing out my room. As soon as she's doing a little better, I'll tell her what I've done. Surely she'll see that it's the right decision.

For Mum's return, Fiona and Emily have baked a nice meal of chicken, potatoes and vegetables. Lorna comes over to play cards, plump pillows, and generally fuss about to make sure that Mum rests and doesn't get upset by anything. It seems to work.

Later on when the boys have fallen asleep, Bill carries them, one over each shoulder, back to the cottage. Lorna helps Mum up to bed, and Fiona and Emily help me tidy up the front room.

'That went well,' Fiona says, keeping her voice low.

'Yes,' I say.

'You'll be OK here... with her?'

'Yes,' I say, more certain than I feel. 'You two go now, I'll see you tomorrow.'

Lorna comes down saying that Mum's in the bathroom and should be fine to go to bed. The three of them leave together.

I finish tidying up the kitchen. I hear the water running upstairs and then the dull sound of *cane, foot, foot, cane*. The opening and closing of a door. It's silly for me to skulk around downstairs. I should go up, say goodnight, begin again as I mean to continue.

I go upstairs. Mum is standing just outside the door to my room. She glances in my direction, her eyes glassy and bright. I know then, that she's discovered what I've been up to.

'Mum?' I say. 'Is everything OK?'

'I... was bringing you a fresh towel...' she says, with a confused stammer. 'I went into your room.'

'OK, thanks.'

Her eyes are those of a stranger as she takes a step towards me.

'You want to cut her out of your life,' she says. 'Pretend she doesn't exist.'

'No, Mum, it's not like that.'

'It's wrong,' she says. 'She's your sister. She's done so much for you. And this is how you thank her for her troubles?'

My breathing quickens with a rising sense of panic. Is it too late to go over and get Bill?

'It's not her fault that you've thrown everything away. All your wonderful talent, everything you worked for. And now, you'll have a baby. You'll be stuck here… Oh, Ginny, how could you do that?'

She crumples against the wall, her face in her hands.

'Mum?' I go over to her but don't touch her. It's as if something inside of her has finally snapped. She's gone, and I don't know how to get her back. I've tried Bill's method of 'not rocking the boat'. That hasn't worked. The only thing I have left to try is the truth.

'Mum,' I say in a calm, soothing voice, 'I've been clearing out some of Ginny's things from the room. Not to forget her, but because it needs to be done. I thought it would help – both of us – to have a clean slate, like you've done with the rest of the house. I won't throw the things out if you want them. But they need to be out of the room.'

Her body shakes. The cane clatters to the floor and she grips the wall. I risk putting my hand on her back to steady her.

'Skye?' she says, her eyes gradually coming back into focus.

I plough on. It feels like now or never. I have to get this out in the open. 'I've learned some things since I've been here,' I say. 'Things that are difficult for me to accept. I know that Ginny resented me. For not listening to her, or finding out what she really wanted. And I also know about the baby. Ginny was going to have an abortion but you talked her out of it. You convinced her to go and tell James.'

'That awful boy…'

'James isn't to blame,' I say. 'Ginny broke up with him, broke his heart. And James wasn't the baby's father. Byron was the father.'

'No,' Mum wails. 'That can't be right. She wouldn't do that.'

I wave that off. 'Ginny did talk to James that night. But he didn't want her back. And it wasn't what she wanted anyway. She was in love with Byron. Genuinely in love, I think. But she couldn't tell me. If she had, then maybe things would have been different. I would have been angry, but I would have forgiven her.

Eventually.' I run my hand in circles on Mum's back. 'And nothing changes the fact that I loved her, even if… she couldn't love me.'

'She did love you,' Mum says. She rubs her eyes as if clearing away a fog. 'But she didn't want the same things as you.'

'She wanted a normal life,' I say. 'I see that now. A husband, and a child. I was the one who acted like that wasn't good enough. That this place wasn't good enough.' I sigh. 'It never even crossed my mind.'

'Oh, Skye…' Mum breaks down sobbing. I take her into my arms, comforting her like a child.

'It's all my fault. I told her to go to the party,' Mum says. 'To talk to James. If she hadn't…'

'And you told me to bring her home. I didn't do that. And Byron…' My anger flares. 'He should have stepped up, taken responsibility.'

'And Ginny never should have been out on those rocks.' She hangs her head. 'It all comes down to that.'

'We can't go on like this,' I say. 'We have to accept that she's gone. But we're still alive. And Ginny wouldn't want us to be grieving after all this time. She would have hated that, Mum. She would have wanted us to keep her alive in our hearts, but not the rest. She'd want us to be strong. To… heal.'

'You're right,' Mum says. She wipes her eyes, her energy clearly spent. 'All this time, I couldn't let go. But you're right. It's time. It's… for the best.'

I pick up her cane for her and help her into her room. 'I'm sorry about so many things, Skye,' she says. 'I never should have made you feel that you were to blame – that's my biggest regret. And I should have told you the truth. But it all just hurt so much.' She sighs. 'In a way, I appreciate what Byron tried to do,' she says. 'Making up that story. I hated him for a while when I found out that it was all lies. But he was right in a way. It was so much better when I thought her death was an accident. To think that she might have... well. It's been terrible ever since.'

'I understand,' I say. The fact that Ginny might have taken her own life has thrown me off-kilter too. 'But remember, Mum, we don't know that it *wasn't* an accident.' I sigh. 'And I guess we'll never know for sure.'

'Yes,' she says. 'You're right. All we can do is put it behind us. Be a family and appreciate what we have.' She squeezes my hand. 'I'm glad you've come back.'

'Me too, Mum.' I'm surprised at how true it is. 'And I'm sorry I stayed away so long.' I sit on her bed as she gets under the duvet, lacing our fingers together. 'That I was a coward.'

'You're the bravest person I know,' Mum says. 'Don't forget that. I feel that my head is clearer now that we've talked it through.'

'That's great, Mum.' Brave or not, my eyes fill with tears.

'Now, off to bed with you,' she says. 'It's only a few days till Christmas. There's so much to do.'

'Yes, Mum, there always is.'

'Now that we're together as a family again, I'm looking forward to it.'

'Me too,' I say.

I kiss her goodnight and Mum smiles up at me. I see love in her eyes, and pride. For a brief shimmering moment, everything seems worth it. Seems like enough.

But as I go back to my room, I think of Ginny's bracelet, I think of Nick Hamilton. I'll go over to Skybird tomorrow. Tell Nick that we're fine, and that he should stop looking into Ginny's death. Send the file back. Forget the whole thing.

I only hope that it's not too late.

CHAPTER 40

The next day, Mum is as brisk and spry as I've seen her. She talks to me at breakfast, even smiling a little. I know now that it was the right thing to do to get everything out in the open, and I feel glad that I finally had the courage to do so.

Mum is doing a crossword and I'm finishing the washing-up when there's a knock at the door. She begins getting to her feet but I stop her. 'I'll get it,' I say.

It's Nick. His car is outside, the motor still running. His face is that of the steely cop. All my hopes shatter to pieces. Mum levers herself to her feet and comes slowly to the door.

'Skye,' he says. He looks past me. 'Good morning, Mrs Turner.'

'Nicholas,' Mum says. 'Is something wrong with the cottage?' She frowns. 'Is the heating working; you have enough wood?'

Nick gives me a quick glance.

'The cottage is fine, Mrs Turner. No worries. I wanted to have a word with Skye.'

'Oh, right.' Mum's hand holding the cane begins to shake a little. 'Would you like to come in? Have a cup of tea? Or there's coffee?'

'Another time, maybe,' he says. 'Skye, are you free now? For a few hours.'

Mum's face blooms into a smile. 'Of course. You two should go. Have a good time together.'

I'm glad that Mum has misinterpreted Nick's reasons for being here. I put on my coat and wrap a scarf around my neck. 'I'm ready,' I say.

'Would you like some sandwiches? A flask of coffee?' Mum seems desperate for this to be a social call, as if she already senses that it's not.

'I've got coffee and food,' Nick says. 'We'll be fine, Mrs Turner.'

Mum looks hopeful and worried, and I want to take her in my arms and tell her that everything is going to be fine. But everything is not fine. I asked Nick to look at Ginny's file for selfish reasons, I see that now: I was hurt and angry, and desperate to put my own guilt behind me. And now, Mum too will have to bear the consequences of my decision. Whatever they may be.

'Goodbye, Mum.' I give her a kiss on the cheek. 'I'll see you later.'

'Yes… um… have a good time.'

I don't reply as I go out the door.

Nick opens the passenger door of the car and I get inside. Kafka is in the boot and gives a welcoming yelp when he sees me. 'Hey, mate,' I say, wishing I could match his enthusiasm. But all I feel is trepidation as Nick gets into the car. Only a few days ago, I was lying on a rug in front of the fire, daring to dream of what could be. Now, though, I feel ashamed of the memory. He seems a total stranger.

'What is it?' I say as we're driving out of the yard. 'What did you find out?'

'Nothing yet.' His voice is matter-of-fact. 'Just that it's about the worst investigation I've ever come across. I've spent two days making enquiries. Trying to get to the bottom of one or two key things that were overlooked. No one has been particularly helpful.'

'That doesn't surprise me.' I take out a tissue and dab away a rogue tear.

'Hey,' he says. He reaches out to touch my cheek. 'It's going to be OK.'

I turn away. Neither of us know that.

When we're through the gate, Nick turns onto the main road. Towards the 'scene'.

'Everything you said about people's statements has borne out,' he said. 'The timings are all vague, and no one saw anything, other than those idiot twins. I spoke to them by phone. They were very reluctant to talk. However, they stuck to their statements. As they would. As for the investigation itself, there wasn't anything untoward, unless you count the fact that it was led by Byron's godfather.' He gives a snort. 'Inspector McVee – sadly deceased – has a brother called Greg, who's married to a woman called Annie MacClellan. Whom I believe you know.'

'"Aunt Annie".' I struggle to make all the connections. 'You beat her other half at snooker.'

'Yeah, I guess we're all mates now.' His voice is full of sarcasm. 'Isn't that odd?'

'McVee was the senior officer on duty. He definitely went the extra mile to make sure this one was wrapped up quickly and efficiently. Open and shut. Technically, the case is still "open" because the body wasn't found. But obviously, it's not an active police file.'

'So there's nothing else to find?' I'm not sure why I feel quite so disappointed.

'I didn't say that.'

By the time we reach the treacherous single-track road out to the lighthouse, Nick has regaled me with almost a dozen things that should have been followed up at the time, but weren't.

'The search area was by the book,' he says, slowing down to let a flock of sheep move off the road. 'They searched the immediate area of the lighthouse and the cliffs.'

'Where else should they have searched?' I say. I feel a little nauseous even asking the question.

'That's what I'm hoping we can find out,' Nick says. 'And there are one or two other points that I'm hoping to clear up too.' He frowns. 'About the car, and your crash.'

'Oh…' I grip the side handle of the door, hoping he doesn't elaborate.

Eventually, we reach the place where I crashed. There are two vehicles parked in passing places. One is a police SUV and the other an estate car with a dog grate in the back. Nick stops with the car still running. He gets out and has a quick word with two men sitting on the tailgate of the SUV, a topographical map spread out before them. I recognise Nick's mate DS Paterson. The other man is older, and he's got a German shepherd on a lead. As Nick comes back to the car, he stops at the back door and lets Kafka out. Kafka barks and runs over to the other dog where there's a playful reunion of fake biting and bum sniffing.

Nick comes back to the car and gets inside.

'Who are they?' I ask, my trepidation increasing.

'Mates. You've met Alain, and Rich is my old boss, retired now. I had to call them in to keep it official. They're looking at the area of the crash. They've been combing the area since early this morning. Bull – that's the other dog – is specially trained.'

'For what?'

Nick doesn't answer.

'It's been fifteen years,' I press, dread thickening in my mind. 'What evidence do they think they'll find?'

'We're just trying to get a complete picture. You said that you think you saw a person running across the road following the crash. And the file confirms that the bracelet was found in the car.' He frowns again. 'The keys, however, were not.'

'What?' I stare at him. 'What does that mean?'

'I'm not sure,' Nick says. 'And obviously we can't rely on your memories alone. But there may still be circumstantial evidence. I want to recreate as nearly as possible what happened that night. Walk through it. Find out who was where and reconstruct the possible scenarios.'

I laugh bitterly. 'Option A and Option B, right?'

'What's that?' He frowns.

'Never mind.' I look away.

'Or we can stop this right now. If that's what you want.'

Option C. I really ought to go with Option C.

'No.' I swallow hard. 'I want to keep going. It's just, I didn't really think this through. How it would affect me, and Mum, and everyone involved. I do want to know the truth – but maybe that's just me being selfish.'

'If we don't find anything, then your mum doesn't need to know. That's why I called in the people I did. I trust them to keep it all off the record. But maybe…' he hesitates '… maybe I was the one being selfish. I wanted you to know that I was taking it seriously.'

'I appreciate that.'

He leans in to kiss me. I turn away.

'I'm sorry,' I say.

'It's OK,' he says. His eyes, though, tell a different story. Confusion, regret, a touch of anger. I don't blame him, but it's as if an invisible wall has sprung up between us. Crushing the green shoots that had started to spring up.

He begins driving again. In a few minutes, we reach the end of the single-track road where it narrows between huge boulders on the way up to the lighthouse. He parks next to the fallen wind turbine.

There are two other vehicles already there. A Nissan and a Land Rover.

Even from a distance I can see two figures standing near the picnic tables below the lighthouse. One big and fair, one shorter and ginger. I feel a surge of anger.

'What are *they* doing here?' I say.

'Helping with enquiries,' Nick says. 'At least, Lachlan is being helpful. Byron, not so much.'

'You should have told me.' I don't look at him.

I get out of the car into the shocking wind. The weather is worse today than it was when I was here last time. But when I think of Ginny's last journal entries, I'm heated by a deep internal rage.

'You!' I scream out over the wind. Lachlan turns. Raises his hand. Byron stays put, staring out to sea. To the burial place of my sister, his lover, and his unborn child. My hair lashes my face as I go to him. He turns as I reach him. I punch against his chest. He doesn't try to stop me.

'How could you!' I shout. 'How could you do what you did? To me. And… to her.'

He grabs my wrists. His hands are warm. 'It was a mistake,' he said. 'It was never meant to happen.'

'Poor you!' I give him a final shove. I'm half-aware of Lachlan standing well-within earshot, and Nick at a distance. I don't care about either one of them – any of them.

'She wanted to get rid of… the baby,' he said. 'I gave her money for the coach fare and helped arrange for my aunt Ellen to help her out. Because that's what she wanted. I'd no idea until that night that she'd changed her mind. That she wanted to keep it. I was surprised when she told me – in the car as soon as we got here.'

'She loved you, and instead of standing by her, you told her where to go,' I shout. 'You told my pregnant sister that it was nothing to do with you. That she was nothing to you.'

'She *was* nothing to me! Don't you see that?' Byron's eyes are as injured as they are angry. 'I loved you. But you were leaving. I felt so… awful. About betraying you, but most of all about losing you.'

'Oh, please!'

'It's the truth.' He turns away.

'And you…' I turn to Lachlan coldly. 'You knew.'

Lachlan looks at Byron, then at me, his eyes hostile. 'Your sister made me sick, frankly,' he says. 'The way she was throwing herself at him. He wasn't interested in her, but she wouldn't leave him alone. "Byron can you help fix the car?" "Byron do you want some sandwiches for the boat?" "Let's go for a picnic," "a swim".' His voice is high and mocking. I feel like slapping him.

'You deserved better,' he says. 'Better than her.'

I take a step towards him. 'And where was I when all this was going on?'

'Working. Writing your songs. In your mind you were already gone.'

Nick comes up to us. 'Skye,' he says, putting a hand on my arm. 'Can I get you to retrace your steps. Starting down at the beach where the others—'

'Leave me alone.' I throw off his hand and turn to walk away. Then, I start to run, stumbling down the rocky path to the jetty. My blood is surging, my pulse thrumming in my skull. The rage is what keeps me going, a reminder that I'm human and that there's a thin line between life and death. I go onto the concrete slab, past the barrier and out onto the rocks. A wave booms before me, soaking me with icy spray. This is where Ginny went that night. She was hurt, angry, just like I am now. I can see her there, the girl on the cliffs. The beam of the lighthouse pulsing against the cloud-dappled sky, her hair a halo, like a dark angel. The bracelet I made her glints in the darkness as she stretches her arms out. She removes her scarf, lets the wind catch it, blowing it into the sea.

She came down here because she was upset. She wanted to get away from the others. Have some time apart to sort through her feelings. And then… I came up behind her, shattering her thoughts. Angry with her in my own right, telling her that I was going to take her home. She fell into her old familiar patterns. Taunting me. Getting me to come and rescue her. To take her hand, pull her back from the brink. And only then, would everything be all right.

Except this time, I turned away. Walked away. I broke the pattern. This is not how she'd expected it to end…

I go out onto the furthest rock. Below, the sea is wild and roiling. Waves crash against the rocks drenching me with spray. This is where she stood. I close my eyes, and for the first time in fifteen years my mind explodes like a firework, the memories showering down with the spray.

'Stop, wait,' my sister yells.

I keep walking.

'Don't go.'

I keep my back to her. 'I've had enough, Ginny. Enough of you manipulating me. It's time you started looking after yourself. I'm leaving Eilean Shiel. And you can stay, or go… I don't care any more.'

'Come on, Skye. Don't be that way.'

'Go to hell.'

'Please. Let's just… go home.'

I turn. I look at my sister. So beautiful. So fragile. She needs me, but nowhere near as much as I need her. She's half of who I am.

'Fine.' I let out a long sigh. 'Let me go back and tell the others.'

'No.' She laughs then, clear and bell-like. 'Let them sweat a little.' She tosses her jumper onto the rocks.

I roll my eyes. 'Stop messing around. Let's just go.'

I walk slowly back up the path cut into the rocks. My sister is beside me, where she should be. We'll leave this place and everything will be fine. We'll leave Eilean Shiel and start our new life.

A dark figure is standing on the viewing platform above. Lachlan. God, he's so creepy. Sometimes I feel like he's stalking me. A girl comes up to him, takes his hand, leads him off. Better her than me.

'Give me the keys.'

'What?' I look at Ginny in surprise.

'You've been drinking. I'll drive.'

'You?'

'Why not?' She shrugs. 'Let's get out of here.'

I toss her the keys.

It feels strange to be in the passenger seat. Strange and uneasy. But I'm relieved to be out of the wind. Relieved that Ginny is off those damn rocks. She drives down the dark, winding road. I sit back. I'm just… relieved. 'Six weeks,' I say aloud. 'Six weeks and we'll be gone.'

'I really hate you sometimes.'

'What?' I look at her. She's not serious, but it hurts anyway.

'I told you. I'm not going.' The icy anger in her voice startles me. 'Why can't you just accept that?'

'Look, Ginny... I know you said that, but—'

'I am not fucking going anywhere! I am staying here. I am going to have a baby!'

'A...' No. 'No... I don't believe it.'

'I don't care what you believe, Skye! It's the truth. And do you know who the father is? Do you even have the slightest clue?'

'What are you talking about?'

'You don't love him. Or me. Or anyone but yourself. You want to use me, you've never asked what I want. You don't care what I want. I love you, but I've had enough!'

Driving one-handed, she unfastens the bracelet from her wrist. And then she turns and throws it at me. It hits me in the face. My cheek stings with the force of it, with the pain of her words. The hurt of what she feels. The bracelet clatters to the floor. The road curves. There's a flashing light. She's looking at me...

'Watch out!' I shout.

Ginny screams.

The road zigs. The car zags. The world shatters. And then... nothing.

I float out of time. It's dark, so dark. The mists are closing in. This time for good. I'll never escape now.

I open my eyes but there's nothing there. Nothing but the pounding in my head. My heart, beating in time with the flashing light.

'Skye! Oh my God.' Her voice. 'Are you...?'

I can't move. I can't see her. I can't respond.

'Oh God! No. Wait here. I'm going to get help. Please, Skye... just hang on...'

No. I want to shout. Stay with me. But I still can't respond. Light flashes in time with the pulse throbbing in my head. One of the car *headlamps is still lit. She runs past it, a dark blur, going in the direction of the flashing light. Dad's voice: 'Always go towards the light.' The light, from the lighthouse.*

'The lighthouse…' I gasp.

'Skye?' Far away, out of time, I'm aware of a voice. A hand on my back. But it's not her voice. It's not her hand. Gradually I come back to awareness. I'm soaking wet. Slumped down on the rocks. Nick… it's Nick.

I try to speak but I can't. I'm gasping and shivering, and sweating all at the same time. My head feels bent like the bars of a cage where a wild beast has escaped.

'I was here with her on the rocks.' The words come rushing out. 'She came back with me to the car. She took the keys. She was driving fast. So fast. And she was saying… things. She threw the bracelet at me. Took her eyes off the road. She… hit the rock.' My teeth are chattering so hard that I bite my tongue and taste blood.

'She thought she'd killed me. So she went off to get help. She went back towards the lighthouse.' *The road of life is full of twists and turns. Best, love, always to go in a straight line.* 'In a straight line.' I'm gasping now. 'Towards the light.'

I'm aware of Nick straightening up, moving away. Leaving me alone, fallen on the rocks. He unclips something from his belt. A walkie-talkie. He speaks into it. 'She might have gone towards the lighthouse. Check the line from the accident site. No – not along the road. As the crow flies. I'm coming now. We need to get the dogs into that gully you spotted earlier.'

He comes back to me. Puts out a hand to help me up. I take it and get shakily onto my feet. He tries to draw me to him. I jerk my hand away.

'No, Nick.' I look away, staring out at the relentless grey sea. I don't ever want to look at him again.

'Take your time,' he says. 'I know this is—'

'You don't know anything. Please, just go away.'

Behind me, he lets out a long sigh. I hear his footsteps on the rocks. And a part of me wants to take back what I just said, what I'm feeling now. But I can't do it. I can never be the woman he sees, the woman he captured in his sketches. That woman was a lie.

I don't know how long I stand there watching the waves beat out their relentless rhythm. I'm aware of eyes on me from above, the same place where Jimmy and Mackie supposedly saw Ginny swept off by the rogue wave; the same place where Lachlan must have been when he saw Ginny follow me away from the rocks. Byron and Nick are standing on the viewing platform. I can't hear what they're saying until Byron raises his voice.

'So if you want me to stay then arrest me.' He takes a step towards Nick, his fists clenched at his side. 'Oh yeah, you're not even a fucking cop, are you?'

'You obstructed a police investigation, mate.' Nick stands his ground. 'You've admitted as much. So I suggest you stick around for now.'

'I'm not your mate.'

'You said in your statement that you found her in the car. But that wasn't true, was it?' Nick presses. 'She crawled out of the car and you found her. You assumed she was alone. That she was driving and had got in the accident. You moved her: put her in the driver's seat – that's why she wasn't wearing a seat belt when she was found.'

'I couldn't leave her in the fucking road, could I? I had to do something. The Jeep had bad shocks. I didn't want to drive her. But I put her back in the car. I even covered her with a blanket.'

'Yeah, you were a real hero in all of this,' Nick says with a sarcastic snort.

'Look, just fuck right off, OK?'

Byron turns and strides off. Nick's teeth are clenched and he tightens his fist. He's got a right to be angry. At Byron and all the other arseholes who lied. And especially at me.

'Skye, do you want a hot drink? I've got a flask in the car. You're shaking.'

I turn, startled. Lachlan is standing there. He's got a blanket. I don't speak, but I let him drape it over my shoulders. We walk slowly back up to the car park. When we arrive, Byron is sitting in the Landy fuming. Lachlan opens the back door of his Nissan and helps me inside. I sit, curled up in a ball. I'm freezing, but I keep the door open.

'Why did you lie?' I say softly. 'You went along with the story even though you saw her come off the rocks.'

He lets out a long sigh. 'I didn't know what happened,' he says. 'Maggie came to find me, and I… well… was otherwise occupied for a while, so I didn't see you or Ginny get into the car.' He blushes a little. 'Then Byron said you were alone when he found you. I assumed that you'd driven away and she'd stayed behind.' He's silent for a long moment. 'I guess, at the end of the day, I thought it was better for you if people didn't know that you'd seen her that night. I figured that you might have found out what was going on with her and Byron, and… well… it just seemed better to keep questions to a minimum.'

I shake my head and pull the blanket closer around me. The others lied to protect themselves, but Lachlan lied to protect me. I don't know if that makes me feel better… or a whole lot worse.

'It was wrong,' he says. 'And I'm sorry. For all of it.'

I nod, but I'm unable to speak. He stays with me for a while, and though I can't express it, I'm grateful not to be alone. Eventually, he goes over to talk to Nick. I don't want to listen, but I can't help but overhear Lachlan's question: 'What are you hoping to find after so long?'

'Bull is a trained cadaver dog,' Nick responds. 'He can find decades-old human remains buried twenty feet underground. You remember that case of the missing girl down Oban way about four years ago? The one who was found down in the old lead mine…?'

Cadaver dog.

I reach out to close the door, trying to shut everything out. But my hand is shaking too hard. It's much, much too late.

'The bottom line is…' Nick is saying, 'we're in a wilderness out here. Even with the dogs, you can't find a body if you're looking in the wrong place.'

As they continue to talk, I stare out at the hazy grey water. I don't know for how long. Maybe minutes, probably more like an hour. Lachlan goes over to Byron, comes back. Nick is on the radio again to his mates at the accident site. A hole opens up inside of me as I hear a crackling on the radio.

'Yeah… would have been able to see the light from here.'

'Sheep trail… pretty treacherous… slow going.'

Another crackle.

'Dog seems to have a whiff down that ravine…'

'I'm coming down,' Nick says. 'There's nothing more I can do up here.'

'Yeah, mate… what's that? Sorry… hang on.'

The voice on the other end of the walkie-talkie goes dead. Nick starts walking over to me. I put my hands over my face.

The radio crackles again.

'You'd better get down here. We've found something.'

CHAPTER 41

Someday, in the elusive, ever-changing strands of the future, I'll unwrap my memories as I did on the coach. Some will be shiny visions of days long gone: Dad putting lights on the tree, the dogs asleep by the hearth, Ginny and me singing songs in front of a crackling fire, Mum's face glowing as she brings in a tray of home-made biscuits. Others will be lonely and empty: stretches of road through desert, dive hotel rooms, a bottle of wine and a five-minute phone call home. And then, there will be the memory of *this* Christmas. Instead of twinkling lights on the tree, it will be the flashing blue lights of the police car. Instead of the patter of children's feet, it will be 'the knock at the door'. Instead of carols and laughter it will be the voice of the young DS as he shows his badge when Bill answers the door, three hours after Lachlan brings me back to the house. 'I'm here to speak to Mrs Turner. Can I come in?'

Bill stands aside. The DS enters. Nick is there too. He comes in just behind the other man. He looks at me, his face grim. I look away.

Mum is sitting at the table with the jigsaw. She presses her lips together in a thin line as she did at Dad's funeral. Her face is lined now and her hair is white. But for all that our bodies have aged, the sense of loss cuts just as deeply. Pain doesn't age.

Mum offers the two men a cup of tea. Bill goes to make it. Fiona has Emily take the boys outside. I pace back and forth in front of the fireplace. The lights on the tree, the glittery baubles, the garlands, the ornaments – they all seem gaudy and garish. Pointless.

The DS sits down on the sofa looking nervous, Nick stays by the door, his arms folded. I wish he wasn't here, wish I never had to see him again. Most of all, I wish that I could still somehow be the woman he'd come to care about, but know that it's impossible now. That *we* are impossible now.

'Mrs Turner, ma'am, I really am very sorry...' the DS begins to speak.

I can't listen or stay in that room any longer. I go into the kitchen and collapse in a chair. Bill stands at the window. He doesn't make the tea or turn around. In the other room, the DS is speaking to Mum:

'... need to do some tests, but the circumstantial evidence is pointing that way. They found a pair of earrings, and a set of car keys.'

'... ran towards the lighthouse to get help. Wouldn't have seen the edge of the ravine in the dark...'

'... fractured skull... probably very quick... wouldn't have suffered...'

'... Give you a call when we're ready to release her remains.'

Her remains. I shudder at the thought of my sister, the girl who wanted to fly, dying alone in a dark hole. Frightened, filled with remorse at what she'd done. Running to get help and not making it. How much better and more fitting a death from the cliffs would have been. Maybe that's why everyone hid what they knew. I don't believe it for a second, but it's a nice idea.

Bill abandons any pretence of making tea and goes back to the other room. I stand up too. Force myself to be strong and follow him as far as the kitchen door. My brother ignores the DS and instead focuses his anger on Nick, laying into him. Questioning him about exactly what was found, why they think it's Ginny, and what's going to happen next.

Nick answers patiently and professionally. I feel a mixture of anger and admiration that he can stay so cool and detached. He repeats what the DS has said about the circumstantial evidence, adding that in his new statement, Lachlan confirmed that he'd seen Ginny come off the cliffs and follow me back up the path. He also confirmed that Ginny was wearing the bracelet and earrings that night. I think of how happy I was when I gave them to her, I think of how much I loved her – love her still – and the loss hits me all over again. I grip the doorframe to steady myself. Nick sees me, takes a step towards me. I shake my head. His face seems to close up and I can see the hurt there, the understanding dawning in his eyes. He masters himself, though, turning back to Bill and answering the question about what comes next. The investigation will be reactivated. The police will need new statements from everyone, and there will be an inquest. They could decide to pursue charges of perjury or obstruction. It's going to be a tough time.

Bill starts in again, but Mum raises her hand. She's been silent all this time, sitting at the table with the jigsaw.

'Thank you,' she says, taking in both Nick and the young DS. 'Both of you. For taking the time to come here and tell us.' Her voice is calm and even. It sounds completely normal.

'Of course, ma'am,' the DS says.

Nick doesn't say anything, keeping his head bowed. This time, he seems to be avoiding looking at me. I want to say something, I want things to be different. But my throat is dry, I'm too numb even to move.

'I hope both of you have a lovely Christmas.' Mum gets up from the chair. She walks with them to the door, slowly, but standing straighter than I've seen her before.

'You too… uh… thank you, ma'am,' the DS says.

'Thank you.' I hear the catch in Nick's voice. His face, though, reveals nothing.

The door closes. It's over. Mum turns. Frowning, she walks slowly over to the Christmas tree, bends down and reattaches a bow that had fallen off one of the presents. 'Well, that's that,' she says.

None of us speak. Mum walks out of the room to the kitchen, barely using her cane at all. Bill takes Fiona's hand and together they sit on the sofa, both looking stunned. I perch on the arm of a chair and stare into the cold black grate of the fireplace.

I don't know what to do. Having cocked things up so completely and inexorably, I simply *do not know* what the right thing is to do. Water runs in the kitchen sink and there's a clatter of dishes. Mum's doing the washing-up. The three of us sit rigid.

Then the boys burst in the front door. 'Muddy boots!' Fiona yells, standing up.

Emily enters behind them, clearly in a strop. 'Jamie kicked me in the shins,' she says indignantly. She turns to her brother, hands on hips. 'Father Christmas is *so* not coming for you.'

Bill stands up. I stand up.

Real life makes an entrance, and as always, it's the star of the show.

*

Grief works in strange ways. I'd expected a pall to be cast over the house, a terrible undercurrent of sadness running so deep that it even affected the children. But instead, with Mum as a barometer, the opposite seems true. It's as though Mum has suddenly become years younger.

Over the next few days she throws herself into preparations for Christmas, and her friends come round one by one bearing casseroles and pies. They give their condolences, have a chat, and generally find out for the gossip circuits how she's holding up. The answer is, pretty well. I overhear her talking: 'Yes, it's good to finally be able to put her to rest.' 'Yes, it's very sad, but it's better to know.' At first it seems strange that the dam of silence is broken and having the subjects-not-to-be-mentioned out in the open. But the thing that makes me the most relieved is that Mum becomes much more normal with Emily, talking with her, baking with her, getting to know her. There are no more breaks with reality.

I, on the other hand, don't know how to feel. I go through a kaleidoscope of different emotions, from sadness to anger, to elation at how much better Mum seems. I need time alone, and yet I also want to be there for my family. Bill, too, seems to be struggling. On Christmas Eve, we have a family dinner. Again I'm struck by how Mum seems like a different person: almost like the person she used to be. But when she launches casually into a discussion of 'what happens next' and asks Bill and me our opinion of whether or not Ginny would want to be cremated, her ashes scattered to the wind, it's a step too far. Bill stands up and pours himself a brandy from a bottle that I haven't seen before. Fiona makes several valiant attempts to change the subject, and even Emily looks a little horrified. Mum eventually seems to notice the silence. 'What?' she says, looking at each of us in turn. 'Do you think I'm acting strangely?' Her brow creases. 'Maybe I am. But I'm just so happy that she's been found. That finally we can lay her to rest. Is that… wrong?'

'No, Mum,' I say, my voice hoarse. 'I guess not.'

She sighs. 'I want it all out in the open,' she says. 'This is the first Christmas we've been together in so long. I want to be able to mention Ginny's name. Relive my memories of her. I just feel… I don't know… relieved.'

'It's going to take time to come to terms with it all,' Bill says. 'I don't think we can just move on overnight.'

She gives him a kindly look. 'You're right, son. I know that. And maybe I'm being selfish here. You and Skye are affected by it as much as I am.'

'I don't know how I feel,' Bill says. 'I'm just worried about you.' He takes in me and Mum.

My eyes fill with tears. 'I'm just so sorry,' I say. 'My timing, as usual, was terrible.'

Mum puts her hand on mine. 'Having you back is the greatest gift you could have given me. And now, in a way, I have her back too.'

'If you think so, Mum,' I say, 'then that's good.' I smile, feeling only love for her.

'Yes, it is,' she says. 'And I'm so grateful. You did the right thing, Skye. For all of us. You brought your sister home.'

CHAPTER 42

On New Year's Eve, the bonfire is lit on the beach. The dry wood crackles as the sparks and cinders fly up into the black sky. The crowd begins to gather in front of the stage where the ceilidh band is set up and ready to go.

I pick up Dad's guitar and tune the strings. The wood is solid in my hands, a reminder of the fact that although I've lost so much, I still have a lot to be thankful for. It's a new year, and a new start. Not quite the one I'd planned, but if there's anything I've learned over the last few weeks, it's that it's best not to cling too dearly to plans.

Nick left on Christmas morning, taking with him his dog, and a piece of my heart. It was another thing that I broke and couldn't fix. Late on Christmas Eve, I'd gone over to his cottage. All I could see when I looked at him was the man who found my sister's remains, the steely cop who knew all my secrets. And after everything that had happened, I knew that his sketches would remain unfinished; that I couldn't be the woman he'd captured on the page. He obviously knew it too, because he was already well on his way through a bottle of wine. He told me that I'd hurt him: the way I'd looked at him, the way I flinched from his touch. He told me that for three years he'd been healing, getting his life back on track. And that the last thing he needed to do was fall for someone: me. And then he'd kissed me. Hard, angry, the lips that had once breathed life into mine were taking it away. He told me to go, and I left. By morning, he was gone.

And I missed him. Once again I'd let the past dictate my future, I'd let my chance at happiness slip through my fingers… I was filled with a new regret, deeper than any I'd felt for any other man.

In the days that followed, I did a lot of thinking and a lot of walking on the beach. I missed the sight of Kafka streaking in the surf, I missed… a lot of things. Lachlan came by, and I was glad to see him – he'd proved himself to be so much more than the 'almost man' by coming forward. We didn't talk much about the past, or Ginny, or the new investigation. Instead, he talked about the future, including his plans to start a traditional music session at the pub. And I'd felt a stirring of something inside of me, something like a dream I could cling to: making music, writing *my* songs, rediscovering my heritage, encouraging young musicians. I've agreed to help him organise it, and it's something that I'm looking forward to.

My second visitor was much less welcome, and yet, someone I also had to face. Byron. He came the day after Boxing Day, looking smaller, penitent. We sat in the Land Rover, and when I'd seen that tartan rug folded on the seat, my anger had crystallised. Anger for myself, but also for Ginny. He'd apologised again, explained again. Hung his head, even cried a little. He'd come clean to the police and was waiting to see if they were going to take it further. I'd listened, unmoved and unfeeling, until he'd told me his news: he was leaving. He was going back to Glasgow to be nearer his son; maybe try to patch things up with his ex. And I'd known at that moment that I didn't want him punished any further – not that it was up to me. I'd wished him luck, and meant it. I told him that I forgave him, and meant that too. Then I'd done something else I hadn't been planning. Told him that I'd play at the festival if it wasn't too late. He said it wasn't; that he could arrange it.

And now, it's time. The rest of the band filters onto the stage, and there's the usual ribbing and banter among musicians. I feel a strong sense of joy that I'm performing here, in front of the home crowd. Old songs that are part of the landscape of my soul, and new songs I've written as a tribute to Ginny.

When we're ready to start, the mayor speaks into the microphone, thanking everyone for coming, and wishing everyone a happy, safe New Year's. He introduces the band and then turns to me. 'And as we're not so good at keeping secrets here in Eilean Shiel,' he quips, 'I think most of you already know about our special guest for tonight.'

I smile and give a little wave. There are a few claps and a lot of whispering.

'She's been a country music star across the Pond,' he continues. (I wince a little at the exaggeration.) The noise from the crowd ramps up a notch.

'But we'll never forget that she's one of us, our own hometown lass from just across the water. So raise your hands and let's give a special welcome to Skye Turner.'

The crowd cheers and the other musicians clap. I stand up from my stool and take a bow. I spot Byron near the pub with a small boy, who has the same square jaw and sandy blonde hair. I feel a slight twinge at what might have been, either for me… or my sister. Mum, Bill and his family are sitting on the rugs in front. Emily's face is shining up at me… so like *hers*.

The mayor hands the microphone to me. I don't have a speech prepared, but I know that there are some things that need to be said between me, and everyone here.

'Thank you.' My voice reverberates through the mike. 'I appreciate your support. Fifteen years ago, I left Eilean Shiel, and most of you know why. I had just lost my sister. Ginny.'

A hush spreads through the crowd when I say her name. 'I've got a lot of regrets,' I continue, 'and the biggest one is that I stayed away for so long. Because home is not just a word, or a house, or a pin on a map. Home is people, and family, and the place where your roots are. The place where the healing can begin.'

There's more murmuring and some more claps. I cue the musicians behind me to get ready.

'So tonight, I'd like to dedicate this performance to absent friends. The ones that we've shared the good times with and the bad. The ones who are part of this place that we call home.' I grip the microphone tightly as my voice finally breaks. 'The ones who may be gone, but live on forever in our hearts.'

I cue the band, pick up Dad's guitar, and begin to play.

Time runs differently during a performance. It seems we've only just started when we get to the last song and the crowd raises a glass and their voices for 'Auld Lang Syne'. Tears run down my face as the words touch my heart. But the deep ache of longing is tempered by a strong flame of hope. A new year... a new start... I've come full circle. I'm back where I belong.

The band gets a huge round of applause from the crowd on the promenade and the people on the boats in the harbour. As we leave the stage, Bill and the boys rush up and give me a hug and a well done, echoed by Fiona and Emily. James and Katie come up to congratulate me, and even Annie MacClellan and her husband come up and shake my hand. It seems an unspoken gesture of truce, one that I am more than happy to accept. Since it looks like I'm going to be staying for a while, I'm hoping that some of my old friends might become new ones.

Mum comes up to me and gives me a hug. I can see from the redness around her eyes that she's been crying. 'It was beautiful,' she says. 'A wonderful tribute. Thank you.'

'Of course, Mum. I meant what I said. About... healing.'

'Yes. I think that now, maybe we can.'

'Oh, Mum.' I put my arms around her. She feels more substantial; more like she used to. A rock in my life. One that I don't ever want to let go of again.

When we come apart, her eyes are shining. But not with the strange, otherworldly look from before. In fact, ever since Ginny's remains have been discovered, she's been firmly grounded in reality. It's too early to hope, but I can't help doing so.

Lorna comes up to us and congratulates me, then asks for Mum's help to sort out a minor crisis involving some duplicate raffle tickets at the WI booth.

Mum takes my hand and squeezes it. 'Off with you now,' Mum says to me. 'Go and enjoy yourself. I'll see you… tomorrow.' She and Lorna exchange a look that I can't quite interpret. I guess it's because I'll be spending my first night in Skybird. I moved in this morning after Mum announced that she wants to have my old room painted. A big step forward.

'OK…'

'Happy New Year, love,' Lorna says. She takes Mum's arm and the two of them go off. As the crowd around the stage begins to disperse, I spot Lachlan with the curly-haired woman from the pub. His arm is around her, and she's laughing at something he said. I feel happy for him: glad that maybe he won't be alone on New Year's. And glad that I will. Sort of.

I pack up my guitar and get ready to head home. I feel an unexpected little pull of dread in my stomach at the idea of spending New Year's in a new place, a new bed. Especially one so recently vacated…

'Skye.'

My whole body jolts with adrenalin at the voice, whispered close to my ear. I turn. He's there, his eyes a deep and intense blue, his face soft with no trace of anger.

'Nick!' I don't care who sees, I want to kiss him. But before I can do so, he holds up a hand, a bemused expression coming onto his face.

'We have a problem,' he says.

'Oh?' I'm so happy he's here that I don't consider his words, and I don't want to. I don't want anything to come between us. Not now… 'What problem?'

His hands slip around my waist. 'I thought you said your mum used to be a maths teacher,' he says.

'Yes,' I say breathlessly. 'That's right.'

'Well apparently, she got muddled up on the dates. I paid for the cottage until the end of January. But now she tells me she's rented it to someone else. In fact...' his look is one of mock horror '... they've already moved in. Now, I know people make mistakes but really, that's just unaccepta—' I stop him talking with a kiss, long and deep on the lips. I feel like I'm going to melt in his arms. Someone whistles but I don't care. I want to stay here, where I belong.

When we finally break off, the laughter fades from his eyes. 'Skye,' he says. 'The way I acted before... I was a complete arse. In truth, I was... terrified. Of what I was feeling and of losing it so easily. That's why I left. I'm sorry.'

I put my hand on his chest, feeling his heartbeat, satisfying myself that he's really here.

'It was wrong of me to push you away,' I say. 'But as soon as you left, I realised that I'd made a big mistake. Again.' I lean my head against him and he strokes my hair. 'I kept thinking...' I glance up at him '... how much I really missed your dog.'

'My—' He gives a hearty laugh. 'Then you might be interested to know that I've already dropped him at the cottage.' He presses himself close to me. 'Though I'm not quite sure what the sleeping arrangements are going to be.'

'Hmm, that's a tricky one,' I whisper in his ear, aware of his heartbeat quickening.

He brushes a finger down my cheek and whispers back. 'When can we go sort it out?'

I put my hand on his and smile. 'How about now?'

EPILOGUE

On a clear evening in late March, Mum and I walk slowly down to the end of the garden. The water below the rocks is black and still, and Orion hangs just above the village of Eilean Shiel. The lights across the water shimmer in the darkness, their reflections, just a little distorted, shine up from the sea. A church bell tolls in the distance, the sound rhythmic like a celestial heart.

When I arrived in Eilean Shiel, I never expected that I would become the person I am today. I was so tired from running, my life wasted before it had even begun, the future a mixture of darkness and shades of grey. But coming back and discovering that my roots were still alive, somewhere deep beneath the frost, has revitalised me. Made me into something better than I was.

Over the last few months, Mum's had her ups and downs, good days and bad days. Grief works in its own time. When Bill and his family left to go back to Glasgow, she looked like she'd aged ten years in a single day. She sat in the kitchen, the kettle cold, her strength dissolved in an unstoppable flood of tears. I was there for her, and later on, Lorna had come round and taken her out for a nice meal. The next morning, she'd been back to normal. Whether that's 'fine' or 'OK' – only time will tell.

I too was sad to see my brother and his family go. I'd got very close to Fiona, and have come to see her as the best kind of sister-in-law, the kind who is also a friend. Emily too has gained a special place close to my heart. When I look at her now, I see my niece, not just a girl who resembles my sister. A girl with her own hopes and dreams, whom I will be proud of no matter what she chooses to do with her life. And I'm happy that I got to tell her just that before she left. That, and the only words that matter in the end: 'I love you.'

Bill and I aren't quite where I'd like us to be, and I know that he still resents my long absence even if he now understands the reasons for it. I'm hoping that I can eventually become an older sister he can be proud of; one who is finally present to make new family memories. Before they left, Bill reminded me of something that Dad used to say: 'if it hurts when it's over then it must have been good'. And in spite of everything, spending time with them has been good. And I hope that this is just the beginning.

Now as Mum and I walk down the dew-fresh lawn, I stop and look back. Nick is standing at the door, a solid, comforting presence in my life. One that I never expected to find, or deserve. It's still early days, and I haven't been the easiest person to be with as the investigation has progressed. Yet he's stuck by me. When I'm with him, I feel a sense of calm stability, like my old soul is already well acquainted with his. He inspires me to be the best version of myself, and at last I'm learning to love and be loved.

Sometimes it feels strange to no longer be a vagabond. But now that I have Mum back in my life, and my family, I know that I'm right where I should be. After a few tense months, the investigation into my sister's death closed. The coroner rendered a verdict of accidental death. No charges were filed against anyone involved, for which I was grateful. The conversations seem freer with everyone in the village now, with the taboo subject of Ginny faced, discussed and cried over. Finally, we can start the process of healing, or at least moving forward. I've thought long and hard about Ginny, the person I thought she was, and the person she wanted to be. The choices she made that took away her future. It was unintentional, and tragic, but it happened.

'Are you ready?' I look at Mum as I unscrew the top of the urn with my sister's ashes. I cling to it for a moment, feeling the smooth weight of it in my hands. Heavy for a jar, and yet so light to contain the weight and memory of a life. Scientists say that energy is neither created nor destroyed, it just goes to a different state. The life force that was Ginny's lives on, not in the contents of this jar, but in the hearts and minds of the people she touched.

'Yes,' Mum says, her eyes shiny with tears. 'It's what she would have wanted.'

I take off the lid. It's as if by opening this vessel, I'm releasing the love, the memories, and the other half of my soul.

The wind is blowing from the north. As I shake the contents of the jar, the grey ashes unfurl in a long stream blowing out to sea. They tumble and dance on the currents of air like playful sea birds unfurling their wings after a long winter's sleep. Finally, my sister is where she would have wanted to be. Part of the sea, part of the wind and the sky. And I'm right there with her...

'Come on,' I say, taking Mum's hand. 'Let's go.'

A LETTER FROM LAUREN

I want to say a huge thank you for choosing to read *My Mother's Silence*. If you did enjoy it, and want to keep up to date with all my latest releases, just sign up at the following link. Your email address will never be shared and you can unsubscribe at any time.

www.bookouture.com/lauren-westwood

My Mother's Silence is a special book for me in many ways. I have always wanted to write a book that expresses my love of Scotland and Celtic music. I grew up listening to *The Thistle and Shamrock* radio show on NPR, hosted by Fiona Ritchie MBE, which is a testament to the power of traditional music throughout the world. When we listen to my Scottish CDs in the car, my children sometimes have to cover their ears when the pipes come in, however, I am proud to be passing on this heritage to them. If you are interested in learning more about this music, I have put together a playlist on my website.

Eilean Shiel and the characters and events in this book are fictional. However, the setting was inspired by the beautiful Lochaber region of the Scottish Highlands. The lighthouse is a composite of three lighthouses I visited on my most recent trip to Scotland while researching this book, and primarily the one at Ardnamurchan, the westernmost point of mainland Great Britain.

I hope you loved *My Mother's Silence* and if you did I would be very grateful if you could write a review. I'd love to hear what you think, and it makes such a difference helping new readers to discover one of my books for the first time.

I love hearing from my readers – you can get in touch on my Facebook page, through Twitter, Goodreads or my website.

Thanks,
Lauren

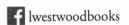 lwestwoodbooks

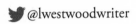 @lwestwoodwriter

ACKNOWLEDGEMENTS

There are many people I would like to thank for their assistance with this book. My agent, Anna Power, my editor, Jennifer Hunt and her team at Bookouture, who were willing to take a chance on my work. I would also like to thank Ronan Winters, Chris King, and Francisco Gochez who have been with me on this writing lark for over thirteen years. I would also like to thank my parents, Suzanne and Bruce Remington, and Monica Yeo for their love and encouragement. Finally, I would like to thank my family: Ian, Eve, Rose and Grace who put up with so much, and are a continuing and much-needed source of support and inspiration.